Charm City Crab Puff

by

Pamela Kyel

Copyright Notice

This is a work of fiction. Names, characters, places, and incidents are either the product of the author's imagination or are used fictitiously, and any resemblance to actual persons living or dead, business establishments, events, or locales, is entirely coincidental.

Charm City Crab Puff

COPYRIGHT © 2023 by Pam Wells

Cover Art by *Tina Lynn Stout*

The Wild Rose Press, Inc.
PO Box 708
Adams Basin, NY 14410-0708
Visit us at www.thewildrosepress.com

Publishing History
First Edition, 2024
Trade Paperback ISBN 978-1-5092-5334-0
Digital ISBN 978-1-5092-5335-7

A Charm City Mystery
Published in the United States of America

The smell of humidity, trash, and car exhaust greeted me the second I stepped outside. The Baltimore Harbor was a quick drive away, and with it, the Chesapeake Bay, which meant humidity was abundant here. July and August found us perspiring faster than a Pimlico racehorse the second we went outside, so I didn't go outside.

Hopping into my car, I congratulated myself again for stopping by the local convenience store and grabbing their second-largest cup. I snagged my drug of choice from the cup holder and slurped down a hefty dose of sweet tea. The sugar rushed in and eased the tight chest and stomach I got from seeing Zach on the table. I would need a pitcher to deal with seeing Desio.

Nothing prepared me for seeing Zach this morning. I knew coming in, there was a good chance it was him, but still—dude, I was not ready. When Colonel Waters couldn't reach Zach once the Air Force notified us, I knew something was up. We even tried Zach's current duty station, but no one there had seen him—at least, that's what they said.

I wrestled into my place in line on I95 and thought about what brought me back to Baltimore. This was my first assignment to bring me home—which I fought for six months. There was nothing but painful memories here, but after I spoke to Colonel Waters, I knew this was what I needed to bring closure. I just wasn't expecting to be confronted with it so soon.

Dedication

To Jeromy, the sugar to my sweet tea. Thank you for following my dreams with me.

Acknowledgments

I honestly thought this day would never come. I've been writing, re-writing, querying, crying, and experiencing the highs and lows that come with writing for years now. I'd almost given up, but my stubbornness wouldn't let me. As a military spouse, I've been in the supporting role, so to do something on my own and put myself out there is new and scary, but it turns out it was well worth it.

I begin with my most important supporters. My daughters Melina and Natania. You guys are the best part of me. You've taught me so much—some of which make it into my books, and some are better left just for us, i.e., "your mom" jokes.

Veteran Special Agent Carolyn Rocco, AFOSI— Thank you for pointing me in the right direction. Your information was as invaluable as your patience with all my questions. Thank you so much. Any discrepancies in my translation of the job of AFOSI are my mistakes—I do not pretend to know all the intricate ins and outs of these highly trained people.

I'd also like to thank veteran Air Force Security Forces and now Fort Worth Patrol Sargeant Erik Lavigne. You're like a younger brother, and to be able to pick on you while also utilizing your brain on all things police further cements your status as an honorary family member. You're doing great things, and I can't wait to see how far you go.

The next thank you is for fellow author Karen Whalen. From the moment I met you, you welcomed me with open arms into this new world of writing. You have taught me so much about writing, publishing, and more things than I can mention here.

Many other encouragers stand behind the scenes, and this is my chance to thank them openly. My brothers Robert and Andy. My cousin Cheryl. My beta readers Deanna and Michelle. I learned in the military that friends are family, and I wouldn't be where I am without my "sisters," Sarah and Arianne.

Last but certainly not least, I want to thank The Wild Rose Press and my editor Dianne for allowing me to be enthusiastic and excited while staying patient with my mistakes.

Chapter One

Men are a lot like sweet tea—they're either too sweet, and you wonder what they're hiding, or there's not enough sugar, and you never finished them. Not to mention when someone did the insane thing of adding lemon. I have met enough sweet tea men with too much lemon to last a lifetime.

The current lemon in the sweet tea was my ex-husband. Zach never spilled his secrets when we married, and a visit to the Baltimore Medical Examiner's Office would soon tell me if his days of keeping secrets were over.

I yanked open the door to the last room in the hallway and was immediately overwhelmed by the smell of formaldehyde. And what was that? Cookies? A scan of the room revealed the source of the formaldehyde, but I couldn't place the cookies—then the coroner greeted me from his desk in the corner. His mouth held half a cookie and the hand he waved with had a plastic bottle of milk in it. The two smells together were enough to turn my already weak stomach.

The partially covered body on the table caught my eye next, and I knew right away it was my ex-husband. I slapped my hand across my mouth to cover my sulfur burp, and instead of returning the coroner's greeting, I about-faced and ran to the women's bathroom at the other end of the hall.

As Special Agent Laci Duvall for the Air Force Office of Special Investigations, I have seen the inside of more bathrooms than I like. My job constantly challenged the strength of my stomach, and admittedly—dead people made me sick.

The bathroom door bounced against the wall to my left when I pushed my way inside—revealing more stainless steel. At the sink, I splashed my face with tepid water and rinsed out my mouth while I drifted in a sea of memories and chrome.

The footsteps in the hallway reminded me where I was, and I stepped into a stall behind me—I didn't need an audience. I rolled my forehead across the door and pinched my eyes shut, trying to block out Zach on the table. My distorted reflection on the door stared back at me while I lowered myself to the toilet.

"What the hell happened, Zach?" I asked.

The last time I saw my ex, we were signing divorce papers. Which was fifteen or so years ago—I think. We were married for five years, and together maybe three and a half of those five. After that, we moved from our failed marriage to our own lives, and I never expected to see him again.

Shit. I needed to get back to the autopsy room. I left my hideout and made the trek back down the hallway—my boots thudding on the floor echoed off the walls and into my head. I couldn't believe I left my tea in the car.

Someone fired up the morgue lights while I was gone, and they blinded me the second I opened the door. I threw my hands over my face, and it slammed shut. A voice inside apologized, and the door opened.

Blinking through the haze—the man holding the

door stopped me in my tracks.

"Laci?" the suit asked.

"Antonio?" I asked at the same time. Yep, that was him, all right. I wasn't ready to see him, so, of course, he showed up. He didn't know I was back, and I wasn't ready for him to know I was back—so much for that idea.

Baltimore City Police Detective Antonio Desio. Charm City heartthrob and the only man I've ever loved. Wow, the years had been good to him. My stomach took that as a sign and rebelled again. Who knew seeing my ex-boyfriend again after twenty years would affect me this way? With an effort of will, I turned toward the center of the room where the body lay. Desio and I reached the table at the same moment, and I stared at Zach spread before us.

"What happened to him?" I swallowed against the bile rising in my throat and turned to breathe in air that wasn't hovering over my dead ex. Instead of the fresh air I wanted, I got a whiff of Antonio's cologne, which made me gag. There wasn't enough sweet tea in the whole world for a situation like this.

"The deceased was fo—"

"Zach." I interrupted the coroner mid-sentence.

"What?" the coroner asked.

"I don't believe we've met." I reached over Zach. "Special Agent Laci Duvall, AFOSI. This man is Zach Wheaton. More specifically, he is Special Agent Zach Wheaton, Air Force Office of Special Investigation. My ex-husband."

Antonio's eyebrows hit his hairline, and thoughts raced across his face. I knew he was putting it all together and coming up with the correct conclusion.

"*Ex*-husband?" Desio asked.

"Dr. Ethan Mann." He hesitated, but then his hand met mine. "Is Mr. Wheaton married?"

"As far as I know, he is." I turned to Desio. "Did your people look for her?"

"I didn't even know she existed, so no," he said. "Do you know her?"

"Yeah, Zach and I weren't that close." I turned back to Dr. Mann. "I definitely wasn't close to his wife. Did you only need me to ID the body? That's what they told me over the phone."

"So, you're positively identifying this man as Special Agent Zach Wheaton?" Dr. Mann asked.

I took another look at the body with the sheet pulled to the chin. The air conditioning in the room ruffled his hair, and a shiver ran through me. There was no more tan from the summers we shared. Instead, he was pasty gray with every bit of life drained from him. I nodded.

"Thank you," Dr. Mann said. "As of now, it's a mystery what killed him, but I'll have a toxicology report and the death cert ready in a day or two. If I have any more questions, I'll be in touch."

I got an eyeful of Desio when I turned from the table and froze. I stood there with my mouth open and nothing coming out. I couldn't help it. I was the deer to his oncoming headlights. Gathering myself together, I snapped my mouth shut and made a break for the door.

"I'm sorry about your ex-husband." Desio opened the door for us to leave.

Hearing his voice after all these years...it aged well like the rest of him. He was a few inches taller than me, and I rested my forehead on his shoulder more times than I remembered. I forced myself back to the present before I gave in to that particular craving and passed him into the hallway.

"Thank you," I said. "We've been divorced longer than we were married. I like to keep my distance from Zach as much as possible. I don't know why I'm here. Do you? I haven't spoken to him since he remarried, which you should look into, by the way." This man rattled me like no one else.

"What do you know about his wife?" He ignored my comment.

"Her name is Samantha Wheaton, and last I knew, they were in Vegas. I don't know how he ended up here. Guess that's one of the things you should ask her when you find her."

He gave me a stern look. "I know how to do my job, Laci."

Whoops.

We reached the door to the parking lot, and I turned to say goodbye. I noticed he didn't have a middle-aged spare tire and still had all his hair but was beginning to gray at the temples. He wore his black suit like a second skin and buffed his Italian loafers within an inch of their life. The dark suit set off his Italian heritage well. Those who didn't know him would expect Italian to pour out, but what they got was a strong Baltimore accent instead.

"Do you think this is work related?" he asked.

"It could be. I don't have enough to tell you one way or the other, though," I said. "My boss, Colonel Waters, has been doing some searching, and so far, no one's talking. He may have found something while I'm down here. I'll let you know." With that, I waved and pushed out the door.

The smell of humidity, trash, and car exhaust greeted me the second I stepped outside. The Baltimore Harbor was a quick drive away, and with it, the Chesapeake Bay, which meant humidity was abundant here. July and August found me perspiring faster than a Pimlico racehorse the second I went outside, so I didn't go outside.

Hopping into my car, I congratulated myself again for stopping by the local convenience store and grabbing their second-largest cup. I snagged my drug of choice from the cup holder and slurped down a hefty dose of sweet tea. The sugar rushed in and eased the tight chest and stomach I got from seeing Zach on the table. I would need a pitcher to deal with seeing Desio.

Nothing prepared me for seeing him this morning. I knew coming in, there was a good chance it was him, but still—dude, I was not ready. When Colonel Waters couldn't reach Zach once the Air Force notified us, I knew something was up. We even tried his current duty station, but no one there had seen him—at least, that's what they said.

I wrestled into my place in line on I95 and thought about what brought me back to Baltimore. This was my first assignment to bring me home—which I fought for six months. There was nothing but painful memories here, but after I spoke to Colonel Waters, I knew this was what I needed to bring closure. I just wasn't expecting to be confronted with it so soon.

Driving the interstate drowned out my gloom because I95 was tough any time, but rush hour posed all sorts of combat scenarios. And don't even get me started on the Fort McHenry Tunnel. In my heart, I knew it was solid and safe, but my head liked to tease my heart by looking for leaks.

Once I reached the office, or Field Investigation Squadron-Operating Location, I dashed the thirty or so yards to the sweet relief that was air-conditioning and made my way down the hall to my office.

With a full roster of cases to occupy my mind, I started my morning by waiting for my computer to boot up. Per the usual government computers, it was a long wait.

****

My chair was tilted at a forty-five-degree angle while I read emails, but it slammed back to ninety, and I jumped a foot when my office door burst open. The door bounced off the wall, and so did my chair when I jumped to my feet. But, in the time it took me to stand up, heart pounding, hands curled at my side, Colonel Waters was at my desk tossing me the latest copy of the *Air Force Times*. It landed facing me.

"Did you see this?" he asked.

"No, sir." I scanned the front page and immediately saw what caused the outburst.

"Jesus and Jessie James, Major, how the hell did they find out so soon?"

"I don't know, sir. Have you checked with PR?" I slapped my hand across my mouth and prayed for a hole to swallow me. The storm was already across his face, and I removed my hand to apologize, but he beat me to it.

"What the hell do you think?"

"I know, sir. Sorry, sir."

He waved me off and stalked to the window, where he stared outside with his back to me. I waited, at attention, for him to speak because I knew he wasn't finished.

"So, it was Zach?" he asked. After my nod, he continued, "I'm sorry you had to see him in that condition, Major. I can't imagine it was easy for you."

In sweet tea rankings, Colonel Waters was Earl Grey—easy on the sugar. He was also quite a puzzle. Part surly drill sergeant and part Easter Bunny, he was a mixed bag, and you never knew what you'd get from him. We've worked together at different points in our careers, and both held memories from our joint deployment that kept us up at night.

"What do you think, Major?" he asked.

"I told the detective at the morgue that I didn't have enough information to call it a suspicious death, and I still believe that. We just don't know, sir," I said. "I haven't had time to dig into his records, and I'm wading through emails as fast as I can. I need access to his files and email. Do you know how I can get that?"

"I'll call his Commanding Officer back—someone at Bolling has to know something. The press is already all over this, and I will not be found with my pants down. We need to know what cases he was working on, and we need to know now." Colonel Waters punctuated his statement with a pointed finger in my face. When had he come back to my desk? "If this is retaliation against him, I have to know yesterday."

The birds filled the feeder outside the window past Colonel Waters's right shoulder. I couldn't name the types, but I thought I glimpsed a cardinal or two. Oh, to be as clueless as a bird right now.

"Who was the detective, Major?" He about-faced from my desk and headed for the door.

"Detective Antonio Desio, sir, Baltimore City Police Department."

He stopped short—damnit—I knew he would remember.

"Not the same…?" He let out a low whistle when I nodded. "Nothing like coming back home, is it, Major?"

I huffed out a laugh. "Touché, sir."

****

The end of the duty day couldn't get there fast enough. Colonel Waters was still drawing a blank on Zach's caseload and went over the CO's head in DC. We needed to know something—anything.

It took me ten minutes to reach home, and my thoughts and memories of Zach filled the short drive. We never spoke, not even in a professional capacity, and it was what we preferred. It seemed like a good idea at the time, but now I knew nothing about what job he was on or if he was still married.

It's strange no one thought to look for Sammie. Maybe they were divorced too, and I was the only one who could get to the ME's office. What about their kids? Oh, just hell, I hadn't even thought about the kids.

Chapter Two

"Hi, sweetie. Do you need to go outside?"

Needles, my beagle, scrambled across the kitchen floor, his claws looking to find a place to land on the linoleum. He stopped where the gate stretched across the kitchen opening. Boo, my cat, and his arch-nemesis slid along the doggy gate in front of him. She liked to taunt him that she was free while he was trapped.

He licked my face when I bent down to kiss his head and open his gate. Boo joined us at the back door, and we all went out. She pounced on things while Needles and I played with a tennis ball.

I surveyed my little slice of heaven—my townhouse in the suburbs, with the small patch of grass known as my backyard viewable from my front door. It was quaint but big enough for Needles to do his thing and Boo to do hers.

During a round of fetch, I heard the distinct ring of the Air Force Anthem and went inside to answer my phone. I hummed along to the tune until I reached the table.

"Major Duvall."

"Laci—"

That *might* have been what she said. There were more tears than words, but I knew in my gut who it was—Sammie, aka Samantha Wheaton. Zach's wife. How did I know this? We spoke exactly once after she and Zach got married and she warned me off. As if I'd needed a reason. I'd remember that voice anywhere.

"Sammie, I'm surprised to hea—"

"La-ci," Sammie sobbed. "Wha-t *scree *muffle muffle* scree* do?"

"Sammie, hon, I can't understand you."

Just then, the doorbell rang—saved by the bell.

"Sam—yes, Sammie, can you call me back? Someone's at the front door—I gotta get it. Okay? Bye."

Hitting end on my phone I pulled the front door open, and there in front of me stood Sammie, with her and Zach's toddler twins on either side of her.

"Samm—"

She fell into my arms, complete with mucus and water and everything. This left me with one arm to awkwardly pat her back while she howled into my shoulder. Backing into the house, with her still attached, I gently steered her to the living room with the kids trailing behind us. I peeled her off and plopped her onto the loveseat and placed a box of tissues in her hands, while I sat on the coffee table waiting for her to tell me why she was there.

Not one to know if kids were cute or not, these looked no different than any others I'd seen. They all had Sammie's hair color, and the little girl had blue eyes that matched hers, while the little boy had hazel eyes, which didn't match Zach's.

Sammie wasn't your conventional beauty at five-foot two inches and built like a brick shithouse. In a previous life, she was a bodybuilder, which how she and Zach had met. Occasionally you would catch glimpses of the body she once had, but two children and ten years of marriage had shown up.

"What am I gonna do now?" Sammie drawled. Born and raised in East Tennessee, she had a southern accent that took you to Tara from *Gone with the Wind* while her stature reminded you of the Shakespeare quote, "Though she be but little, she is fierce."

She hiccupped and covered her face with her hands. The twins turned to look at her and then scrunched their faces and let out an unholy screech. It didn't even phase Sammie.

Above the sound of the kids and Sammie, I heard a howl. There in the backyard, sat Needles, with his nose straight up in the air and a perfect "O" on his lips. I would have laughed if it were happening to anyone but me.

"I'm sorry about Zach," I said, turning my attention back to Sammie. What the hell was I going to do now? Why was she even here? But she didn't hear me, let alone the twin sirens sitting next to her. I reached over and clasped her wrists in my hands, and said her name, but again, nothing.

"Sammie." I slightly squeezed her wrists this time.

"What?" She peeked through the fingers covering her face.

I pointed at the screaming kids trying to climb into her lap. "Your kids." When I raised my voice for her to hear me, a gray blur raced up the steps.

She took her hands down and raised her eyebrows—surprised to see her twins next to her. "Ana. Ryan. Stop." They didn't stop. I rolled my eyes in non-surprise.

"Do they need something to eat?" I shouted to her over the noise.

I stood up to hunt out some snacks in my kitchen, but Old Mother Hubbard had nothing on this single officer. She waved me off and I sat back down on the coffee table.

"Why are you here?" I asked. There was a sense of impending doom gripping my insides. Something in my gut told me I already knew the answer, but I needed to know for sure.

"Why, to live with you, of course," she said. "Zach told me to. He said if anything happened to him, we're to come to you."

There it was. The real reason she was here. If Zach weren't already dead, I would have killed him. What a guy.

"Did he tell you to come live with me?" I asked. "Specifically, I mean. Did he mean for you to move in with me?"

"No, but—"

"When did he tell you this?" I asked.

"About six months ago, right before our anniversary." She stared past me out the back window. Her eyes took on a faraway look while she remembered things I had no interest in hearing, filled with insight I would gladly gouge out with an ice pick if I could. "We went to a local B&B, and my parents watched the kids for—"

Yep. "Why aren't you staying with your parents?" I asked.

"They can't handle the twins full-time," she said.

"What happened to your apartment? Why aren't you staying there?" I asked.

"We moved back in with my parents. Again," she said.

"Why?"

Her eyes fell to her hands and the color rose in her cheeks. "Zach insisted we needed to save money and what better way to do it than live in a place for free? It was awful. Having to ask my parents if we could live with them again."

I let that sit for a minute, trying but failing to feel guilty about the thoughts I was having on Zach at the moment. "What about Janis and Floyd?" I desperately threw people at her to stay with, even Zach's parents. Anyone but me. I didn't want roommates—especially ones that cried.

"You do remember his parents, right?" she asked.

"Yeah." That was all that really needed to be said about them. "You *can't* stay with me. I need my space and my quiet. Plus, I'm still in the move-in phase." I glanced around me and saw a settled house. "Sort of."

Tears welled up in her eyes as she stood up which dislodged Ana by her side. The little girl fell over on the couch, replacing Sammie in her seat. "Okay. Fine. Then on to Plan B." With Ryan asleep on her right shoulder, she reached down for Ana's hand and strode to the front door.

I didn't know what "Plan B" was, but my insides were climbing the walls as she walked past me, poker straight, with her shoulders squared. She continued to the front door then stood waiting for me to catch up and open the door for her.

I felt lousy, but I knew this would end badly if I gave in—I just knew it. I was a loner and had been that way for the past fifteen years. What on earth did I even have to give the wife of my ex-husband?

Once I opened the door, Sammie pushed onto the

small front porch. She took Ana's hand again and strode for the red sedan parked at the curb. I closed the door before they reached it.

Leaning my back against the door, I could see Needles standing in the backyard with a tennis ball in his mouth. His head was tilted to the side in question. I groaned, scrubbed my face with my hands, turned back to the front door, and thunked my head on it. Repeatedly. Then I grabbed the knob and wrenched it open.

"Sa—" Sammie stepped from the left into my line of sight, wrapped me in a bear hug, and dissolved into tears again.

I escorted them back into the house and to their previous spots on the couch. I reconned in the kitchen to find food, but then stood staring at an empty refrigerator before I ordered pizza.

Later, once dinner was finished and Sammie and the kids were settled into their room across the hall, I sat on the side of my bed. I stared at Boo, but I didn't see her where she lay less than two feet away. She raised her gray head off her paws and gave me a disparaging look which revealed how she felt about the noisy visitors. She blinked, and I could hear as plainly as if she'd spoken, *What have you done, woman?*

"I couldn't leave them to starve now, could I?" I asked.

I wish to hell I knew what Zach was thinking sending them to me.

****

Clearing the brush from the path in front of the Humvee, I heard the siren going off. I dropped and rolled one way—flattening myself to the ground under

15

the vehicle while Zach rolled the other.

I was searching for the cause of the siren when my bedroom light flicked on, and Sammie stood inside the door with an outraged Ryan in her arms.

"What the hell?" I asked. I clamped my hands over my ears from my prone position on the floor. I couldn't believe the noise coming from such a small person.

"Why are you down there?" Sammie asked.

"What?" I yelled.

I couldn't stand up while my hands were over my ears, but I didn't want to take them down because of the siren—I mean crying. With no other choice, I placed them on the floor and vaulted to my feet, then clamped my hands back in place. Sammie walked into the room and didn't stop until she was inches from me.

"He won't stop," she said. She was doing that whining thing again. "Do you have any children's pain medicine?"

"Why the he—ck would I have children's pain medicine?" Her face fell in misery, so I changed tactics. "But I can go get some—the drugstore is just a few minutes away."

Her face lit up, and I did a mental head slap, but I pulled on my bunny slippers anyway. Why on earth did I volunteer to go to a pharmacy at night for the wife of my ex-husband? With Sammie's detailed medication list in my hand, I grabbed my bag from the front table and headed into the night.

The pharmacy was a few blocks away and you could see the lights announcing its presence almost from my front door. When I entered the sliding glass door those same lights hit my senses like a police line-up. It reminded me of my visit to the morgue today and

I felt my stomach flip over and felt a sigh rush past my lips thinking of Desio.

I shook my head to clear it of the images coming through and went down the first row I reached. There was chocolate, soda, chips, and everything else you could possibly think of as far as the eye could see. *Where the hell is the kid's medicine?*

Several aisles later I realized I was completely lost. So, I went back to the first aisle and started reading the signs hanging from the ceiling this time. I reached the one marked children's medication, and someone spoke behind me.

"Cute shoes."

I wiggled my toes, looked at the woman in uniform in front of me, and smiled. "Yeah, well, I like bunnies. Do you know where they keep the kid's medicine by any chance, officer?" I asked.

She flashed a grin and pointed at the aisle behind me. "You was almost to it."

"Thanks." I turned and walked down the aisle and she came with me. "Did I do something wrong, Officer…?"

"Davis. My name's Cassy Davis, but my real name is Cassandra Davis. No, you didn't do anything— This here's the medicine section. Whatchu need?"

"I wish I knew," I said. "I have a kid screaming its head off at my house, but his mother doesn't know why."

"This here is universal. Takes care of lots of things." She reached past me, grabbed a pink box of children's medicine from the shelf, and handed it to me. I assumed it was kid's medicine since there was a cartoon kid on it.

"Is this the only thing they make?" I asked.

"Nah, they make all kinds. This one for headaches and the like, this one for gas, and this one here for when they can't poop, and thi—" She stopped when she glanced at me.

"Do kids really need all this?" I asked. My arm was spilling over with medicine for all sorts of stuff that I didn't know a damn thing about.

"Not all at once, no, but it's good to have it around in case of emergencies. Plus, it cuts down on trips to the drug store at midnight," she said with a wink and a laugh.

"Gotcha, then we'll take them all. What do kids eat? I don't have kids' snacks at home, either."

She blinked at me and then walked away. I stood and stared, not sure if she wanted me to follow, but when she reached the end of the row, she turned to see if I was behind her.

"You comin'?" she asked.

I shuffled after her, my bunnies silent on the shiny floor, and reached her in the next aisle. She stood with a box of o-cereal, which she handed to me when I reached her. I juggled all the medicine and the additional tube of fruity stuff while she grabbed a pack of what looked like baby wipes. I raised my eyebrows at her final addition.

"These help clean up all sorts of things," she said. "I think you all set now. I'll help you to the register."

We headed to the front of the store, passing more boxes of cereal, fingernail polish, and walls of candy. The sound of her gun belt creaking when she settled her hands on it contrasted with the sound of the elevator music playing around us.

"How do you know all this?" I asked.

"Comes with the job."

"Are you married?" I asked.

"Are you?" she asked, avoiding my question.

"I was once, twenty years ago," I said. Too late I noticed Cassy stopped and I ran right into the back of her.

She turned to look down at me. "Damn, honey, you musta been a kid."

I laughed despite myself as we approached the register where I laid everything on the counter. The clerk looked like we woke him from a nap somewhere, but he silently went through the motions of checking out the goods while Officer Davis and I chatted.

"We were, yes, and I think that's why it didn't work out. What about you? Are you married?"

She sobered up, her eyes turning serious. "I almost was. Made it to the altar before the asshole left me."

"Well, that sucks," I said handing my credit card to the cashier.

"Yeah, that's one way of puttin' it."

"So, tell me, did karma bite them in the ass, and they're living with momma now?" I asked while gathering my plastic bags from the counter.

"Nah, karma skipped him. He went to California and joined a dot-com start-up and is worth millions now, and I'm still here. Same job. Same everything."

"That's not true," I said. We walked out the sliding doors, and I found I enjoyed talking with her. "You probably learned how to spot an asshole from a mile away."

She tipped her head back and let out the best laugh I'd ever heard, and I found myself laughing with her.

With a chuckle, she said, "You're funny."

"Thanks, I'm not usually this open and honest, but with the day I've had, I've given up giving a damn." I glanced at my watch. "I have fifteen more minutes before I have to care again tomorrow."

"Now that sounds like my job. What do you do?" she asked.

"AFOSI." When she looked confused, I explained it more. "Air Force Office of Special Investigations, like the FBI, but for the Air Force."

She let out a whistle.

"Yeah, well, it sounds more impressive than it is. Mainly it's paperwork followed by random bits of terror thrown in there."

Again, she threw her head back, and again I laughed with her. She had a great laugh and I found I couldn't stop myself. She stood beside me at my car, and I had to look straight up to see her eyes. Her boots weren't platforms, but she was easily six feet even in flats and gorgeous. Her dark skin revealed an African-American heritage, and she spoke with a hint of Hip-Hop to the rhythm of Little Bo Peep.

"I'm Laci Duvall. It's nice to meet you."

"Likewise," Cassy said and placed her hand in mine. She eyed me for a second before pulling out a business card from an outside pocket on her pants leg and grabbed a pen from her sleeve. She wrote something on the back and handed it to me.

"Here's my number. Call me if you need to get out of jail or just want to party it up with another crazy ass chick."

This time I threw my head back and laughed. "Oh, Cassy, if you only knew how totally unlike me that is.

But if I ever feel wild and crazy, I'll let you know. Here, take my card too." I reached into my car, took one from the glovebox, stretched my hand out for her pen, and wrote my cell number on the back.

"Here's mine in case you need a boring night at home."

She took the card from me and chuckled while she walked away. I got in my car and drove home; my fifteen minutes of not caring were just about up for the day.

Chapter Three

The siren wail from last night woke me up faster than the coffee in my cup the next morning. Needles' ears perked up, and he whined a bit, and I reassured him as best as I could. "Don't worry, boy, I'm putting you in my room today. You and Boo don't need the stress."

"Here," Sammie said.

Turning around, I received Ana as best I could, but I didn't know how to hold kids any more than I knew what to feed them. Lucky for me, she was a pro and wrapped her legs around my waist and held on for dear life. Her small hand grabbed my Operational Camouflage Pattern (OCP) shirtfront, right over the rank, and my hand automatically went to support her diaper-clad bottom. I smelled baby shampoo on her and leaned my nose against the wisp of hair with a pink bow stuck to it.

"You going somewhere?" I asked.

"Oh, yes—Ana and Ryan are in daycare, but I think I'm gonna keep Ryan home today, bless his heart. I think he's getting a cold or something. I'm fixin' to call the pediatrician, since he's got a fever of 100.2. I need someone to look at him today."

"Oh, they're in daycare?" I asked.

"Oh, yes, there's no way I can do this on my own all day long," she answered, gesturing between her and the twins.

I thought Needles was slurping his water but turns out Ana found her thumb and was going to town on it. "Is one hundred the magic number or something?" I asked. I traced my finger up and down Ana's cheek. *She's so soft.*

Sammie's tinkling laugh brought my attention to her hand across her mouth. "Bless your heart, you really don't know a thing about kids, do you?"

"Nope, not a damn thing." My cell ringing upstairs caught my ear, showing how off my game I was. I never forgot my phone. "I need to go get that."

"Okay," she said. But she didn't make a move to take back Ana. Instead, she went for the coffee pot with Ryan still in her arms.

Skipping every other step while I ran upstairs, I heard a gurgle and looked down into smiling baby-blue eyes. I guess she liked that.

"Major Duvall," I answered.

"Is this Laci Duvall?" Dr. Mann asked.

"Yes, that's me, Dr. Mann. How can I help you?" I said.

After a second, he asked. "How'd you know it was me?"

"I have a gift for voice recognition. Did you need something?" I asked.

At the top of the steps outside my room, I juggled Ana in the hopes of not dropping her while I walked down the stairs. I pulled my phone away from my ear at the continued silence on the other end.

"Dr. Mann?" I asked.

"Voice recognition?" he asked.

"Yes, I'm a super voice recognizer. It's part of my

job."

"Uh-huh," he said. "We've been unable to locate the wife of Special Agent Wheaton, so I am sharing my results with you, seeing as how you were co-workers. I'm also assuming you're investigating for the government. Are you free to go over the results right now?"

I debated for a hot minute whether I should confess that I knew where Mrs. Wheaton was, but I needed to know the information he had.

"Sure, give me a second, though," I said. I turned to Sammie in the kitchen. "I have to take this, but we need to talk. It's about Zach."

"That's fine. I'll be back directly if I don't get through to the doctor. Iffin I do, I'll go see him. I need to get these guys dressed and us out the door—they don't like it when you're late for drop-off. Something about messing up their day or schedule or something. How much can it be affected? I mean really, it's only two kids. It's not like I have half the class out with me. I swanny, they'll just have to deal with having one today, because I need to find out what's going on with Ryan. I don't need Ana catching whatever it is he has, you know?"

She finished by reaching for Ana and I handed her over, though I missed the small weight and her sweet smell. Sammie easily toted everyone upstairs and disappeared around the landing.

"Hello again." I greeted Dr. Mann, grabbed a sweet tea from the fridge, then left the kitchen for the front office, where I kept my sticky notes.

"Hello," Dr. Mann said. "I wanted you to know that Special Agent Wheaton had marijuana and alcohol in his system. There are tests still being run, but I'll let you know when those results are in."

"Zach struggled with alcohol when we were married," I said, "and he has a history of recreational marijuana use. I wonder if he quit his meetings. Was his blood alcohol high?"

"Mmmm, it was .05, so no, he was below the legal limit."

Sammie walked by my office while I was spoke with Dr. Mann. The sound of the front door closing echoed into the now-empty house. When I peered through the blinds, I saw her getting everyone in their seats and seatbelts. I guess we'd catch up later.

"Do you know the regular habits of Mr. Wheaton?" Dr. Mann asked.

"Not any of his latest ones, no," I said. "Zach and I didn't work or associate with each other. It was what we both preferred. Our divorce wasn't messy, but it wasn't friendly either, you know. I haven't heard from him since he and Sammie were newlyweds."

"Speaking of Mrs. Wheaton, please alert us and the police as soon as possible if you hear from her. I can't release the death certificate to just anyone."

"Will do, Dr. Mann. Thank you again."

Colonel Waters might know what Zach was working on, so when I got to the office, I'd talk to him. For now, I placed a call and received Desio's voicemail, but I didn't leave a message.

****

My office was a Field Operations Investigation Squadron, which meant we weren't attached to a military installation. In fact, if you didn't know we were here you would miss us all together. Our parking

Pamela Kyel

lot was empty this morning—we came and went as we pleased here. We had no schedule to keep as long as we came in and did our job.

Opening my office door, I could almost see my desktop under all the paperwork I needed to get busy on. They liked to tell us if there was no record it didn't happen, and I needed to make sure people knew stuff happened. I've investigated everything from suicides to sexual assaults, drugs to child pornography, and everything in between. It could be a heavy job, but I love puzzles, and all my cases are puzzles needing to be solved.

Once my computer was booted up and my sweet tea cup was in place, I went to the Defense Central Index of Investigations (DCII) and plugged in Zach's name to see what would happen. There were more pages than I expected on Zach. The first few were investigations of Zach holding stock in marijuana. In addition to a Letter of Reprimand (LOR), the Air Force strongly compelled him to sell his stock. It was either that or he would have his security clearance revoked, and trust me, no one wanted their security clearance revoked.

I clicked on the LOR link, but nothing came up. I'd get a copy from Colonel Waters the first chance I got. I got sidetracked by an internal email popping up and before I knew it my phone was going off with Indiana Jones's theme song. I snagged it before it went off.

"Major Duvall," I said.

"We've been in a car accident," Sammie gushed.

"What?" I asked. Surely, she didn't say what I think she said.

"I swanny Laci, someone ran us off the road.

We're on our way to the emergency room right now—I'm so glad I didn't have Ana with me. They bashed in her side of the car, and I know she would have been hurt if she'd been in her seat. It's amazing Ryan didn't get hurt." She ground to a halt, took a deep breath, and burst into tears.

I couldn't get a word in, so I just propped the phone on my shoulder and finished the email I was writing. It's not that I didn't care about her and Ryan, it's just that I needed to get things done. Her crying eventually turned to hiccups, and I saw my chance.

"Are you okay?" I asked. "Is Ryan okay?"

"I think so," she sniffed. "We're almost to the ER. Can you come? Please?"

"Why are you going to the ER?" I asked. "Since he's okay, I mean."

I fought my immediate instinct which told me to stay away and instead glanced at the clock on my computer. It was 11:45, which meant I could take a lunch break and be back to work by two.

"Because when they hit me, I banged my head and left a spiderweb crack on the side window. I tried to tell them I was fine, but I think I may have stumbled a bit when I was walking around with Ryan. I swanny I do not need this today."

"I'll be there as soon as I can," I said.

I shut off my computer and grabbed my purse on the way out while Sammie rattled off directions to the hospital I already knew how to get to. Lord knew why I felt compelled to keep an eye on her when she was my ex-husband's wife, but something told me it would help me find out what happened to Zach if I stuck with her.

Winding my way through Middle River, I reached

Franklin Square parking lot in no time. Lucky for me a spot opened in the far-off corner as I got to it. A quick jog to the building entrance left my back drenched under my OCP, and when I took my hat off to go inside, sweat dripped into my eye.

Reading signs and directions as I went, I reached the front desk and asked the receptionist where I could find Sammie. She informed me I couldn't see her because I wasn't family. So, I reversed my tracks, went back to the entrance, and called her. She picked up on the fifth ring.

"Sammie, it's Laci; they can't tell me where you are. Can you meet me at the front desk?"

"I can't right this second," she stage-whispered. "The doctor is here staring at me while I talk, and he's not thrilled about me telling him to hold his horses. It looks like I'll have to meet you in the waiting room when we're done."

With nothing left to do but wait, I hung up and turned to go back to the reception area.

"How is it out of all of Baltimore I run into you?" a familiar voice spoke behind me. "I mean, you're cute and all, but why can't you be six-foot-three and play pro basketball. You know what I'm sayin'?"

I laughed and turned toward Cassy with a huge grin on my face. Today, she wore denim cut-off shorts, an Orioles T-shirt, and tennis shoes. "I wouldn't have recognized you if you hadn't said hello first. What are you doing here?" I asked.

"I came to have lunch with a friend. She's a nurse in the ER. Why you here?"

"Ex-husband's wife was hit by a car this morning, and since we're not related, I'm waiting for her."

"Ex-husband's wife?" she asked. "This the same one with the kid who needed the medicine last night?"

"Yep—one and the same," I said.

"Hunh—lemme see what I can do. What's her name?"

"Samantha, or Sammie Wheaton. She has her son Ryan with her," I said.

"Gotcha, I'll be right back."

I nodded and turned right where she turned left to go into the Employees Only area of the ER. There was a kid's magazine on the table to my right, which I flipped through while I waited. My legs were crossed at the knee, but they jumped while I impatiently waited for Cassy to come back.

I didn't know tiger urine smelled like buttered popcorn. "I'll never look at Orville Redenbacher the same way," I wondered out loud.

"Say what now?"

"Tiger urine—it supposedly smells like buttered popcorn." I turned the magazine for her to see, and she roared her laugh again, and I found myself grinning. "Have I told you how much I love your laugh?"

She stopped laughing. "No kidding? Hunh, people always picked on me because of it. I used to try and change it, and then I thought, what the hell, you only live once. I came to getchu to go back and see your ex-husband's wife."

"Really? They let you do that?" I asked.

"Sure, why not? They know me—I know them."

Cassy was right; they knew her here, and she said hello to every single one of them. From the doctors and orderlies to the nurses and seniors in candy stripes—they all greeted her by name.

29

"You don't know a stranger, do you?" I asked.

"Nah, people's people no matter where you are. Some want to talk, some want to tell you their life story, and some want you to mind your own damn business. You don't know who falls into what category until you say hi."

"That makes total sense. I think I would fall in the latter category."

"Really? You don't strike me as not friendly."

"I didn't say I wasn't friendly, just that I'm not keen on talking to people."

"Ahhh, you one of them introverts?"

"Oh, yes, very much so. I've seen enough people in the last two days to last me the rest of the month."

She chuckled but didn't throw her head back and laugh like before. I trailed behind her, and we reached the end of the hall and ran out of curtained area, until we turned the corner to the left, where they kept going.

The nurse's station was a hub of activity and there were party balloons behind the desk indicating someone's birthday. The smell of the birthday cake co-mingled with the antiseptic they used in the hospital, and together they created a mix that turned my stomach a bit—I would never get used to the smell of hospitals.

"Sammie?" I called.

"Laci?" I heard a frantic voice call from the curtained wall in front of me. A moment later, down on the left, the drapes parted, and Sammie's bandaged head poked out and the rest soon followed. "Laci! Oh, my Gawd, there you are!" She wrangled me into a full hug and then got a good look at Cassy. "Who are you?"

"I'm Cassandra Davis. I met Laci last night at the drug store then ran into her again out front of the ER.

You the ex-husband's wife? Hunh, how old were you when you got married, honey, sixteen?"

"Samantha Wheaton, this is Cassy," I said. "Cassy, this is Sammie."

"Well, I'll be. You're the first of Laci's friends I've met. It's nice to meet you."

"We just met last night at the pharmacy," I said. "Like she said."

"Do what now?" Sammie eyed Cassy again. "What?"

"Yes, Officer Cassandra Davis here helped me find all the stuff I brought home last night. If it weren't for her—I would probably still be there. Where's Ry?" I asked. She pulled the curtain back, and there curled up on the hospital bed was Ryan. "Wore him out, did you?" I deadpanned.

"No, I didn't wear him out. Being here has done that—bless his heart. We never made it to the pediatrician, and I had to call them and tell them he was in a car accident with me, and we wouldn't make it. I hope to raisins they don't tell the insurance company. That's all I need is to get a bill for something I didn't even get to do. Which reminds me, how long do you think I have insurance from Zach? I need to call them, I guess. It looks like I'll be the one to tell them about the canceled appointment this morning. I swanny, they'll flip when they hear about the trip to the ER." Sammie unloaded on us without taking a breath.

"You do need to find out about the insurance, but I know ours covers ER visits for dependents. Once you have the death certificate you can call them. How much longer do you have to stay here?" I asked.

"The doctor is supposed to be coming back. He

was here once and left while shaking his head. I don't know what in the Sam Hill for, but he told me he'd be back in a few."

"Are you okay? Can we talk about Zach for a second?"

Sammie touched her bandaged head and glanced at Ryan who was still dead to the world then nodded that we could go on.

"Do you know if Zach was drinking much alcohol lately?" I asked.

"Not that I know of, at least around me he wasn't. Why?"

"Dr. Mann at the Baltimore City Medical Examiner's office gave me the toxicology report this morning," I said.

"Toxi-whosis?" she asked.

"The report that details what was in his system when he died. Stuff like alcohol or drugs, except in this case it was marijuana."

"Why you?" she asked.

"What do you mean?"

"Why'd they call you and not me?" she asked.

"I might not have told them where you were," I said. She stared at me, and I gave her my best Cheshire cat grin mixed with what I hoped was the look of innocence I saw on Needles when I came home, and the trash was all over the floor.

"Why on earth didn't you tell them?" She placed her fists on her hips and stared up at me.

"Because I didn't know how things were going to pan out with you and I didn't want to be left in the dark. This way we both know—because I'm telling you. I knew I would find out eventually, but this way I hear it without going through all the hoops. I'm sorry. I did try and call the detective on the case and tell him, but he didn't answer."

"Did you leave him a message?" Sammie asked.

"I might have forgotten to do that," I said.

"Who's on the case?" Cassy asked.

"Desio," I said. She let out a whistle and I turned toward her. "What?"

"That man is fii-iine," she said.

I stifled a hysterical giggle and turned back to Sammie. "I can try and call him now if you want me to." I pulled out my phone only to realize I had no reception back there. "Did you know Zach had been doing marijuana?" I asked. I shook my phone like an idiot, somehow thinking that would give me the bars I needed to make the call.

"He always hid that type of thing from me," she said. "What else is in the report?"

"I don't know yet. He's sending it to me," I said.

Just then the curtain parted, and a man came through wearing a lab coat over scrubs telling me this must be the doctor. He raised his eyebrows in surprise when he saw us. He was around my age and competent looking, and then I saw his footwear—emerald-green Converse.

Before the curtain closed behind him, Desio, emerged through the opening. Surprised to see him, I took the opportunity to get another good look at him. What I saw only confirmed that he got to skip the line in the sweet tea department. This man bypassed tea and went straight to fine wine.

When he entered, his cool gray eyes caught mine, and I was transported to that fateful day all those years ago. I had asked to meet him, and he agreed to see me outside his parents' restaurant in Little Italy.

Desio's parents owned a restaurant in Little Italy on South High Street. He put in his time working in the kitchen before he was allowed to serve tables to get himself through college. He was a third-generation Italian American and had two brothers, Giancarlo, who was older, and Dante was younger. They used to fight over the girls before I came along. They had respected Antonio and not fought over me, despite me having met Giancarlo first. It was either that or Desio was the only one who wanted anything to do with me.

My voice shook as much as my hands that day when I turned from Antonio with tears pouring down my face. It wasn't that I wanted to leave, but I hadn't any other choice then.

His gaze held mine and he knew I was remembering. The stone of his face softened a bit, but it wasn't with pity, it was in understanding. My life changed when I walked away from him that afternoon.

An elbow dug into my right side, and I looked up at Cassy's shit-eating grin as she glanced between the two of us.

"Mrs. Wheaton," the doctor began, "Detective Desio was here regarding another issue, but I asked him to join us. He's agreed to speak with you, but first, I must tell you Ryan has a case of chickenpox. It's been making the rounds this summer, which is strange since school isn't in session. I've had numerous cases appear. Have you been vaccinat—"

"Oh, hell no," Cassy said.

I jumped in surprise and turned to see her backing away from us while making an x-sign with her fingers as if she could ward us off like some evil spirit.

"I take that to mean you've never had chickenpox?" I asked.

"No, I ain't had chickenpox, and we for sure didn't get shots for that shit." Her eyes were as big as saucers as she backed through the curtain. "I'm out."

One look at Sammie and it was clear she was in the same boat. "You either, huh?"

"Mrs. Wheaton." The doctor cleared his throat to get her attention. Such an old man move for someone so young. "It's not painful, just annoying, and only if you do catch them. There's a reasonable chance you won't suffer any repercussions from the virus. I suggest you stop and get lotion on your way home to help alleviate his itching. Of course, the best thing to do is to not scratch, but we all know how that goes.

"I'm assuming his sister hasn't received the vaccine either?" Sammie shook her head. "Then she'll need to stay at home also. If she's in daycare and they find out she brought them to school, it will create a messy situation. Just keep them comfortable and well-hydrated. Anything you can get in them—popsicles, juice, water. Follow up with your regular pediatrician when they've passed. Do you have any questions for me? Concerns? If not, the nurse will be in to discharge you in a few minutes."

Sammie mutely shook her head and he left. Then, as a unit, we turned our attention to the man remaining in the room. Detective Antonio Desio.

Chapter Four

"Can you tell me what happened with the accident?" he asked.

"There's not much to tell, really. We were on North Point Boulevard by Eastpoint Mall, where their daycare is. I was fixin' to turn off the road—" Sammie turned to me to continue. "Oh, that reminds me, Laci, they weren't none too thrilled with me splitting the twins up like I told you this morning. They wanted me to take her with me if you could believe it, but I told them, 'Y'all, I can't manage them both at the doctor's office.' I mean, can you imagine what could have happened if Ana had been in the back? The car that hit me—hit me on her side. It would have been awful."

Sammie's face scrunched up, and she started crying just thinking about it. My gaze slid to Desio to see how he was taking it when his eyes met mine. He raised his eyebrows, and I rubbed Sammie's back in reassurance. I couldn't imagine what she was feeling.

"So, the car that hit you hit you on which side?" Desio asked.

"It was on my side in the back." She touched her bandaged head again and this time I noticed she blinked her eyes when she touched it.

"Is your head hurting?" I asked. "Did they give you something?"

"Yeah, they gave me some ibuprofen for the pain

when they wrapped it up. I swanny I don't know why I needed to come here in the first place, but here I am."

"Did you get a good look at the appearance of the other vehicle? Maybe color or size? Were you able to see the driver?" I asked. Desio turned to look at me and raised his eyebrows. "Or, you know, anything he wants to know," I mumbled, then waved in his direction.

"By all means, answer…" He turned back to me. "Why are you here again, Duvall?"

"Detective Desio, may I present Samantha Wheaton, my ex-husband's wife?"

For two beats he gave me a hard stare. *Uh*-oh I was busted. "You two are friends?" he asked.

"We're getting acquainted after news of his death." I glanced at Sammie, who was looking at the floor and biting her thumbnail. "Sammie showed up at my house yesterday, through an invitation from Zach."

He nodded while keeping his eyes steady on mine. Then he turned to Sammie. "I'm sorry for your loss, Mrs. Wheaton."

"Thank you. It's been quite a 48-hours. First, Zach is dead, and then to read his letter telling me to come to Laci's. Then Laci didn't want me, and then she did, and then she went and got us medicine at midnight last night. Then this morning we were on our way to the doctor and instead we got hit. I swanny y'all it's about more than a body can take." Her face scrunched up again, and more tears tracked down her face.

"Did you see the car?" he began again.

"It wasn't a car, actually," Sammie answered, wiping tears from her face. "It was a truck, but not one of those big ones. This one was older and smaller, and the color was gray, but there were bits of it missing, and you could see the rust underneath. My daddy had a car that he was rebuilding, and rust covered its back. Come to think of it—it may not have been gray at all. It could be the putty you put on when you're getting ready to paint it after covering up the rust—you know the stuff I mean?"

Desio glanced at me in confusion, and I could tell we were of one mind on this. I had no idea Sammie even knew what the stuff was.

"Anything on the driver Mrs. Wheaton?" he asked.

"He wore a green trucker hat with yellow letters and dark sunglasses like Laci has."

He glanced at me again, this time looking for an answer.

"Aviators," I volunteered.

"Okay, since I have you here, can I ask you some questions about your husband?" Sammie nodded, and he went on. "When was the last time you saw your husband alive?"

"Well, I think it was Saturday morning. I say Saturday because I remember asking him where he was going since it had been a while since he was gone on a weekend."

"Did he mention what the job was?" I asked.

"Oh, my lands, no; he never confided to me about his job. Said it felt like I was questioning his manhood. Y'all, if that don't beat all. I mean really, I'm his wife. Shouldn't I know what he's doing for his job?"

"When did he get back?" I asked.

"I don't know. His side of the bed looked slept in Saturday night, but it was empty when I woke up. I caught him in momma's kitchen when he was heading out the door. I just figured he was on another case. Is there any way to look it up and see what he was working on?"

She and Desio both turned to me for an answer.

"It's not as easy as all that since we're not based at the same location. My boss and I are getting in touch with Zach's commander, and Desio, I'll let you know if I find anything. Were you up with the twins any Saturday night, Sammie?" I asked.

"No, I haven't been up with them since they turned two. It's a dream not having to get up with them at night, I tell you what. Zach always complained when I asked him why he didn't get up with me in the middle of the night. I mean, he made them too, you know?"

"Did he have any friends in the area?" Desio asked.

"Not any that I knew of—he was kind of a loner, wouldn't you say, Laci?"

My mind went blank, but I scrambled for something to say. "He didn't have many when we were married. I think I can count on one hand the number of times we went out with friends. He never had anyone over either, at least none of the male variety." Desio's eyes bore into mine as he processed what I had just said. I could see him filling in the gaps and coming to conclusions. I wasn't going to slam Zach in front of Sammie though. Glancing past him at Sammie I could see I needn't have bothered with the code; she was staring off into space.

"Did you know of any enemies?" he asked. Sammie shook her head, and so did I when he looked at me. "Well, if you have any more information that you can remember, you can call me at my number. I'm glad you and your son weren't hurt." He handed her a card, which she took and stared at. He surveyed me head to toe, taking in my entire uniform. Then he parted the curtain and walked out.

"What did they do with your car?" I asked. We were waiting for the nurse that would come and release Sammie and Ry from the ER.

"It was towed. I called Daddy, and he's going to pick it up and take it to his house to look at."

"Speaking of your dad, why didn't he come to get you?" I asked.

Sammie gave me "the look," and I conceded. I was the better option.

The nurse came through the curtain a second later and let us go with written instructions of the doctor's orders. Sammie picked up Ryan, who had slept through the entire ordeal, and followed me as we snaked our way through the hallways to the entrance of the ER.

One step outside and I remembered why I hated outside. It was hot. It was humid. It was Baltimore in July. "I love my city. I love my city. I love my city," I mumbled when stepping into the sun, and it's a damn good thing I did, or I would have asked to be stationed in Alaska where it's cold.

"Do what now?" Sammie asked.

"It's nothing," I said, "just trying to remind myself why I'm here. Anyway, I'm way back there by the exit. Do you want to wait here, and I'll pick you and Ry up?"

"Oh pshaw, I'm fine. I got this." But it was clear she was anything but that. Halfway to the car, she switched Ryan to her other side and almost went down with him. I reached over to take him from her, but she turned away, with him in her arms. "Laci, I'm fine. I don't want you to get sick."

"Don't worry about me. I had chickenpox when I was a kid. My older sister brought them home from kindergarten and gifted them to me. Let me have him— you look ready to drop." He didn't weigh as much as I thought he would, and we weaved our way to my car in the heat. We were almost to it when I slammed to a halt. "Shit," I exclaimed.

Sammie bumped into the back of me and mumbled, "What?"

"No car seat."

"Ughhhhh." Sammie clapped both hands down on the top of her head, but we kept walking.

I moved Ryan to my left arm so I could pull my phone from my back pocket and opened it to contacts. Who on earth could I call that would have a car seat they could run over to me? The closer we got, the faster I scrolled and the more my anxiety grew as I ran through the list of people I knew who could bring me a car seat. Right before my row, I realized an angel was my new friend.

"What?" Sammie stepped out from behind me this time to avoid running into my back when I stopped in front of her again. She looked past me to where I was staring. "Holy cow."

"No kidding," I said.

"Where did it come from?"

"One guess? Cassy." I pulled the note off the car seat. " 'Figured you'd need this. C—' Now that's the understatement of the year. I'm dying for a sweet tea. Have you eaten this morning?"

"I wonder why no one stole it. I can't go in anywhere with Ryan." She buckled him into the backseat while I started the car. I cranked up the air in

41

the hopes of freezing my ass off in the next few minutes.

"Hello, drive-through? There's a Groovy Hen a few blocks away. How's that?"

She nodded, and I put the car in gear before pulling onto Route 7, headed for the Groovy Hen or Groov's for short. The drive-through lane was empty and littered with napkins, but I placed an order for a Hen in a Handbasket, three sides, and sweet tea all around. What? I was hungry.

Once we had our food, I pulled into a spot behind the restaurant and divvied up the goods. The grease on the chicken never failed to make me salivate and today was no different. I washed it all down with a swallow of sweet tea and took a minute to appreciate the flavors. One glance at Sammie found her staring into space with tears pooling in her eyes.

"What's wrong?" I asked. My mouth was again full of chicken, and I may have spit some on her leg, but I wasn't sure. The smell of grease filled the inside of the car, but Ryan slept through it all.

"Did Zach cheat on you?" she asked.

Blinking at her a few times gave me a minute to gather my thoughts. She surprised me—I didn't think she understood or even heard what I'd said in the hospital.

"Yes," I said.

"More than once?" she asked.

I nodded instead of a reply. My chicken turned heavy in my hand, and I dropped it with a thud in my lap. I wondered where she was going with this. After a minute of silence, I plunged in.

"Did he cheat on you, Sammie?" I asked.

"Yes," she whispered, "but he swore it was only the one time. I didn't believe him."

"I'm so sorry, Sammie. Was this before the twins or after?"

"Before," she said. "Momma and Daddy warned me not to marry him, but I did it anyway."

"Hunh—I think we both reached Zach with the same mindset." I huffed out a laugh. "Did you have a good wedding at least?" I asked.

"We got married in Vegas," she said. She sounded embarrassed.

"We went to the courthouse," I said. "Did you pick a fun wedding chapel?"

"The guy who married us looked like Elvis, but when Elvis wasn't looking too good toward the end, you know? Why?"

"Do you have your wedding license?" I asked.

"My what?" she asked.

"A wedding license," I said, "is what you sign to be able to get married."

She was shaking her head before I had finished. "I don't have one of those, and Zach never mentioned it. Why do you need it now?"

"Because it may also give us a clue why the ME's office called me and not you. Did you sign anything before you got married?" I asked. "Or after?"

"Yes," she sniffed. "I signed a prenup."

"A what? Zach made you sign a prenup?" I asked.

"Well, yes, he said he wanted you to sign one, but you refused."

I bit my lip. There had never been any such discussion between us. The only thing we took into the marriage was baggage and burdens. We eked out five years, but half of those we weren't living in the same house, let alone the same city.

Sammie realized the truth when I didn't say anything. "He didn't ask you to sign a prenup, did he?" I shook my head. "Why would he lie?"

"Now, that is a good question," I said. "Did Zach ever have people over to your apartment?"

She shook her head, blotting her tears with a paper napkin, then blowing her nose. "But then I wasn't always there; I worked part-time for half of the year."

"Did he never tell you what he did for his job?" I asked. "Did he talk about it at all?"

"He always told me the same thing: that it was top secret. Once, when the twins were babies, I tried to ask, but he got mad to the point where I was scared. He didn't like me questioning his word."

"Yeah, Zach never liked his authority questioned, which made our marriage so much fun. He didn't like to think of me as an equal at work and that carried over to his view of me at home. I don't know about you, but I'm ready to go back to the house. I want to trade this uniform in for a pair of shorts and my back porch," I said.

"Don't you have to go back to work?" Sammie asked.

"I called my boss on the way to the ER, and he told me to take the rest of the day to get done what was needed. I just need to be there early tomorrow."

My townhouse was around the corner from the hospital, so we were home in a few minutes. Sammie dropped me off, then took my car to pick up the car seat from her car at her parents' house, and then get Ana from daycare. We were in for a fun-filled few days.

Boo met me at the bedroom door with a meow when I went to let Needles out of his mini prison so he could go outside. The princess's bowl was empty, and she made sure I knew it. I changed clothes, let Needles out, then collapsed on the couch.

****

Babbling and a warm body woke me up. I cracked open my eyes and looked down into familiar blue ones, and a smile crossed my face. One glance at my watch told me I only slept an hour.

"Hiya, toots," I said. I hauled Ana up the rest of the way, and she sat with me when Sammie went upstairs with Ryan. Her thumb was in her mouth, and she fought to keep her eyes open.

Needles came in through the hanging screen on the back door with his tennis ball and dropped it at my feet, where it bounced across the floor. Ana thought that was funny and giggled around her thumb.

Needles brought me the ball again and I left-handed it across the room for him to go get it, which he did. He brought it back and dropped it again. This time I put it in Ana's hand, and she threw it, but instead, it bounced off my knee and bonked Needles on the head, and she giggled some more.

We were immersed in our game when Sammie came downstairs with an envelope. She pushed it into my hand and then sat across from me on the coffee table.

"This is what Zach gave me when we got married."

"Did you go with Zach to get the license before you were married?" I asked. I took the papers out and smoothed them against my shirt front next to Ana, then glanced the length of the page.

"No, he told me he would take care of it all," she said.

Damnit, Zach—how could you do this?

"That's bad, huh?" Sammie asked.

"In order to be married, you apply for a license. You said that Zach wanted to take care of everything, and while that's nice, he didn't take care of everything. So yes, the license is official, but it wasn't certified, which is required by law." I waited to see if she would figure it out on her own.

"So, what does that mean?" she asked.

"It means, according to the state of Maryland, you and Zach aren't married."

"But how can that be? We have Ana and Ryan. How is that possible? Are you sure?" She was firing questions at me but not waiting for an answer. Suddenly, she slapped her hands down on her lap. "No, it's not true. We were married. This right here tells me we were married." She snatched the papers from my hand and waved them in front of my face. "We were married at the top of the Eiffel Tower. With Elvis. We came down, and he and Zach signed everything, and Elvis told us we were good to go.

"No, he wouldn't do this to me." She plodded on. "You're just jealous because he loved me and not you. You should hear all the things he told me about you. You can tell me we weren't married until the cows come home, but I know better. I know we were married."

She snatched Ana from me and marched upstairs to their room without saying anything.

"What the hell just happened?" I asked Needles. He tilted his head and cocked his ears in question, but

Boo chose that moment to swat him. She took off running with him hot on her heels up the stairs where I heard him baying at her in my bedroom. She must have gotten where he couldn't reach her.

I didn't know what Zach chose to tell Sammie, but I gathered from that little tantrum that it wasn't good. That's fine with me; I had plenty to tell her about the dearly departed, but I was taking the high road. No matter how much it creamed my corn.

I sat debating whether to go and reason with Sammie when my phone went off in my bag on the hall table. Hauling myself up off the couch, I went to answer it.

"Special Agent Laci Duvall?" Dr. Mann asked before I spoke.

"Yes, this is she. How can I help you, Dr. Mann?"

"I'm sorry to bother you at home, but I needed to let you know that something has happened here at the office."

"What's wrong? Is everyone okay?"

"Yes, Major, we're fine. Unfortunately, someone broke into the lab overnight and stole all the files and photos of Special Agent Wheaton."

"Oh, shit."

"Yes, and that's not all."

"What the hell else could there be, Dr. Mann?" I demanded.

"Well, uh, Mr. Wheaton's body is currently MIA."

"*What*?" I screeched. "How the hell do you take off with a body?"

"Well, as for that, we don't know yet. We—"

"What about cameras?" I asked. "Forget that. Why are you just now telling me about this, Dr. Mann?"

"We've been trying to track him down to avoid this kind of conversation, Major Duvall. Whoever they are, they seemed to have known about the cameras and disabled them before removing Mr. Wheaton."

"Oh no, no, no, no, no." This couldn't be happening. I pushed my knuckle to my forehead to ward off my oncoming headache.

"Detective Desio informed me you know the whereabouts of Mrs. Wheaton. Do you know how I can get in touch with her?"

"I'll tell her."

"I think it'd b—" I hung up on him before he finished and raced up the steps. Skipping every other one, I broke the landing with my chin when I tripped and fell on the last stair.

Sammie opened her door the minute I fell. Ryan was in her right arm and Ana in her left, and there was a diaper bag slung over her right shoulder. Looped on the same arm carrying Ryan was a reusable grocery bag stuffed with clothes and diapers.

"Sammie, where are you going?" I hauled myself up and put my hands out to stop her from going down the stairs. "It doesn't matter. I need to tell you something."

"We're leaving. My parents are coming to pick us up."

"Sammie, wait…Sammie, I have to tell you something." She walked around my waving hands, and I put them down so I didn't smack one of the kids. I was desperately trying to get her to listen, but every time I called her name, she started singing the first line of "Nuthin' but a G Thang," and I stopped in my tracks in shock. *How the hell did she know Snoop Dogg?* She was still singing when she reached the bottom of the stairs and turned right for the front of the house.

She yanked open the door with enough force that she staggered a few steps. Once she recovered, she picked Ana up and sailed through the door with her chin held high.

Her parents were early, and her mother rushed to gather Ana from Sammie, while also giving me a look that should have filleted me alive. This brought me crashing back to reality. If she wanted to go—she could go. Zach never asked for my thoughts on his wife and children coming to my house—hell if I was going to make her stay if she didn't want to.

"Okay, Sammie, you have fun," I said. I waved her off, and her mother gave me the middle finger. *Wow.*

Chapter Five

Propped up at my desk the following afternoon, I gulped down sweet tea like a Bojangles test kitchen. I needed the medicine of caffeine and sugar to help me wake up—the silence at the house was deafening. Somehow, I had grown accustomed to the crying of toddlers and the baying of beagles. My heart missed them like crazy—especially Ana. When had she wound me around her little finger?

Last night, I was so lonely I wandered into Sammie's room and found a pacifier she'd left, and the bow Ana had stuck to her hair that first morning. I won't lie, I have the bow inside my chest pocket.

Every sound in the night had me jumping and peering out the window, while Boo snored on her pillow next to my head. Her little gray ass was ready to eat at four in the morning, and I told her where she could stick that perkiness.

A knock on the door was all the warning I got that someone was coming in before the door swung open. I swiveled away from the window I had been staring out and found Major Mitchell strolling through the door.

Major Keith Mitchell and I have worked together for three of my last five assignments as well as a deployment. He told everyone who would listen just how awesome he was, but his administrative skills were atrocious. Plus, he was always losing things. His keys, his Common Access Card (CAC), his hat—you name it.

In the world of sweet tea, Major Mitchell was the tea bag you used multiple times because it's your last one. I didn't like diluted tea and I didn't like Major Mitchell. He let his jealousy rule his head too many times in our relationship.

How did I know he was jealous? A few months ago, I got the Outstanding Special Agent of the Year for an Officer award, for the second time. Major Mitchell hasn't gotten it once. At the awards ceremony in his introduction to the speaker, he alluded to everyone in attendance that I only got it because I was female, and the Air Force felt compelled to give it to me because of it. Major Mitchell was second only to Zach in his hatred of losing to me. After that day we moved back to a semi-professional relationship, but I bite my tongue around him.

He was of average height while still being taller than me, and his eyes were brown like his hair, which was thinning on top. He was also going soft around the middle—all of this was a huge contrast to what I had seen with Desio yesterday. A rumor circulated a few months back that Mitchell's wife had left him and run off with an airman, but I didn't know how accurate that was.

"Colonel Waters wants to see you, so I thought I'd be the happy messenger," he said. He sported a car salesman smirk and rocked back on the heels of his boots while he waited for me to join him.

"I'll have to meet you there. I'm waiting on a phone call." I lied, but my phone dutifully rang anyway, and I fought the urge to appear surprised.

"I don't mind waiting," he said.

"It's a private call, so if you'll excuse me," I said.

Once out of my chair I paced him to the door, where I stood with my hand on the knob ready to close it once he was out. I stuck my head out the door to make sure he was gone then I closed and locked it before I ran back to my desk to answer my phone.

"Major Duvall."

"Hello, Major," Dr. Mann greeted me. "I wanted to let you know that we received a ransom note for Zach's body."

"Wait, what?"

"Yes, exactly. I'm suddenly questioning the intelligence of the people who took him. I wanted you to be aware they might contact you or his wife."

"Yeah, well, it turns out I'm the only wife he had," I mumbled.

"They weren't married?"

"Not unless there's a notarized marriage license we don't know about. Have you alerted Detective Desio of this new development?"

"I'm calling him next to catch him up on everything," he said. "When I get him back, I can get the death certificate ready for you then."

We hung up, and I made my way to Colonel Waters's office. I took a deep breath and knocked on the door—the bark from inside was my command to come in. Major Mitchell was already there, sitting across the desk from Colonel Waters.

"Have a seat, Major Duvall," Waters said, gesturing to the seat next to Mitchell. He stayed behind his desk and addressed us across it.

In what could have easily been an email, we spent over an hour processing the details surrounding Zach. I caught them up to date on the disappearance of his body and how Dr. Mann received a phone call trying to ransom his body.

"Who is the lead detective on the case?" Mitchell asked.

"His name is Desio. He's a veteran with the BPD. If anyone can get it done, it's him," I said.

"How do you know that?" Mitchell asked.

"I just know." He stared at me as if he didn't believe me and I honestly didn't care. Colonel Waters knew my association with Desio and he's the only one who mattered.

****

My townhouse sat about fifty yards off the main road so it's hard to miss when things are different in the yards. Today it happened to be a blonde with two kids camped out on my front porch.

Ana was ecstatic to see me and toddled over and raised her arms for me to pick her up. Once she was up, she wrapped her legs around my waist and assumed the position—this time laying her head on my shoulder and putting her thumb in her mouth. Everything in me turned to goo in an instant. I'd missed this.

"Hi, Sammie, how come you're back?" I asked.

"Momma didn't cater to Ryan and Ana's noise, so she threw us out." This last part came out in a mumble. I knew it must have cost her a lot to come back, so I didn't rub it in.

"How long have you been here? Come on in. Everything's in the same place it was when you left." I picked up her new suitcase, and she followed me into the house with the car seats. "How's Ryan feeling?"

"Momma had to get her hair done so she left us out

here a few minutes ago. Ryan's fine, though the spots have started showing up, bless his heart. Momma swore he had the plague or something despite how many times I told her what it was. She said there ain't no such thing as chicken pops, except in the grocery store, whatever that meant. I tried to reassure her they were an actua—"

"Pox," I said. "Chickenpox."

"Ain't that what I said?"

"No, you said pops. No wonder your mother was confused."

I put the suitcase at the bottom of the stairs and set Ana beside it. She shot off for Needles and reached over the kitchen gate to pat his head. I put him back in the kitchen this morning since no one was there.

"Anyway, I assured her they were an actual thing, and she got upset with me for bringing them into her house. It's not like I didn't tell her about it before she came to get us, but I think that, along with his crying, was too much for her. Daddy just putters around in the garage and the yard and ignores everything else. He's been like that since I was little, though. Except when Zach and I lived with him; then he would sit in his room and watch TV. It was weird."

"Did you talk to them about Zach and the wedding stuff?" I asked.

I plopped down on the sofa with Sammie next to me. She faced me with hunched shoulders and downcast eyes. "Daddy yelled at me, and he ne-ver raises his voice. I showed him what I had, and he said all sorts of not-nice things. Momma just tells me I spent my years living in sin with the same breath she talks about how much of a b-word you are."

"You don't believe her, do you? About either of

54

those things?" I snorted.

She looked at me like I'd grown a head in front of her and we burst out laughing.

"I swanny you should have heard her," Sammie said. "She ranted for a good ten minutes about Zach and his character. Then she started on you, and I got up and left. I mean, we're not friends, but I hope we can be, you know? You've been nothing but great to me. I mean look at today. Even after I stormed off in a huff you took me back in without rubbing my nose in it."

"I think we're going to be good friends. Are you okay if we talk about Zach for a second? Again? First, I have to tell you something, and then can you answer a few more questions I have?" Ryan climbed in her lap, and Ana moved to pat Needles on the living room floor. He was in heaven with all the attention. "I got a call from the Baltimore City Medical Examiner's Office yesterday. I tried to tell you before you left, but there was some miscommunication at the time."

She gave me a rueful smile, and I knew she remembered ignoring my attempt at talking to her on her way out the door.

"You know, you'll have to tell me how you know the words to that song sometime." I grinned as she laughed. "Anyway, the ME called me to tell me that Zach's body is missing. Someone came in and stole it."

Sammie's mouth fell open in surprise, and then thunder crossed her face.

"They what!" she shouted. Ryan covered his ears with his hands and Sammie brought her voice down an octave. "How in the Sam Hill do you lose a person? I mean, it's not like he's a small book that you can misplace—this is an actual person. They ain't small. I swanny, when I get my hands on that Medical Example, I'm going to come un—"

"Examiner—Medical Examiner," I corrected, and then she turned the thunder my way. I lifted my hands in mock surrender. "The ME's office has already received a ransom phone call asking for money to get him back."

"They did what now?" she asked. Ryan crawled off her lap and joined Ana in mutual adoration of Needles.

"The people that took him are asking for money for his return," I said. "Do you know why anyone would take him?"

"Not that I know of, but I'm beginning to see there was a lot about him I didn't know," Sammie said. "I can see now that I trusted him too much, and he took advantage of that trust. I think that's what upsets me the most; I trusted him, and he lied to me."

"I bet from here on out you'll be able to spot the same in someone else and more than likely will have learned your lesson. We do a lot of stupid things when we're in love, and I'm just as guilty as anyone."

"I bet you made sure your license was signed and certified, though," Sammie mumbled.

"Yeah, but I trusted him with money. I paid bills with an empty bank account more times than I can count. He was always bad with it and spent it like it was growing on trees. That's what most of our fights were over. As two lieutenants in the Air Force, we brought in quite a bit every month, but we had nothing to show for it. He would also go to those payday loan places and borrow at astronomical interest rates, where paying it off would be more than the original loans. Oh, yes, I learned many hard lessons, but just because mine were different, doesn't mean they weren't any less embarrassing."

****

Ryan was currently in the middle of chicken pox. Ana got them but Sammie didn't—at least not yet. Last night was especially rough with all the crying he was doing. Sammie tried to let Ana sleep by taking him downstairs, but sound carried in the house, and he was just as loud downstairs as he was upstairs.

It was because of this that I sat with my elbows on my desk, leaning my head in my hands, and downing sweet tea like it was the answer to all my problems. The knock at the door jarred me out of my haze and I turned bleary eyes to Major Mitchell approaching my desk.

I squelched a groan when Colonel Waters, hot on his heels, strode in next. I stood up for Colonel Waters, and my eyes stayed on him. I wasn't sure if his surly expression was for Mitchell or me.

"Good morning, Colonel Waters, sir," I said.

"I wish to God it was," he grumbled. "I have been given a reprimand that you and Major Mitchell are working too slowly on this thing with Special Agent Wheaton. It came down from Quantico. We need to haul ass if we're going to find out what's happened. Moses and Mary Magdalene, Major, we should have known yesterday where he was and what the kidnappers want. Do I need to step in and take over?"

"I know there are many things on your plate right now, sir, and I don't want to add to it. Major Mitchell and I can put our heads together to learn everything we can. We'll let you know the second we have something."

"Have you been able to speak to the detective in

charge?" Colonel Waters asked.

"I keep calling him, sir," I said.

"Sir, if Major Duvall is too busy to be the lead on the case, I'll be more than happy to spearhead it," Major Mitchell said. He turned his car salesman smile on Colonel Waters, and it was all I could do not to growl at him.

"We only met on this yesterday, sir, I need a little more time. I have called Detective Desio and will again once you leave. I'll be prepared to meet on this in another day or two. Would you be available for a meeting of information exchange early next week, sir?"

"I can do tonight," Mitchell said.

I stared at him for a heartbeat. Did he even listen when I talked? "I suggest first thing on Monday morning." I turned toward Colonel Waters to finish. "We can meet in the conference room and exchange information there."

Colonel Waters nodded, then he and Major Mitchell turned and left my office. Major Mitchell looked at me over his shoulder while he walked down the hallway. I didn't know what that was about, but instead of dwelling on him, I marked the meeting down on my calendar, then got to work funneling emails into lists.

They say hindsight is 20/20 and I see the wisdom in that now. I wish Zach and I had stayed in touch more—maybe then I would have a better answer for Colonel Waters and Sammie. Like maybe the answer to who would take his body and what they wanted with it? Did they expect money? Did they expect government information? Maybe Zach had something they wanted. Sammie didn't know anything and neither did I, so who would know?

I straightened in my chair. His parents?

Running with that, I picked up my phone and dialed Desio. Luckily, he was there this time, and after a bit of convincing, he finally agreed to let me come along when he went to see Zach's parents tonight. I told him I could give insight into them and if they were telling the truth. Time would tell if mine was the lie or theirs.

There was no sign of Colonel Waters or Major Mitchell when I left the office later. I wasn't intentionally avoiding them, but they had questions I didn't know the answers to. Yet.

Needles met me at the front door when I walked in the house from work; he was getting spoiled by being out during the day. Ana also greeted me at the front door with her thumb glued to her mouth. I grinned and reached down to pick her up, and she giggled when I tossed her above my head.

I walked into the kitchen with Ana settled on my hip, where Sammie stood at the stove. "Has she always been a happy baby?" I asked.

"Oh yes." She turned and smiled at Ana. "I swear she came out grinnin'. Ryan, bless his heart, has always tended toward the hangdog. So, that's how I knew he was Zach's."

"Did he question whether they were his or not?" I asked.

"Not to me, he didn't." An interesting response.

"Do you have their birth certificates with him named as father?" She turned back to the stove and wouldn't look me in the eye. "Sammie? Who's listed as their father?"

"I didn't know when they were born, whether we would be together much longer," she mumbled. "We hit a rough patch, and Zach kept threatening to leave me. We did the DNA test after the twins were born, which showed him as their daddy. I never went back to get his name added to it." She gushed to finish, then finally turned to face me.

"Well, it's nice to know I divorced him for a good reason—it doesn't sound like he improved after I left him," I said. "Speaking of Zach, guess who I get to go see tonight?"

At her blank look, I filled her in on my visit to Zach's parents.

"Oh, Gawd," she groaned, "please don't make me talk to them. More highfalutin a folks I have yet to meet, I swanny."

"Don't feel bad—they hated me, too. We're hoping to find out what kind of things he was into that may have led to someone killing, kidnapping, and now ransoming him. I asked Desio if they had any leads on where to find Zach, but he's drawing a blank too. The only one to be contacted so far is Dr. Mann, and he didn't get anything we could use to find him. On top of all this, my boss lectured me today that I'm moving too slowly and need to make progress asap, or he'll find someone else to run the case. There's nothing I want less than another agent trying to figure this out. We don't need the drama."

"What's your relationship with the detective?" she asked. She blindsided me with her question.

"What do you mean?"

"There's obviously a history between ya'll. I mean the air vibrates when you two are in the same room."

"I think you're imagining things," I said. Now it was my turn to avoid looking her in the eyes. I set Ana down and trudged up the stairs and Needles ran up in front of me, but I sent him back down with the kids. They would run him out, so he slept tonight.

I flopped across the bed without taking off my uniform. Taking a shower could wait until later. Boo jumped on the bed, with a question in her meow, and curled up on her pillow at my head.

Zach highly underestimated females, and Sammie was no different. Is that all he thought of her? Just a weak female who couldn't fend for herself. *Boy, was he wrong.* I would have to watch myself around her. There was more to her than met the eye.

****

Something was tickling my ear. I turned my head to the other side, but it continued on that side, too. Somewhere in my mind, it occurred to me what it was. Or rather who it was. Boo. It was her reminder that her food bowl was currently empty. I jostled her off and she hopped on the floor and went into the bathroom where her bowl was.

Trailing after her, I fed her then jumped in the shower to get ready to go meet my ex-husband's parents alongside my ex-boyfriend. *Oh boy.*

I settled on black pants and heels with a black tank covered by a black lace T-shirt. All in all, not workwear, but also not something his mother would find offensive, though I'm sure she'd try.

My curly hair went up into a messy bun with respect to the humidity that came with a Baltimore summer. Then I grabbed my shoes and headed downstairs.

Ryan was on his toes beside the couch trying to reach Boo when I came down; she was hissing at him. "I wouldn't do that if I were you, Ryan," I said. He turned to look at me with a huge grin behind his pacifier—or sucker as Sammie called it. Boo took the opportunity and was off like a shot—racing back upstairs and under the bed more than likely.

"You ready to see Janis and Floyd?" Sammie asked. She sat on the floor in the living room with Ana, bowling with a ball and some plastic bottles. Her voice held laughter, but her face only showed concern.

"No amount of dressing up can get me ready enough for them," I said, "but I'm trying my best. You have my cell phone number. Call if there's an emergency."

I waved to Lisa, my next-door neighbor as I left my parking spot in front of my house. The Bradleys were from Ohio and Georgia and had a little girl named Rosemary. Lisa stopped over when I first moved in and brought banana bread, which I admit I scarfed down standing over the kitchen sink. Don't judge. It was really good.

Her gift was a reminder of life when I lived in base housing and a next-door neighbor brought over blueberry muffins when I moved in. Things like that were a regular occurrence on base, so it was nice to experience it with my first home off base.

Chapter Six

Zach's parents lived on a golf course and had ever since I'd known them. His dad, Floyd, played every other day and probably was just as bad at it now as he was then. His mother, Janis, wasn't the warm, nurturing type—instead, she spent her time with friends at the clubhouse. Neither one touched alcohol and looked down on people who drank even the smallest amount. Which, of course, was why Zach went off the deep end when he left home.

Joining the military had settled Zach down a little, but there always seemed to be darkness lingering right under the surface. I tried to remember what it was that attracted me to Zach in the first place. He won the lottery in the looks department. Trouble was, he knew it. Women constantly hounded him. When we first got married it made him uncomfortable, but the longer and further between our living together, the more comfortable and encouraging he got with it.

Desio and I were meeting at Glendale Park where I would leave my car and ride over with him. Pulling into the lot I saw him in his ancient work sedan which they should have retired when Mayor Schaefer did.

"Riding in style tonight, I see, detective." I leaned down to the open passenger window and peered at him propped up in the corner of the driver's seat.

His mouth twitched the same way I had seen

hundreds of times before, and it still affected me like it always did. It was odd to feel butterflies again at my age. He watched around us, his eyes taking in and cataloging everything he saw. I knew he was doing it because I saw that same look on myself.

The sun was moving to the west of us behind the park where parents wrangled kids and settled them in car seats, while other families rode home on bicycles on this sticky night in Charm City. My suit jacket stuck to me in the heat the instant it met the faux leather seats in the sedan.

This took me back to the numerous times Desio and I sat in the front seat of his old car. He drove his dad's old sedan back in the day and there were many times we cursed the center console.

"What's the rundown on Zach's parents?" He brought me out of my trance with a thud back into reality. Oh yeah. My ex-husband.

"It's tough summing them up in a few sentences— you have to experience them to see it yourself. They're polite, but not nurturing, which means I don't expect them to show any emotion about the loss of Zach. The only thing we *will* see is hostility at the sight of me. We didn't get along very well. So, don't expect them to give answers voluntarily."

Desio displayed his uncanny ability of raising one eyebrow to express surprise without saying anything. He probably remembered how much his family loved me.

"Glad you brought me along?" I grinned.

"Sometimes it takes getting them off-center with the unexpected to get anywhere."

I nodded my head, recognizing a tactic I used to

my advantage on several occasions. It helped to surprise people sometimes. They say things they wouldn't ordinarily say when you shake them up.

"Are you nervous?" he asked.

"N— Why?" I asked.

"Because you're bouncing your leg so much, I'm worried you've worn out my carpet," he said.

I cut my eyes to him, but he didn't look at me, and I stopped the motion of my leg.

"It's no secret that Zach's parents didn't want him to marry me," I said. "They had someone else in mind, but he saw it as a chain to them, so he asked me. For all his faults, it wasn't his that I said yes." I knew I was opening old wounds, but it needed to be said. "I don't know what Zach told them about us. I only know that I signed the divorce papers a few miles from here, and while he crashed at his parents' house before his next assignment, I went back to an emptied-out house in San Antonio."

We followed traffic to the turn-off for the front gate of the golf club community in silence. Desio gave the guard the information of where we were going, and yes, they were expecting us.

The houses on the course were well groomed and large, and the Wheatons' house was no exception. Georgian majesty clashed with modern vibes at the top of their circular drive. Wings, the same white as the house, settled on the lawn to the left and right of the main building. The windows were sparkling and edged with shiny black shutters that matched the black double doors on the front of the house. Behind the house would be the empty mother-in-law suite in addition to the pool and cabana. They had all this house, and it was just the two of them living there.

Hexagonal pink bricks greeted us on our walk to the front door, where Desio knocked and then rang the doorbell. I looked at him with amusement which he caught and did his eyebrow thing.

"You're one of those, huh?" I asked.

"One of what?"

"You could just ring the doorbell, but you choose to knock *and* ring the doorbell. You don't have to do both," I said. My grin stretched from one side of my face to the other. I don't know why this struck me as funny; it just did. Maybe it was nerves, but whatever it was, I let out a snort, and Desio swung his head to look at me. Which made it even funnier, so I snorted again. All the while he didn't even crack a smile.

A maid opened the door during my brief dip into insanity, and Desio did the formalities. He placed his hand on my back and guided me inside when she gestured for us to enter. I fought the shivers that threatened me to my toes. He hadn't touched me in twenty years, but my body remembered it.

The wood floor was covered with a large Persian rug in blue and ivory hues. Delicate instrumental music played from small speakers in the wide entryway where an ivory-colored round table stood sporting a gigantic bouquet of coral roses. I couldn't resist a sniff, so I leaned over and inhaled. The smell hit my senses at once, and my eyes flew open, where Desio's gaze met mine.

I snapped to attention and followed him and the maid into the study where Zach's parents were waiting for us. This room always reminded me of the studies I'd read about in my Victorian romance novels growing up.

I could picture the hounds lounging by the fire in the middle of a snowstorm on some far-off English country estate.

The ceiling was high, and the bookshelves ran all the way to the top. There was a nifty ladder that ran the course of the room and was tall enough to reach the top shelf. Zach and I played on that thing one afternoon and when his parents walked in on us, you'd have thought we were the antichrist instead of the twenty-year-olds we were.

Floyd stood by the fireplace at one side of the study, and when he saw me, he pulled himself upright in dismay. Janis caught sight me of at the same time and gasped from the wingback chair she was ruling from beside the window that faced the golf course. Not exactly the English countryside, but it worked for them.

"Thank you for seeing us, Mr. and Mrs. Wheat—" Desio began.

"We agreed to see you, Detective; we did not agree to see her." Floyd's jaw was clenched as tight as his ass was.

"I understand your concerns, but in this, I need the insight I get from Special Agent Duvall if I'm going to discover what's happened to your son."

Desio led me to the couch and sat next to me. You could feel the resentment in the air, and it showed in how they held themselves and watched me with contempt.

"Please tell me everything you remember from the last time you saw Zach," Desio asked.

"Detective, we have not seen Zach in several years, so I fail to understand what that has to do with this?" Floyd said.

"When was the last time you saw him?" Desio asked.

"I can't recall the exact date, detective, just that it's been a few years."

"Was it before the twins were born?" I asked.

Nothing. No acknowledgment that I spoke or anything. Though I did see a muscle twitch in Floyd's jaw. So, I knew he heard me.

Desio waited to see if they would answer but after a minute he pressed on.

"What friends did Zach have in this area?" Desio asked.

"Zach had no friends outside of his wife and children," Floyd said.

"No friends?" Desio asked.

Janis opened her mouth to speak, but Floyd froze her with a look. "No," Floyd said.

"Any extended family? Cousins? Uncles?" Desio pressed.

Floyd shook his head but didn't speak.

"Okay, what about his enemies?" Desio asked.

"The only enemy we knew about is your associate there," Floyd said.

"Hey—" I began.

"Let's just keep to the task at hand," Desio said. I couldn't tell if he was talking to them or me.

Floyd flicked a disgusted glance at me, then addressed Desio. "He didn't speak of his job with the government to us, and we never asked."

"So, you didn't know what his current case was?" I asked. Floyd ignored me again and kept his eyes on Desio, who didn't bother to wait to see if he would answer this time.

"Zach's body has been removed from the Baltimore City Medical Examiner's office. Did you know about that?" Desio asked.

Janis opened her mouth to speak, but nothing came out. Floyd wasn't so shocked. "Are you accusing us of stealing our own son? Why would we take him when we could have easily had him legally removed in the first place? Why don't you ask Ms. Special Agent of the Year here, what she did with him? Her kind has ways of disposing of inconveniences."

I opened my mouth to respond but was too shocked to say anything. I didn't even know they knew about my award. Desio had no such hesitation—he knew exactly what he wanted to say.

"Are you finished?" Desio demanded. He laced his voice with the steel I always dreaded. "I asked because the ME's office has received a ransom phone call, and I wondered if you had."

"I'm going to go use the restroom," I said to no one in particular. I stood up, purse in hand, and left the study for the hallway, where it was quiet. The only sound was my heels tapping on the hardwood floor. Once in the hallway, I stepped onto the large Persian rug, hoping to disguise my steps so they didn't know where I went. I aimed for the kitchen to see what I could discover there.

The voices faded behind me, and when I entered the kitchen, the maid was polishing silverware. Her gaze met mine and her hands stilled on a fork.

"I just needed a drink of water. Is the sparkling water still in here?" I asked.

She nodded her head but didn't say anything. I grabbed the bottle from the stainless-steel fridge and cracked it open then sat at the bar in front of her. I used my persuasive voice to see what I could get out of her.

"Have you been with the Wheatons long?" I asked.

After a moment's hesitation, she nodded but didn't speak.

"Did you know Zach?"

She cautiously nodded again, still not taking her eyes off what she was doing.

"Have you seen him around here recently?"

She shook her head immediately.

"Do you like working here?"

She didn't answer.

"I didn't mean to put you on the spot. I'm sorry." I finished up my water and placed the bottle on the counter. "I don't know what they do with the bottles when they're empty."

She put the rag and fork down, grabbed the bottle, and took it to the corner of the room, where she opened a door and placed it with a bunch of other things.

"I'll just be going. If you ever feel like talking, here's my number." I placed my card on the counter next to the silver, then turned and made my way back to the study, where the drone of voices was still going.

While I crossed the threshold of the room, my phone went off in my bag. I reached in to answer it, fumbled, and dropped it on the wooden floor of the study. The Indiana Jones theme song rang through the room and off the chandelier which hung over the room. Bending down, I picked it up and hit connect and speaker at the same time by accident. I put it up to my ear, but it came out over the speaker.

"Laci Duvall, is this you? Damnit, woman, where the hell are you?"

"Cassy? What's wrong?" I asked. I fumbled with the phone, trying to get it off the speaker, but instead, I turned off the screen.

"What the hell do you think is wrong? I got the chickenpox, woman."

I snorted.

"What was that noise?" she asked.

"I'm sorry, Cassy," I said. Laughter was bubbling up, and I couldn't keep it in, and it erupted in little hiccups and snorts. I tried again to turn off the speaker, only I dropped it again, and this time it slid across the floor. Cassy was still speaking while I chased it to the coffee table in front of Janis.

"Are you laughing at me? You and that crazy-ass woman gave me chickenpox, and my roommate kicked me out until they gone. What's your address? Imma come live whichu until they done. They won't even let me work, man."

I finally snatched the phone up, rattled off my address, and turned it off. Then I glanced at the faces in front of me. *Yikes*.

"I believe we're finished," Floyd said with a sniff.

"Thank you for your time, Mr. and Mrs. Wheaton," Desio said. He grabbed me by the elbow and propelled me down the hallway. You could hear our shoes reverberating on the floor as we skirted the rug on our way out.

He hustled me to the car, but I couldn't tell if he was upset or just in a hurry to get out of there. I had the insane thought of what did he think seeing the parents of the man I married instead of him.

I went around to my side, and Desio followed to open my door. I slid in and shut the door while he got in his side and cranked the engine over. No sooner was his seatbelt on than he put it in gear, and we hauled ass out of the neighborhood.

"I'm sorry about that," I said. The silence was unbearable, and I needed to know if he was angry with me.

He looked at me, but his eyes were unfocused. "About what?"

"About what? Did you miss that part where I had a crazy woman ranting at me on my phone?"

"No, that would be hard to miss," he said. "What's going on? Who was that?"

"You remember the other day at the ER when Sammie was recovering from her accident? Well, that brief interlude with Officer Cassandra Davis apparently was enough for her to get chickenpox." I couldn't help it, and giggled again, but I brought myself under control by recalling the house we'd just left. "I don't think I was much help tonight, aside from entertainment value. Did you learn anything from them that's important?"

"How do you know Officer Davis?" he asked.

"I met her the first night Sammie was here when I had to go get medicine for Ryan right before midnight."

"I won't be sure until I check, but I think they gave me some ideas," he said.

He'd always done this—hopped around to different subjects, leaving me to play catch-up. You'd think I was used to his silence, but it seemed like whenever I wanted him to talk, he stayed quiet, and when I wanted quiet is when he wanted to chat. Now was no exception, and I waited for him to tell me what it was he learned. He stared out the window as we pulled up beside my car while I stared at him…waiting. Then, finally, he glanced at me in surprise and saw me watching him.

"You going to tell me what it was they said?" I asked.

"It wasn't what was said, but rather what was left unsaid."

"Well, that clears it up for me," I said with an eyeroll. His mouth twitched, but he still didn't elaborate. "I guess that's my cue. When you decide to divulge, you know where to find me."

"Have you eaten?" he asked when I reached for the handle to get out.

I turned toward him in surprise. "Today, or just tonight?" I slapped my forehead. *Ugh.*

He just fixed his gaze on me and didn't blink.

"No, I haven't eaten, but I have a woman with chickenpox on her way to my house, and the only one there is the one who gave it to her. I need to head home to foil her plans of killing the other one," I said, with laughter in my voice.

"You lead an interesting life, Special Agent Duvall."

"Oh, you don't know the half of it, Detective Desio. Can I give you a rain check?"

He nodded, and I reached to let myself out.

"Was he good to you?" Desio asked.

I wasn't surprised he asked. It had been between us since I saw him standing in the coroner's room peering at Zach, and in every conversation since.

"He tried," I said. "I'm sure you would have done better, but that's the choice I made."

My words dropped into the intimacy of the car like small grenades. I glanced at him to see his reaction. When there was none, I got out, walked to my car, and slid in. I rested my forehead on the steering wheel and expelled the breath I had been holding in all night. Then, raising my head, my eyes collided with Desio's, and the hairs on the back of my neck rose. Instead of jumping him like I wanted to, I lifted my hand to wave and pulled from the spot.

Traffic on the beltway was usually sparse this time of night and tonight was no exception. That was fine by me—it kept them out of my way. I thought back to the brief conversation I'd listened to at the Wheatons' and wondered what had been said or unsaid after I left.

I met Zach's parents at brunch at the country club on the golf course that borders their backyard. Halfway through the meal, we told them we were getting married, and it went downhill from there. What I told Desio was true—they planned someone else for Zach, someone who could add to their already fat bank account, and I wasn't it.

As for Desio's question, the very fact that he asked it led my mind and heart to a place I'm not ready to go yet.

Chapter Seven

A white, two-door classic muscle car sat parked in front of my house, with no one home. I entered the house expecting World War III, but instead, there was a whole different kind of excitement going on.

Cassy and Sammie were at war all right, but it wasn't the kind I thought it would be. Instead, they were playing some sort of video game where they got to shoot targets with the other's face on it. The twins must have been in bed because I didn't see them anywhere.

"What are you two doing?" My voice carried over the din of the TV noise, and the two partiers screamed and dropped their remotes at the same time, in their effort to protect themselves. Cassy looked like she was ready to karate chop me while Sammie was rigid with fear. "We have got to work on your self-defense skills."

Needles came to greet me, and I bent down to say hello with a rub of his velvet ears and a cold nose to my palm.

"How'd it go?" Cassy asked, and I raised my eyebrows in question. "Sammie here done told me what's been going on."

I shrugged. "Okay, I guess. I didn't stay for the entire conversation, and Desio wasn't forthcoming with information. He asked me if I had eaten, but I told him I needed to be here to prevent World War III, but I see my anxiety was for nothing."

"He asked you on a date?" Sammie asked. Cassy let out a whistle in response to Sammie's statement.

"I thought I sensed something in that hospital room," Cassy said.

"No, I think he wanted to compare notes on the information we had gathered, but Zach's parents are Zach's parents. You remember how they were, don't you, Sammie?" She nodded, and I was off and running. "They pretended I wasn't there the entire time, and when I did ask them a question, Floyd ignored me. We sat there in awkward silence waiting for him to answer, but nothing. I zoned out after that and left the room. Found the maid and tried to talk to her with no success.

"I was back in the study when I answered Cassy's phone call but pushed the speaker button by accident, and then I dropped my phone." I giggled, just thinking about it again. "While I tried to get it off the speaker, you could hear Cassy cursing at me." I snorted. "Then I dropped it again, and it slid into the middle of the room. I chased after it and picked it up and finally got it off the speaker, but the damage was done." When I finished, we looked at each other and burst out laughing.

"How did you get the pox so fast, Cassy?" I recovered enough to ask her.

"Member the doc tellin' us he seen cases of it a lot this summer? Turns out my nieces had it when I seen them a coupla weeks ago. My doctor gave me a shot this morning to help with the symptoms. I tried to tell my roommate that, but she wasn' havin' it."

Well then. "All right, ladies, since that visit drained me, I'm going to bed. You guys can continue to party if you want to. Cassy, I have a spare bedroom with a yoga mat. Will that work for the time being? It's a room with a door that locks out toddlers, and you can sleep in tomorrow."

"Sounds great; count me in, coach. I got my lotion right here," Cassy said. She patted the polka-dot bag at her hip, which I assumed carried all her gear.

Sammie turned off the TV, and we headed to our separate rooms. I put Needles in the kitchen, where he plopped on his bed and let out a loud sigh. Upstairs in my room, Boo raised her head off the pillow and gave me the evil eye.

I brushed my teeth, but I was asleep before my head hit the pillow. I was instantly awake when my phone rang, though. I looked at the time—2:30 a.m.

"Hello?" I grunted.

"You want your husband back?"

The fog cleared instantly. "Actually, I'm not married." I played along to see what they'd say.

"Yeah, you are. I got your husband right here."

"Well, I have divorce papers that say otherwise. Who the hell is this?"

"What—she says she ain't married to him." I heard muffled voices in the background. Glancing at the number, I took a screenshot before I hung up on him.

I figured I'd given him enough to think about, so I turned the volume off on my phone, closed my eyes, and went back to sleep.

"Lac—" My fist connected with something. "*Owww,*" Sammie howled.

I snapped the bedside light on and found Sammie standing a foot from the bed, with her hand clasped over her nose. She was blinking her eyes trying to clear the tears.

"What are you doing in here?" I asked. "Oh, hush, I didn't hit you that hard."

"Someone called me and said they had Zach." It came out all nasally as she bent her nose back and forth. "I told them we weren't officially married, and they said, 'what the hell is up wit' you dames? I got the body of a guy named Zach who I thought was married, but now he ain't?' I tried to find out why he had him in the first place, but he hung up on me. So, what's going on?"

She did a surprisingly good copy of the man I spoke to earlier. "I'll explain in the morning. There's nothing to worry about tonight."

I lay back down once she was gone and was soon back to sleep, but four in the morning found Boo up again, only this time she was meowing at the window from the bottom of the bed. I threw a pillow at her, but she didn't budge, which I knew wasn't typical behavior for her, so I got up to look.

A black SUV was sitting beside the mailboxes with their parking lights on. After watching them for a few minutes, I shrugged and climbed back into bed. Boo was fed up with the disruption to her beauty sleep and took off for parts unknown. I burrowed under the comforter and tried hard to get to sleep, but now my mind was spinning.

We received our first ransom call, and I had a number I could use to track them back to Zach. I needed to call Desio and fill him in on the latest development. Desio...my mind drifted to the question of whether he was asking me out on a date or if it was business, and with that in mind, I fell into a dreamless sleep.

****

A noise from the front door interrupted my getting the toaster from under the counter the following morning, so I stuck my head around the corner. The flurry continued as Sammie came through the front door pushing the kids in a tandem stroller, and the scream I heard was Ryan laughing and giggling when Sammie tickled him.

"You're awake," she said when she spotted me in the kitchen. "I thought you could use the quiet this morning."

Once Sammie released Ana from her cushy prison, she ran to me, and I swung her up in my arms while she giggled. The three of them resembled cheetahs, with their light-pink spots matching perfectly.

"How was the park?" I asked.

"It was good. Nice and quiet this time of the morning, and the heat isn't too bad yet," she said. "Though the people there kinda gave us the side-eye."

I laughed and went to answer my phone with Ana in my arms. "Major Duvall."

"Listen, lady, I got this body, and you gotta take it."

"But I don't want it—you keep him." I figured it couldn't hurt to play devil's advocate to see what information I could get.

"No, no—no, no, no. You're supposed to want him back," he said. "Why don't you want him back?"

"Why did you take him?" I asked.

"How's it that I go from two wives to demand money from—to begging someone to take him? I ain't got time for this lady." He didn't answer my question.

"Wait, his second wife didn't want him?" I asked.

I stepped into the living room, placed Ana on the floor, then gestured for Sammie to come here. Ana toddled off to pet Needles, and I held my finger up to my lips to keep Sammie quiet while she approached; then, I pressed for speakerphone.

"Naw, she said they wasn't technically married, whatever the hell that means. Listen, lady, how bout I give you a deal? How bout I pay you to take him back?"

"You'll pay me to take him back? How much?" I asked. I glanced at Sammie who was chewing on her bottom lip looking worried. I laid my hand on her arm to reassure her.

"I think I can spare a grand," he said.

"You're kidding, right?" Disappointed and amused despite myself. "You know how much it costs for funerals these days?"

"Yeah, yeah, considering what he took from me, the most I could swing is two grand, take it or leave it."

"Took from you? What do you mean?" I asked.

"You mean you don't know?" he asked.

"Why the hell would I ask you if I already knew?" I asked. Instead of the reply I wanted, I got the dial tone. I asked Sammie, "What does he mean took from him?"

"Beats me," Sammie shrugged.

"Did Zach ever mention owing somebody something?"

"Mmm, not really, but like I said before, there was a lot he didn't share with me. He said it was better if I didn't know. I thought he was talking about y'all's jobs."

My toast popped up just then, and I went to the

kitchen to get it. What could Zach possibly have taken from someone? Was this a case from work, or was it personal?

"Is Cassy up?" I asked.

"Her roommate called and told her someone was waiting for her at the apartment," Sammie said. "I don't even know who they are, but why are they paying us to take Zach back? I really would like him back, you know."

"Did the roommate say who it was?"

Sammie shrugged. "If they did, she didn't say."

"We're going to get Zach back, I promise. I want them to sweat for a bit, so they'll be more forthcoming with information. Only now I've got more questions."

I grabbed my bag, got my tea, and bid Sammie goodbye. It was Friday, and the empty end-of-week reports I needed to get done called my name. I also wanted to find out what Zach's current caseload was.

I mulled over this new information while I made my way to the office. Colonel Waters was in his when I walked past, and I could hear him yelling at Staff Sergeant Ballou. "Cheese and grits, sergeant, I could find out that information on my own..." I kept walking. I didn't want to know what had set him off so early this morning.

I knocked on Major Mitchell's door, instead of heading to my own. Hearing the signal, I entered and found him on his hands and knees beside his desk. He was sweeping small bits of paper up with a brush and dustpan.

"You okay?" I asked. "What's Waters upset about?"

"He's mad at me. I didn't have the information he

wanted, and he ripped up my leave request. This is what's left of it." He raised the dustpan for me to see before he pitched it.

"Sorry he denied it. Where were you off to?"

"Yuma. My family is there. It's my yearly trip, and I already had everything planned."

"Well, don't give up yet," I said. "He's likely to change his mind."

I left him in his office and went to mine to get to work. I planned on taking a longer look at the Defense Central Index of Investigations (DCII) for Zach. I closed my door behind me and locked it so I wouldn't be disturbed.

The database was handy because it was a treasure trove of information on investigations conducted by Department of Defense (DoD) investigative agencies. The first thing to pop up again was the LOR, which I printed out. Scanning my computer, my attention was caught by three letters, CDI. *Uh-oh,* this was a Command Directed Investigation, and it was no joke.

I clicked on it, and it launched a new file. Going back about seven years, the Air Force launched an investigation on Zach for an unprofessional relationship he was having with a co-worker. Zach's boss submitted it at Malmstrom Air Force Base (AFB) in Montana. It named the woman he was involved with, and she was a subordinate within the OSI. She also happened to be the ex-wife of one Major Keith Mitchell. *Oh shit.* I had no idea Major Mitchell's wife had been Active Duty, let alone involved with my ex-husband.

I hit print then jumped out of my chair and went back to his office. I entered after I knocked, not giving him a chance to answer before I went in. He turned to look at me from his computer the minute I stepped inside.

"Major Mitchell, what happened with your ex-wife and Zach?" I asked.

"Why do you want to know?" he asked.

"I noticed Zach's CDI from Malmstrom. Did you know about it?"

"Yes, but it wasn't me. It's nice to know someone cared enough to try and curtail his extracurricular activities. He and Samantha were only married a few years at the time. There were no children, but I knew she was trying."

"Did you meet Sammie?" I asked.

He shook his head. "I saw her at various functions we had, but we never officially met. After his affair with Anne, I decided to spare her and kept my distance."

"How long was the affair?"

"It was a year when I gave her an ultimatum—him or me. Seeing how he was married, she chose me."

"Why did you guys divorce?" I asked. It didn't have anything to do with Zach, but I was curious.

"She couldn't limit her affections to just me. After the situation with Special Agent Wheaton, we were never the same, and their affair became one of many."

"I'm sorry that happened. I can relate. When I was gone, Zach always found someone else."

****

I ate lunch at my desk and spent the remainder of the day getting paperwork done and sending out emails. The commander who filed the CDI was retired, so tracking him down was a no-go. I went down the chain of command until I found someone who was still in and sent an email off to him.

I had other cases I was juggling and made a pass at them, but Zach was the priority for everyone in OSI. It's different when it's one of your own.

Shutting down my computer at the end of the day always meant waiting a few minutes for it to catch up to my commands. Sammie might remember seeing Major Mitchell all those years ago; she might even remember Anne. I wonder if she had any idea of the affair and the ongoing investigation. Passing Colonel Waters's door, I noticed it was open and stuck my head in to say goodbye.

"Have a good weekend, Colonel Waters," I said.

"What?" he barked. "Oh, are you leaving already, Major?"

"Yes, sir. I've got some information I'm chewing over and someone I need to interview when I get home. I'll be ready for the meeting on Monday, though, sir."

He returned his attention to his computer, and I was dismissed. I hoped Sammie had information that was worthwhile for me to bring back on Monday. I would formulate a mental list on my way home of things to ask her.

****

I wasn't home ten minutes, when I realized the SUV was back beside the mailboxes again. I yanked open the front door and surprised Cassy when I smacked into her. She fell backward, half on the cement entrance and half in the grass, with me splayed on top of her.

The SUV started its engine, and I struggled over Cassy and bolted down the sidewalk in the blink of an eye. Once I reached the mailboxes, all I could see were the taillights where they turned onto the road in front of the complex. *Damnit.*

Back in the house, Cassy lay spread eagle on the couch with a dazed look on her face.

"Are you okay?" I asked.

"Damn, woman, you about killed me."

"I'm sorry. That SUV was here in the middle of the night, and now here it is again. I was trying to see who it was. I swear I've seen it somewhere before and not just parked out here."

"You know the car company made more than the one, right?" Cassy asked with a twinkle in her eye.

I flipped her off as Sammie came down the stairs. Ana and Ryan followed, with Ana scooting down on her behind and Ry grasping the railing and making his way down carefully.

"Who was it who showed up at your apartment?" I asked.

"My BPD partner. He was checking up on me. I told him before that I was fine, but he wanted to see for hisself. My roommate freaked when she saw him— thought I was in trouble."

"Did he show up in uniform?" Sammie asked.

"Yeah, that's what freaked her out. She thought something happened to me."

With everyone hanging out, I decided now would be a good time to call Desio about the ransom calls. He was out, so I left a message. I sat in the wing chair and tried to fit the pictures together in my head, but instead of getting work done, I fell asleep. I came crashing back to earth when my phone blared from the desk.

"Hello?" I answered.

"Duvall, it's Desio. You called?" I could hear the

commotion in the background, but it was hard to say exactly where he was.

"Yeah, we got ransom calls, and I wanted to let you know."

"Okay, I can't talk right now, but I can meet later. How's that?"

"Yep, where and when?" I asked.

"Tonight, at Pizza John's at six. We'll discuss."

This gave me some time to burn before meeting him, so I decided to wake myself up by going for a run. I changed into shorts and a T-shirt and left the girls a note telling them what I was doing.

It was strange having to leave my whereabouts with someone else. Strange but also comforting. These were people who cared and would look out for me if I needed them. This was a novelty to me, and I remembered the fight I put up when Sammie came to live with me.

Shaking my head but with a smile on my face, I pulled the door closed and took off across the parking lot. I ran the roads I knew from growing up. Back when all that was along this road was JCB selling construction equipment and a few houses. I ran Route 7 toward Middle River Road, but I wasn't sure if I would cross Pulaski or turn around and run back when I got to the bottom by Royal Farms.

Farther down Middle River Road heading toward Middlesex, sat the High's convenience store where I used to get fresh served cookies and cream ice cream, every Sunday. The church farther down the road had its steeple torn off by a passing airplane back in the '70s.

I decided to cross at Royal Farms and run against traffic back up the way I came down. Once at the top, I slowed my pace, since this was the last leg of the journey. Humidity was high today despite no rain in the foreseeable future, causing my shirt to stick to me like a second skin. I could also feel my hair frizzing with every step I took. I passed someone mowing their lawn on Route 7 and the smell of the fresh-cut grass mingled with the smell of the diesel from a passing truck.

My street was in my line of sight when an SUV popped up in front of me. I didn't pay much notice, until the sound of a gunning motor drew my attention. In hindsight, I realized I never stood a chance when they crossed into the narrow path on the side of the road and came at me head-on. They jerked the wheel at the last second, but I still met the front bumper of the SUV.

The grass on the side of the road caught me once I bounced off their right side. I landed on my face but turned my head to catch the plate. Of course, they had something covering it, so I couldn't see it. It was a black SUV, and if I didn't know better, I would swear it was the one parked in front of my house as recently as an hour ago.

I brushed the freshly cut grass off my face and moved my toes inside my shoes. Everything seemed to work fine as I rolled over, propping myself up on my elbows and looking down at my legs. True, I moved a bit more gingerly, but nothing seemed broken.

"Well, I'll be. Laci, I thought I recognized you," a familiar voice said. "What happened?"

My neighbor Lisa approached me in the grass with every step pounding through my brain. Behind her, I saw her white SUV parked in the nearest driveway with her hazard lights on.

"I tripped," I lied. "Can you help me up?"

"Are you sure you should be getting up? Should I call 911?"

"Lisa, it's fine. Right now, I just want to get home—I have somewhere I need to be." I looked at her, and she looked like she needed some more convincing. "If you help me stand, I'll show you I can walk just fine."

She reached her hand down, and I clasped it with one of mine, and she hoisted me to a standing position, where I proceeded to go right back down again.

"Maybe I need just another minute or two," I said.

"Uh-huh," she said. I looked at her from her feet, and she had that look her daughter Rosemary got when she was going to disobey her mom.

"I'm fine, I promise. Let's try again."

Lisa walked around and bent down behind me, hooked her arms beneath mine, and lifted. "Up and at 'em," she said. This time I stayed standing, and she came up beside me, looped her arm through mine, and guided me to her SUV. I clambered in and we were off to the townhouse. She side-eyed me and bit her bottom lip the entire two minutes it took to get home. I knew this went against every southern manner she had been taught, but I just wanted to be home.

Once she pulled into her parking spot, I threw open my door and got out on my own. I was halfway to my house before she noticed I was even gone.

"If you need anything, y'all just holler," she yelled. I waved my hand at her behind my back. My goal was my house and getting inside. I silently prayed that no one would be downstairs when I walked in.

"What happened to you?" Sammie asked.

Damnit, she spotted me the minute I walked in the

front door. Needles came from behind her and approached me with his tail between his legs. Even he knew something wasn't right.

"Nothing. Why do you ask?" I tried to get it to come out normal, but I squeaked a bit at the end.

"Nothing?" she asked. "Have you seen yourself?"

Either she was getting louder, or something was up with my ears. I shook my head and did an about-face to the downstairs bathroom. I swayed to the side as everything in my head shifted and I caught myself on the wall. I didn't recognize myself when I got to the bathroom.

There were gravel bits mixed with more grass on the left side of my face from my jawline to my temple, and my hair had worked itself loose from my bun and was down next to my ear.

Sammie joined me in the bathroom, and I saw the mutinous curve to her mouth. *Oh shit*, I knew I wouldn't get away with brushing this off.

We were analyzing the pattern of the chickenpox lotion dots on Sammie's arm, and I was running out of distractions when Cassy came looking for us. I knew it was only a matter of time before she showed up. That's the reason for the distraction.

"We're in the bathroom!" Sammie yelled. Her voice ricocheted off the small room right into my head, and my hands flew up to cover my ears. "Oh, sorry."

Cassy appeared behind us, and I saw her eyes grow large when she saw my face.

"What the hell happened to you? Did you fall while you was running? You know that happened to me once. I still pick gravel out my face on occasion—and that was months ago. What'd you do, trip over your

89

shoelaces? Yup, been there done that." After she contributed this, she about-faced out of the small room, and I could hear her slamming around in the kitchen.

"Yes, I fell." I looked Sammie in the eyes and lied. Again. "Lisa got there right after I fell and gave me a ride home. I wasn't there long. Now, I just want to take a shower before I meet Desio."

I tiptoed into the kitchen and grabbed something for my head, then went up the stairs to start the hot water. Boo was curled up in the middle of the bed when I walked in, so I slid into the bathroom, being careful not to wake her up.

Standing underneath the spray, I brought up the image of the SUV and tried to recall any details I could. Did it look like the one parked out front? It was hard to say when I saw a different angle of it on each occasion. The size and shape were the same and the age could be too. I wished I could get another look at it.

When I finished, I lay across the bed still wrapped up from my shower. Boo raised her head when she felt the bed move and came over and lay against me. Two seconds later—I was out like a light.

The banging on the door woke me up, and I looked at my watch. *Shit.* I hopped up and opened the door to Cassy on the other side.

"I wondered what happened to you. Fall asleep?"

"Yeah, but now I have to go."

She stepped inside and shut the door behind her, then folded her arms across her chest. One look at her face and I knew she knew I had lied. "Thas fine, but first you can tell me what happened. I won' tell her."

I debated for half a second on whether to lie to Cassy, but my gut told me she would see right through it like she had the one downstairs. "A black SUV hit me while heading home from my run. During my shower I racked my brain to see if it matched the one I'd seen out front of the house. Did you notice anything about it?"

"Not really, no, jus' thought it was someone getting their mail, you know?"

"Yeah. How'd you know I didn't tell the truth?" I asked.

"Ain' my first rodeo, you know that. You gonna tell Desio about it?"

"I was thinking about it, but I haven't decided."

Chapter Eight

Pizza John's is an icon. You can't live in Baltimore and never pass through its doors. Desio and I went there on our first date, right after they finished one of their major renovations. It was the best place for good pizza.

Desio's work sedan was in the lot when I pulled in and I slowly got out of my car and made my way to the front door. When I opened it, the chatter and laughter and the sweet aroma of pizza slapped me in the face. My head was especially sensitive tonight—so it was all I could do not to put my hands over my ears.

Desio leaned against the front counter speaking to the owner, so I dodged the crowd and joined him. He saw me coming and stood from his lean—scanning me from my toes up. I knew he'd remember what I wore if I asked him in a month. He was dressed in jeans, a white button-up, and loafers with a sports coat, and I saw the lines around his eyes and the day-old growth on his face when I got closer.

"Have you been home anytime lately?" I asked.

He didn't answer but his gaze focused on the left side of my face. I told you he didn't miss anything. I put several coats of foundation on trying to cover up the scratches, but I knew better. He reached out and grabbed my chin and pulled my face so he could look at it straight on. I fought him for a second but caved on a sigh.

When he finally let go, his eyes remained on mine, and suddenly I felt my headache coming back. I reached up and rubbed my eyes and leaned against the counter.

Desio took my elbow and guided me to a booth in the back corner. He helped me onto the faux leather and stood waiting for me to scoot over, which I did. I closed my eyes and leaned my head against a picture of Cal Ripken Jr. on my right. I felt Desio watching me, and I rotated my head toward him and found his eyes on me.

"You wanna tell me what happened?" he asked.

"Did you order already?" I asked.

He nodded, and my eyes dropped to the tabletop while I debated what to say. I knew I wouldn't lie to him about this, but I didn't know where to begin.

"I was hit by an SUV while out running. My gut tells me it's the same SUV I've seen parked outside my house a few times."

"There's been an SUV outside your house?" he asked. I told him about the prior occasions where I'd seen it parked by the mailboxes. "I'd trust your gut," he said. "When was this at? Is that why you were late?"

"It happened right before I turned into my subdivision, and yes, it's why I'm late. That, and I fell asleep after I took a shower. It took more out of me than I realized. Cassy guessed what was up, but Sammie doesn't know—at least I don't think she does. She's surprised me with her perception on a couple of occasions so far."

Our drinks arrived, and I filled him in on the ransom phone calls. He listened and asked questions, the same ones I'd had.

"Tell me about Floyd and Janis. What did you

gather from the conversation I missed?" I asked.

"When you left the room, I asked them again when they had seen Zach last. This time there was a pause before anyone answered me. Janis began to speak, but Floyd cut her off and corrected what she was saying. Does he ever allow her to speak?"

"Not when he can do it for her has been my experience. I often wondered what our relationship would have been like if I could have gotten her away from him. She can't sneeze without asking him first. What was Floyd's answer this time?"

"He told me they hadn't seen Zach since Easter two years ago when he and Sammie had stopped by with the twins. Has Sammie mentioned the visit?"

"She probably would if I asked her—they didn't like her either. There was some initial confusion when the kids were born about who the father was. Sammie did the DNA tests, but she said Zach was never close to them before or after. It was like he doubted the results of the tests, you know? I think Zach probably shared his concerns with his parents, which led to further hostilities. Tack that on to the fact that they were never legally married, and you have a match made in heaven."

"Or hell," he said.

"No, that would be my marriage to him. Sammie says theirs was pretty good, and by all accounts, it was." I turned and asked him what I had wondered since I saw him again. "Did you ever get married, Desio?"

"No," he said with no room for questions.

Okay. "Zach took it upon himself to do all the marriage paperwork for him and Sammie, including the prenup." I glanced over at Desio's grunt. "I know, right? He told Sammie that he and I had one, but there was no way in hell I would ever sign something like that, but she believed him, bless her heart. She believed him in everything. He told her he was taking care of the wedding license when all he did was fill everything out and *sign it for her*, but it was never certified. I'll just say the day I filed for divorce was one of the best in my life, but I would never tell her that."

"How did she end up with you? It's an odd choice."

"Another of Zach's doings. He invited her to stay with me until she got back on her feet. I also found out today that Zach had an affair with the ex-wife of one of my co-workers, Major Keith Mitchell."

Desio let out a low whistle. "While you were married?"

I shook my head. "No, he saved that for others. This was when he and Sammie were first married. She mentioned it briefly, and I could tell it was embarrassing for her, so I didn't ask anything."

"He did that to you?" Desio asked.

"Oh, God yes," I blurted out. Desio's eyes turned flint in anger, and it occurred to me that even with our history, he would still hurt for me. I laid my hand on his arm. "It's okay, Antonio." My voice dropped to an intimate level. It was strange talking to him about my relationship with Zach. "He made many mistakes, and so did I. The difference is, I learned from mine, and he didn't."

The pizza arrived then, which kept me from saying anything more. Instead, I slid my hand from his arm to remove pizza toppings—it was much safer on my food.

I might pull him close and kiss him otherwise.

The olives came off first, then the mushrooms, and several pieces of sausage, and then I picked it up and flicked off the ground beef sticking to the surface cheese. I watched it skate across the table and stuck my thumb in my mouth to get the grease off when I noticed Antonio wasn't eating next to me, and he was watching me, and I froze. I saw the amusement in his eyes, then they slid to my finger in my mouth, and my stomach turned squishy, and I pulled it out of my mouth with a pop.

"Still like plain pepperoni pizza?" he asked, and his eyes were still on my mouth.

I nodded then took a bite.

****

Needles was in the kitchen, and all was dark when I returned from my trip to Pizza John's. I wasn't in a hurry to get home after leaving Desio. He was a puzzle. Memories of our time together seeped into our conversation over dinner. The intimacy and camaraderie that we'd shared twenty-odd years ago had enveloped our little booth, and it was like no time had passed.

Boo was on her pillow when I entered my bedroom. I brushed my teeth and changed clothes before sliding under the covers and was asleep in a matter of minutes. Needles' baying downstairs woke me up and I glanced at my phone—three in the morning. A time when all creatures should be sleeping, so what woke up mine?

Holding my phone up for light, I silently opened my bedroom door, stuck my head out in the hallway, and quickly brought it back in. I repeated this before I stepped into the pitch-black hallway. I strained to hear anything from the kitchen, but it was quiet.

Creeping downstairs, I reached the stair landing and peeked around the corner. The light above the stove was on, and I could see Needles sitting in the middle of the kitchen with his head tilted, listening for something. I came around the landing corner and took the rest of the steps slowly.

I realized I forgot my weapon upstairs at the same time Needles growled. Too late now. I continued down while formulating a plan. When I was almost to the hallway, I jumped from three steps up and yelled as loud as I could—holding my phone in front of me like some kind of weapon.

The scream that erupted from the intruder was like nothing I had ever heard before and one I would never forget. I hit the light switch next to me, and there stood Cassy with her hands over her eyes, mouth still open, emitting a shrill screech. I reached over and ripped her hands from her face, but her eyes were screwed shut, and she was still screaming.

"Cassy," I said *sotto voce*.

Nothing.

"Cassy," I yelled this time while shaking her arm.

Her eyes popped open, and she stopped, but then we turned at a new noise. About twenty steps up at the top of the landing to my right stood Sammie holding a gun, aimed directly at us. I dove for the living room floor, and Cassy stood there, eyes wide open.

"What the hell, Sammie?" I yelled.

"It's not loaded," she said.

I jumped up and made my way over to Cassy, who had not moved. "Cassy?" I waved my hand in front of her face, and she finally blinked down at me.

"What the actual hell, woman? You scared the shit out of me." Cassy's shaky hand went to wipe her upper lip.

"I'm sorry," I said. "I didn't know it was you. How on earth were you a cop if you can't handle someone sneaking up on you?"

"Hey, you show me one person who doesn't react like I just did when they snuck up on. I dare you."

I nodded my head, giving her the point, and glanced over at Needles, who was watching the play-by-play with his tongue lolling and tail wagging. "What were you doing down here in the first place?" I asked.

"Dinner upset my delicate balance, and I didn' want to use the can upstairs. So, I came down here."

Sammie snorted from beside me, then slapped her hand over her mouth, but her eyes were still dancing. Her other hand hung by her side, and the gun was still in it. I reached out for her to place it in my hand, which she did, with the muzzle pointed directly at me.

"Holy shit," Cassy exclaimed and knocked it out of Sammie's hand. It went flying down the hallway, where it skidded to a stop and went off against the front door.

"*You said it wasn't loaded.*" I didn't mean to shout at her—it just sorta happened.

"*I thought it wasn't,*" Sammie yelled back.

"Oh, my God, my neighbors are going to call the police on me."

They both started talking at once, and Needles bayed again. "Hey," I yelled into their chaos. "You guys go upstairs, and I'll stay here in case the police show up." I went to the front door, grabbed the gun from the floor, emptied the magazine, then handed it back to Sammie—grip facing her, barrel pointed to the floor. "Do you even know how to use a gun?" I asked.

"Ummm, I know which side the bullet comes out."

Cassy shook her head and rolled her eyes, and I slapped my hand to my forehead in disbelief. "First thing tomorrow, we're going to a shooting range to teach you," I said.

"Do you have a license?" Cassy asked.

She nodded. "Oh, yes, Zach made sure of it."

"I'll need to see it to make sure it's legit," Cassy said.

Figured Zach got her a gun license, but not a marriage license. Is it any wonder we're divorced?

Needles joined me in my search for the bullet, but only a screwdriver or pliers would get that out of the bathroom door frame—something I wasn't doing right now. So instead, we lay down on the couch together and fell into a restless sleep. My dreams were full of gray-eyed men who didn't say much.

****

I jerked awake to Ana standing in front of me with a grin and two teeth showing. She tried again to put her thumb in my mouth, and I pretended to suck on it by making slurping noises, which caused more giggling.

I sat up and pulled her onto my lap and turned on cartoons for us. Those pesky kids were on, and they were my favorite. Watching TV allowed my mind to roam freely, and I stayed busy making plans. First things first was getting Sammie capable with a firearm.

The sun was climbing, and the sky was brightening minute by minute when the kids pulled the mask off the villain. Sammie descended the steps holding Ryan, swiveling her head from side to side. "Ana?"

"She's here, Sammie," I said. "We've been catching up on our cartoon time."

She came over and sat down next to us and placed Ryan on the floor. He toddled over to the loveseat across the way and climbed up. Sammie then reached over and hugged Ana, who was camped out on my lap.

"I don't know what I would do if anything happened to one of these guys," Sammie said.

Ryan was now sitting opposite us with his feet stretched out in front of him and a pacifier in his mouth. His hair was as rumpled as his pj's, and he giggled at the brown dog on the TV.

"You're a great mom, Sammie."

Her eyes welled with tears when she turned toward me. "Really?"

"Has no one ever told you that?" I asked. She shook her head no, eyes as big as saucers. "Not even Zach?"

"Oh, God, no, he was not forthcoming with compliments, as I'm sure you remember."

"You know," I said, "it's a wonder he got anyone at all, let alone two hot women like us."

"Now, ain't that the truth? He was lucky to have us," Sammie said. "I miss him, though, and I love him when all is said and done, and I have his children. What kind of mom would I be if I didn't look for their daddy?"

"Do they ask for him?" I asked. "Do they remember him, you think?"

"You know, I don't know." Glancing at Ana, then at Ryan, her eyes welled up again. "They didn't really bond with him. A part of me wondered if he was getting ready to leave us."

"You said that Zach was unfaithful to you," I began. "Did you know who she was?"

Sammie dropped her eyes to her lap and nodded her head.

"We lived in Montana," she said. "She was a co-worker."

"Did he know you knew?"

"Oh, yes, he didn't hide the fact that I was inadequate. She was the one to break things off, that much I know. Zach came home angry and spent the night drinking. When I asked what was wrong, he filled me in. Trust me—he didn't leave anything out."

"How did you recover?" I asked. "I know the first time it happened to me, it felt like someone ripped my guts out. By the time we got to the third affair, I didn't care. It was over."

"It wasn't easy, but I reckoned if I loved him, I needed to work for our marriage. We went to counseling for a while, then Zach quit, but I kept going. It's tough living in a marriage when you're never sure if they'll find someone else."

"Momma—" Ana said.

I looked down at Ana, who was reaching for Sammie, and I gladly gave her over as Sammie burst into tears.

"Do you need some chocolate while we're out today?" I asked.

She laughed, hiccupped, and nodded her head. "Oh, yes, I could use some this week. So, we're still going to the shooting range?" she asked me while she nuzzled Ana's neck.

"Your parents still okay watching the twins?"

"Oh, yes, Momma doesn't mind as long as she

knows I'm coming back to get them, and Daddy loves them to pieces."

****

Cassy and Sammie were in the kitchen checking out each other's outfits when I came down after lunch. They had gotten new clothes that morning after breakfast and were dressed in the day's uniform.

Sammie insisted on a camo theme for the shooting range, so I showered and donned an old uniform from fifteen years ago. Don't ask me why I still had it—I was just happy it still fit. Sammie wore camo capris, a black T-shirt, and black flats, and Cassy sported a white T-shirt under a camo romper with black high-top sneakers, something only her long legs could pull off.

The duffel bag we put all the necessary paperwork, guns, and ammo in was by the front door. I grabbed it on our way to the car, while Sammie loaded the twins in the back and got in with them. Then she gave me directions on how to reach her parents' house.

Once the kids were dropped off, we drove north around Baltimore on I-695 then I-795. Traffic was low this time of day and we made the drive easily.

After we checked in, we walked the path to the hundred-yard range—the security pistol center was our destination. I handed out ear protection and targets when we got there. While we waited for the cease-fire, Cassy and I went over everything with Sammie, including identifying the parts of the pistol and quizzing her on them. It was a good refresher course for Cassy and me considering it had been a while since I held a firearm, let alone shot one.

I stepped to the side while Cassy showed Sammie the mechanics of the pistol she would be firing today. I glanced over the gallery down the line of people firing their weapons when suddenly tunnel vision closed in on me, and I was hiding in a hut being fired at by members of Al Qaeda.

I was mistaken for a local militant, and the hut I was in shuddered under the weight of all the gunfire. I stared above me at the ceiling, wondering how much longer the roof would hold when suddenly it fell on top of me. I yelled, and my hands flew up to cover my head from the worst of the damage. Before I recovered, someone grabbed my arms. I could hear voices speaking to me over the mad beat of my heart, but they were far away and sounded like radio static.

My eyes opened to Desio's face inches from mine. His hands were the only thing holding me up. Glancing at movement behind him, Cassy and Sammie stood there, their eyes as big as saucers. I collapsed into Desio's arms and buried my head in his chest. I tunneled into his heat, with my teeth chattering.

He sat down in the middle of the gallery and pulled me into his lap. His mouth was next to my ear, and he ran his hand up and down my spine while he spoke. "Was this leftover from last night?"

I shook my head. "No, stuff sneaks up on me sometimes. One second I'm here, and the next I'm a sitting duck, taking on fire from Al Qaeda. It hasn't happened in a while, but it can start anytime. I've never had it happen like this before."

"I'm sorry," he said. His voice was deep and pleasant. I realized I could listen to him talk all day. He glanced behind me, and I turned my head to where the girls were watching us. He used that opportunity to gather himself up and disappeared down the gallery to the group gathered there. There were a few BPD cadets in the group. It must be a training day.

"He's like the wind—don't stay around when things get interesting," Cassy said.

"Yeah, I guess, places to go, people to see." I grabbed Cassy's offered hand and got up.

"You still insisting there ain' nothing between you two?" Cassy asked.

Instead of answering her, I put on my ear protection and approached the small table that held the weapons. Cassy glanced from me, to where Desio disappeared, then back at me. I could practically see her mind working to figure it out.

Trying to get her mind off me and Desio, I handed Sammie a Ruger LCP, a compact, double-action handgun. We loaded the magazine with hollow points—we didn't need to take anyone out; we just needed to stop them.

"Now, you gotta keep your fingers out from in front of the gun. Otherwise, you shoot your finger off that way," Cassy said. "You gotta be careful of a 'phantom reset' where you think it's ready to go again, but it's not. That's why we practicing—to avoid that. Now, you ready to shoot. Two hands on the gun and feet shoulder-width apart."

While it wasn't possible in the heat of the moment to stop and make sure your position was correct, it was good to have the fundamentals down as a starting point.

After Sammie shot the Ruger, we handed her a Glock 43 to see which one she liked better. She was hauling around an old Smith & Wesson 9mm, and I wanted her to try something not as bulky.

"This here's a Glock 43 and consists of a SAFE

ACTION System that lets you shoot all your bullets at one time if you want," Cassy said. "This way, you can pay attention to what you shootin' at and not worry about releasing and firin' again. It also means you can shoot wild, so you gotta pay attention to where it's going. Got it?"

Sammie turned and gave me a deer in the headlights look but she stepped up and fired anyway. She might have gotten half of them on the target.

Cassy was next and put up an impressive showing in everything I gave her. "I'm very impressed," I said.

"Yeah, well, it don' put food on the table, and guys frown at a woman who can shoot better'n they do." Cassy nodded at our looks of disgust. "Someone, please explain that to me."

"Men have fragile egos?" Sammie asked.

"Damn skippy," I agreed.

Taking the Glock out of Cassy's hand, I got in position for my turn at the targets. I glanced out of the corner of my eye to where Desio's group was. While those not shooting stood in a huddle talking to each other, Desio was the outlier and stared at me. I swallowed my nerve and began firing.

The next hour was spent rotating turns between us, but by the time we were finished, it was clear Sammie wasn't comfortable holding a gun. We discussed an alternative form of defense with her, and a pawn shop specializing in these things was a couple of miles from our exit, so we stopped in on our way home. I could see walking in that there were plenty of opportunities for us to get distracted.

"We want to see your tasers and stun guns," I said. The woman behind the counter skimmed her eyes over us and returned to me.

"Okay, what kind are you thinking?" she asked.

"I'd like to leave that up to you, but it's for this lovely lady right here," I said. "Now, don't let her looks deceive you—she is small but mighty." I winked at Sammie, but I could tell by her death grip on the counter she was only taking in half of what was said.

"Do you prefer one or the other? A taser means you don't have to be within arm's distance to shoot it, but with a stun gun, you have to be all up in their business and have a good grip on it to deploy it. We also have one that if you don't disable with the taser, you can use it as a stun gun."

"Sold!" I said.

"It's a bit pricey, but to me, it's worth it." She finished her pitch and turned to grab the goods.

"It's fine; the price doesn't matter; safety matters. Also, can you pack up four or five extra cartridges for us?"

Before we left the store, I gave Sammie the chance to hold the stun gun in her hand and test its weight to see if she was comfortable with the feel of it. You could tell it was foreign at first, but I thought with some more experience of handling it without the charge, she would be okay. Time would tell if that was accurate or not.

****

Colonel Waters sat beside me at the head of the table and rechecked his watch; impatience radiated off of him.

"Cellphones and cyborgs, Major, I'm giving him five more minutes, and then I'm going about my day."

The meeting was for 0800, and we were approaching 0815, and there was still no sign of Major

Mitchell.

With thirty years under his belt, Colonel Waters had served longer than anyone I knew. The Air Force denied him the chance to work in Washington and rub shoulders with the brass and instead sent him here—close enough to peer over the fence but too far away to matter.

It was hard to say if he was disgruntled over the current assignment and how the Air Force had treated him or if it was just his nature. This was his last assignment in a long career. I know he would have liked to have gone out with a bang, but instead, he had to settle for a whimper.

Seven more minutes of staring at the clock on the wall passed when Colonel Waters erupted at 0820 and left the room without looking back. I followed him at a more sedate pace and was almost to my office when Major Mitchell came strolling by.

"What are you doing? Meeting's in ten," he said.

"That was twenty minutes ago, and you were a no-show, so we adjourned the meeting."

"You can't leave…so what if I'm late? You have to be here." His face quickly turned an angry shade of red and he put his finger inches from my nose.

"I was here at the time of the meeting, and you weren't. I'm pretty sure my presence has been noted and is no longer required. But you can go see Colonel Waters and explain why you came strolling in late and expect us to comply with your demands."

"I suggest you get your ass back in the conference room for the meeting." Now his face was inches from mine, and he was spewing demands. He even poked me in the shoulder with his finger.

"What the hell is wrong with you?" I asked. Instead of answering, he grabbed my arm when I turned away from him. "Major…" I continued, "I'll give you five seconds to remove your hand, or I'll remove it for you."

"You ca—"

"One. Two." He was staring me down to see if I would flinch first. "Three. Four." *Shit.* "Five." He didn't remove it. So, I did it for him.

Grabbing his wrist with my left hand, I quickly placed my other hand next to it. I raised my elbow up and over his arm, stepped back, and twisted his wrist while turning away from him—yanking his wrist up in front of my chest, all at the same time. I could feel him trying to free himself behind me, but I wasn't budging, so neither would he. I counted to five again, then I let go and backed away.

He stared at me, and his nostrils flared while he tried to get air in his lungs. The standing armbar was quick and effective. I kept my eyes on him the few steps it took me to get to my office.

I sat at my desk and dropped my head in my hands—trying to still my rapidly beating heart. I hated confrontation. I laughed at the irony of being in the military and hating confrontation.

Shaking off the moment, I booted up my computer so I could immerse myself in Zach's history again. I wondered about his connection to Mitchell's wife. A quick search on her gave me her name—SSgt Anne Mitchell née Parker. She retired from the Air Force shortly after her affair with Zach—she was never penalized for the affair. Her record indicated that she changed her name back to Parker following her divorce from Mitchell and moved back home to Columbia, Maryland.

I jumped in my chair when the door to my office bounced off my wall, and Colonel Waters stalked through and stopped an inch from my desk. I made it to my feet as soon as possible, but it did little to appease him.

"Major, you want to tell me what I missed in the hallway?" he demanded.

"Nothing, sir, just a small incident with Major Mitchell and myself. We took care of it and have moved on. Why?"

"It was brought to my attention by SSgt..." here, he ground to a halt and snapped his fingers, trying to recall the name. "Anyway, everything's taken care of then?"

"Yes, sir."

He about-faced and strode for the door without a goodbye, and the door slammed shut behind him.

I dropped into my chair and pulled my hair from the ponytail—I needed a second to regroup and refocus. After a minute or two I grabbed my phone and searched for Anne Parker's phone number. Nothing came up.

I smacked myself on the forehead when I remembered my late-night phone call from the people holding Zach, and I went looking for the screenshot. I quickly found it, but it wasn't a local number, so who knew what I would get.

"Benny's Mattresses, home of the pillow-sheathed queen mattress. You need it—we got it. How can I help—" I hung up. It didn't sound like the guy who called me.

I dialed from my desk phone this time.

"Baltimore City Medical Examiner, Dr. Mann speaking."

"Dr. Mann, have you received any more ransom calls?"

"Good morning, Major Duvall. I haven't heard anything else since we spoke last. Why?"

"I kept the phone number from my ransom call, and it goes to Benny's Mattresses," I said.

"It's more than likely a front for something else."

"Well, yeah, but mattresses?"

"Better than nothing, I guess," Dr. Mann said.

I did a quick look-up of Benny's Mattresses, which was on Edmonson Avenue. "Three guesses as to where their office is," I said, then I rattled off the address to him.

"West Baltimore, which only stands to reason since that's where we found him."

"That's where they found his body?" I asked. "Can you tell me what happened?"

"We had a student call 911. She was standing with a group of her friends, and a cab pulled up. Someone pushed a body out the back door, and it landed at her feet. They were leaving Pratt Library when it happened."

"What time of day was that?" I asked.

"We received the 911 call around ten, howev—"

"It's them." I interrupted Dr. Mann when my cell phone went off, and I looked at the display. "They sure took their time in calling me back. Hang tight, Dr. Mann." I answered my cell and put it on speaker. "Major Duvall."

"You ready to do a trade?" he asked.

"Nah—I just wanted to see if the number you

called from actually went to something."

"Listen, lady, I ain't gonna keep him much longer. He's taking up too much room in my freezer." The man spoke with a distinct accent. He dropped his "r's" at the end of words. So, what should have been, "longer", instead sounded like, longuh, and "freezer" sounded like freezuh.

"Well, just be sure and say a few words for him when you do away with him." I hung up. "Dr. Mann? Are you still there?" He was silent so long I had to double check if he was still there.

"How are you so cool when talking to them?" he asked.

"Oh, that? That's nothing. I've talked to worse. Of course, with kidnappers, you can't let them know your true feelings, but in this, my feelings aren't so far off. The more I learn about who Zach turned into after we divorced, the less I miss him."

My cell rang again, so I had Dr. Mann wait again.

"Major Duvall."

"We have discovered who has Mr. Wheaton," Desio said.

"You have?" I asked. "Are you out getting him?"

"He's in Western Baltimore, though I can't reveal the location at this point. Unfortunately, I can't get him yet because there are steps I have to follow."

"Why did you call me then?" I asked.

"Because I was under the impression we were working on this together. Am I wrong?"

"No." I accidentally yelled at him. "No, Desio, you're not wrong. Thank you for letting me know."

He hung up, and I stared at my cell phone while I thought about that.

"How come you didn't let him know you already knew who had him?" I jumped when Dr. Mann's voice came across the speaker. I completely forgot he was there.

"Old habits are hard to break, Dr. Mann. I play my cards close to my chest, and this time is no different. I don't believe Detective Desio is being a hundred percent honest with me either—we just have to see who will break first. Thank you for your help."

Chapter Nine

"Duvall?"

"Jesus, Desio, what do you want?" I asked. It was the middle of the night and being woken up by Desio wasn't high on my list of wants. Unless of course, he was here with me. Wait, what? Where di—

"Can you come down to the morgue for me?" he asked.

"Right now?"

"As soon as you can," he said.

"Seriously? You do realize the sun's not even up."

"Since I've been here most of the night, I'm perfectly aware of where the sun is."

"Fine, I'm coming. Do you want to tell me what this is about?" I asked.

"I wish I could, Duvall. Meet me at Dr. Mann's office."

I hung up and left Boo sleeping on her pillow at the head of the bed when I rolled out only to land flat on my face, my head barely missing the bedside table. I fumbled with the closet door, tripped inside, and landed on a pile of laundry. It wasn't a strange occurrence in my line of work to be called out in the middle of the night or early morning hours—and this time was no exception. The only difference was who was doing the calling.

The sun was approaching the horizon, and the sky

was lightening when I exited west off I95. I turned left at the end of the ramp onto the road that would take me to the ME's Office. I honestly thought I had finished with the place.

The front door swung open easily in my hand when I pushed inside and entered the hushed building. There was no echo from my footsteps this morning, which was a stark contrast to my last trip to the morgue. Approaching Dr. Mann's office, I pulled open the stainless-steel coated door to meet Desio.

"What's this about, Desio?" I demanded.

He gave me a silent come-hither action with his two fingers, and we walked from the office area, back into the hallway, and into the examination room next door where they autopsied the bodies. I drew up short, with my stomach clenching and palms sweating. I wiped them on the front of my shorts.

From a safe distance I saw a man with brown hair lying on the table with his lower half under a sheet that contrasted with his pale and gray skin. He had the same ligature marks I had seen on Zach after his autopsy.

"I don't understand," I said. "Who is he?"

"You don't recognize him?" Desio asked.

"No. Why? Should I?"

Desio looked thoughtful for a moment and considered what I had told him. "You're certain you've never seen him before?" he asked again.

"As certain as I can be."

Desio joined me at the door to the room, and we stood staring at the man on the table. When we turned to leave, Desio kept up the conversation.

"His alias is Thomas Thornton," Desio said. "His actual name is Thomas Wheaton." Desio watched me, and I'm sure he was waiting for a reaction.

"Is he related to Zach?" I asked.

"That's what we're trying to find out."

"Where was he found?" I asked. "How did he die?"

"He was found at a local strip club called the Purple Peacock. He was out back in the dumpster. We're not sure how he died. Dr. Mann is still running tests."

"Why did you call me down here for this?" I asked.

"Because you knew Zach, and I thought you would know Thomas. You never heard of him before?" he asked. "Your ex never mentioned him?"

I shook my head. "I can ask Sammie when I get back. She may recognize the name. Did you ask Zach's parents?"

He shook his head. "I haven't had the chance to. It's on my to do list with about a million other things."

We parted ways at my car on the street in front of the ME's office. I pulled onto the road and followed my GPS which directed me back to the interstate—You would think I knew my way around the city, but the one-way streets always got me turned around. My luck I would go down one going the wrong way.

Five yards from my turn, a black SUV rushed up behind me and rear-ended me. My face bounced off the steering wheel, but the motion of my car continued along the curb, pushing us up onto the sidewalk. The vibration from the SUV on the rear panel resonated throughout the car while the entire right side of my car slid along the newspaper boxes, pushing them farther into the sidewalk and knocking most of them over. I never even knew they still made them.

The SUV reversed and took off when I stepped out

of the car. Again, I couldn't see his license plate, but this time I was sure it was the same one from our previous meetings. Thankfully, it was too early for bystanders to gawk at me surveying the damage to my car. The newspaper boxes had done their worst along the entire right side—front to back. The driver-side taillight was busted, but the bumper was still attached which I was thankful for.

I got back in and cranked the ignition to see if it would go—it rattled, but it worked. A glance in the rearview mirror showed I had a trickle of blood coming out of my lip. I grabbed a tissue from my bag and blotted—yep, I could see the teeth grooves. *Damnit.*

Slowly, I got back on the road, and stopped at the red light. I dialed Desio and left him a voicemail telling him what happened. When the light turned green, I turned and followed the street to the interstate. A half-hour later I was home and Sammie spotted me the minute I walked in the door. This woman had the best timing of anyone I knew.

"What happened?" she asked.

"Why?"

"Bless your heart, you're walking like you're eighty, your lip's bleeding, and there's blood on your hand."

"Oh," I said, "yeah, someone ran my car off the road while I was in Baltimore."

"What?" she asked. She went past me to the front door and peered outside.

Leaning against the kitchen counter, I waited for her to come back; I knew I wouldn't have to wait long. Ana came over for me to pick her up, and I was leaned-down to get her when Sammie came rushing back in.

"Don't pick her up," Sammie said with a firm set to her lips.

"I promise I'm fine. Just sore. Where's Cassy?"

"She's meeting her partner, Amaré."

"Okay, I'm going to go upstairs and lie down."

"*No*," she yelled. When I cringed, she whispered, "Nooo. You may have a concussion. You're not supposed to sleep with one of those."

"I give you permission to come up and check on me every thirty minutes, but I will not be responsible for my actions." I winked at her, remembering the last time.

"Fine." She crossed her arms over her chest, a mulish expression on her face. It was the same look I had seen on Ana.

I lay down without bothering to wipe my face off. I didn't expect to fall asleep, but the feel of the pillow against my head was too delicious not to take advantage of. Before drifting off, I remembered I didn't ask Sammie about Thomas Thornton. I would do it when I woke up.

****

"What the hell happened to you?" Cassy caught me at the bottom of the stairs after my nap. She slammed to a halt outside the laundry room with her hands on her hips.

"You mean Sammie didn't tell you?" I asked.

"Told me what? I just got home, and I had a hella lotta soda today, so I had to pee."

"Someone drove me off the road this morn—"

"What?"

Then she too rushed to the front door to gawk at my car. "She'll be right back," I told Sammie. Sure enough, she erupted from the hallway.

"What the hell, woman?" Cassy asked, "Did you report it?"

I was standing there when it hit me like a ton of bricks, and I felt the breath knocked out of me. These people changed my whole world. How horrible a person was I to try and send Sammie away that first day. I loved these people, and they loved me, and when the tears gathered in my eyes, Sammie and Cassy rushed forward.

"Do we need to call nine-one-o—Whas wrong?" Cassy demanded.

Sammie was standing to my left and took my hand and held it.

"I'm fine, really. I'm fine. I just got emotional. You guys, I never planned on you guys. I mean, wow. It's just been me for so long. I'm sorry I tried to send you and the kids away, Sammie. I see how wrong I was. I've forgotten what it's like for someone to care about me. I mean. I mean." I hiccupped. "I don't know what I mean. You guys leave me speechless—you know?"

"I feel the same way," Sammie whispered. "I thought once Zach was dead, my life was over, but it's not. My life *has* taken a big turn, and I feel good about myself for the first time in my life. I…am an amazing mom," she said more firmly and with a touch of confidence. "I am doing this. But I don't want to do it without you guys." She finished in a whisper.

"I'm so proud of you," I said. I gripped her hand in mine and held on tight.

"Me too," Cassy said. "You got the best kids I ever seen. Yeah, you a crazy-ass white chick, but if I ever get in a fight, I want you on my side. After you check your gun. And you"—she turned to me—"I mean damn, if I hadn't helped you at the pharmacy, my life would be totally different, and I must say, I like it better now. You'll have to pry me out of here with a crowbar."

"You're welcome to stay as long as you want," I laughed. "I love having you here. I can't believe I said that. I love having a house full of chaos, toddler giggles, and midnight screams. Though, I'm not sure I'm up to making lunch right now. Do you guys have anything you can fix?"

Out of the deafening silence, Cassy volunteered, "I can make toast."

"Ooh, and I can make eggs and fry up some bacon," Sammie piped in.

"It all sounds wonderful. I look forward to tasting your results," I said. "I'm going to go and sit down again for a little bit."

Sammie held my elbow, and we trailed after Needles to the couch where Needles and Ana fought over my lap. I ended up with Ana in my lap and Needles in hers. I leaned my head against the back of the couch and watched my family in the kitchen and smiled. I knew I needed to talk to them about what happened at the morgue, but I was exhausted again. I would explain it when we ate.

I couldn't believe I fell asleep again. The TV was on an old *Love Boat* episode, but otherwise the house was silent. I didn't know what woke me up until I heard knocking at the front door. Gingerly getting up from the couch, I took my slow gait down the hallway, where I pulled the door open and found Desio on my front step.

"Desio? I should have known when I heard the

knock," I said. "What are you doing here?"

"I got your message, and I'm here to take it all down."

"Wha's goin' on, Laci?" Cassy asked. She stopped before reaching us. Then she got a good look at who was at the front door.

"Desio's here because of the run-in with the SUV I had with my car. Are you going to take everything down from the SUV hitting me while running the other day too?" I asked.

"Did you ask her about the man from the morgue yet?" he asked.

"I didn't get a chance to," I said.

"Do what now?" Cassy asked.

"There's a man in the morgue with the same last name as Zach. I was called down and questioned about him by Desio here. I was on my way home when the SUV hit me."

Cassy let out an f-bomb that could have leveled the house, but it didn't even phase Desio.

"You want to do this at the station?" I asked. He paused but then nodded. "Then can I get a ride with you?"

"We can fill out a report for you on the hit and run, both of them, while we're down there," he said.

"Why it gotta be right now?" Cassy asked. "I don't like this. Uh-unh, I don't like this at all," Cassy said.

"I know you don't, but I have to do it anyway, and Desio's here and can take me. I won't be gone long," I said.

The drive to the station was quiet, with neither of us feeling particularly social. Finally, we arrived, and I put my mask of indifference in place. Desio walked the hallways with authority radiating from him like the sun off a summer street. We were in his arena now and I had to play by his rules.

I followed him through an area of cubicles, crammed with men and women in police uniforms who poured into the walkways. When they saw Desio coming, they parted like the Red Sea. I was met with open curiosity and here and there a little hostility. But instead of hanging my head in shame, I held my chin up and refused to be intimidated by him or anyone else in the building.

We took a sharp right in a large room with more desks and more uniforms and walked down a small hallway painted white on the top and blue on the bottom. There were a few people in cuffs being led by a uniform or two. No one I knew or recognized.

The door to Desio's office was nondescript, and it matched the space well. It was painted gray, with a wooden bookshelf on one wall and a large window on the opposite side of the room. His desk sat in the middle of the room, where it was piled with stacks of paper in varying stages of chaos. The picture was complete with a couple of folding chairs parked around it. Another officer joined us when we sat down—ready with a notepad and recorder.

I was surprised to see someone else in here when all we were doing was looking over my statement and signing it on the SUV hit and run. Desio ran through the gamut of questions we covered last night, asking for a few more details here and there.

"Can you tell me the last time you saw your ex-husband?" Desio slid the question across the table like a gambler with the winning cards.

"What the hell does that have to do with this?" I asked.

"Some new evidence has surfaced regarding your ex-husband's murder, and I'd like to know when the last time you saw him was." He didn't raise his voice. He never raised his voice.

"The last I saw my ex, aside from IDing him at the morgue last week, was fifteen years ago when we signed the divorce papers at the courthouse. I've told you this before. Why the sudden interest?"

Desio locked eyes with me and I recognized the hard line of his jaw. He didn't want to tell me anything more, but he would do it anyway. "We've had an anonymous tip that says otherwise."

"It's funny how anonymous tips pop up at opportune times. So, now I'm supposed to believe you when you could be making the entire thing up?"

"Why would I make it up?" he asked. Something in his tone led me to think I may have hurt his feelings. *Hardly*.

"Why the hell would I?" I asked.

"Were you able to ask Samantha about Thomas Wheaton?" he asked.

"No, I saw her briefly this morning before I fell asleep. Being in a car accident takes it out of you," I said.

"Tell me about the SUV that hit you," he said.

"I think it's the same one that hit me when I was running earlier this week. It looks the same, but as Cassy also said, it looks like a lot of black SUVs are out there. This one just happens to always know where I am."

"What else do you remember from the SUV?" he

asked.

"It has limo-tinted windows, and something covers the license plate." I closed my eyes, taking me back to what I witnessed. I opened them to continue. "I couldn't see if there were little bits of me all over the front, but they might have transferred to the back of my car since that's where he hit me. I didn't think about that until now."

The muscle in Desio's jaw ticked, but I couldn't tell if he was mad at the person who hit me, or me. I know who I hoped it was.

Before he could come back from that, we were interrupted when someone tapped on the door. The officer got up and opened the door, and I heard Cassy's raised voice outside. Anger flashed through Desio's eyes, and a wicked grin flitted across mine as Cassy pushed the door open. She stood just inside with her arms crossed over her chest and gave Desio a stare-down.

"You ready to go?" Cassy asked. She didn't take her eyes off him.

"I don't know. Am I, Desio?" I asked.

"Am *I* ready for you to leave?" he asked. He switched his gaze to me, and I felt it to my toes. "No, I'm not ready for you to leave. I have an ex-husband and a relative of his both dead and both with a connection to you. Then there's the black SUV problem. What do you think, Duvall? Do you think I'm ready for you to leave?" He jerked his head and motioned the officer over. After a quick scan of his notes, he turned back to me. "We'll have the reports typed up for you to sign tomorrow. You're free to go—but don't leave town."

Chapter Ten

A scream pierced the quiet morning, and I promptly fell out of bed. Again. Scrambling for the door, I raced down the steps with Cassy a heartbeat behind me, which meant it could be Sammie screaming.

At the bottom of the stairs, I glanced toward the front of the house, and Sammie was leaning against the door sobbing. I ran to her and began checking her for injuries. She couldn't control the amount of shaking she was doing, so I helped her into the home office and set her on the wingback chair by my desk.

"Sammie? Sammie? What's wrong? What's happened?" I asked.

"Z— Zach— Zach—"

"What?" I asked. "What about Zach?" Her teeth were chattering, and she lifted her finger and pointed at the front door.

Cassy was immediately on her feet and looking outside. "Holy shit," she exclaimed.

I reached her in six strides and there in front of us on my small front porch was a giant block of ice with Zach frozen inside.

"Now, how the hell do you think they did that?" Cassy asked. I shushed her and pointed to Sammie. "Oh, yeah. Sorry. I'mma go call this in."

Cassy had a good question, how on earth did someone do this? I tilted my head to the right trying to

124

take it all in. I probably resembled Needles when he looked at something, confused as all get out.

It was hot as hell out there already, which meant he must not have been in place long. There was a small water trail off the porch, but otherwise, you couldn't tell it had begun melting.

"Good morning, Dr. Mann," I called, "I have Zach."

"Good news then?" he asked.

"I guess you could say that."

"Okay, I'll leave now. What's the address? Have you alerted the police?"

I rattled off my address and went inside to stay with Sammie, who was as white as a sheet.

"They sending someone over now," Cassy said.

"Sammie, do you need a drink of water? Juice?" I asked.

"I'm gonna go an' take care of somethin' real quick," Cassy said.

She walked by a few minutes later carrying one of my moving blankets from the upstairs linen closet. The front door opened and closed, and I knew what she was doing. We didn't need to bring more attention to the house than we had already. Ten minutes later, Cassy walked through the front door, and five after that, the doorbell rang.

"Hello again, Desio." I greeted him at the front door.

He was giving the blanket-covered ice block the side-eye. "Is this why I'm here?" he asked, gesturing to the block. I nodded and closed the front door behind me. I lifted the blanket so he could see what it was. "Is that?" he asked.

"Yes, I found Zach for you."

"He's…"

"Yes, yes he is."

"Have you called the ME?" he asked. "May I come in and speak to whoever found him?"

"Yes, Dr. Mann is on his way, and his wife found him," I said. "Sammie? Desio wants to speak to you. Do you want to talk in here or in the front room?"

"Anyplace quiet is fine." He spoke in a hushed voice. Good to know he had some manners.

"You can use the office. I've got the kids, Sammie. You go on." She got up from the couch, and with shoulders drooping, handed me Ryan, then followed Desio into the front room.

Needles, Ana, Ryan, and I went through the screen and sat on the back patio. I threw the ball for Needles, and the twins giggled when he brought it back again and again.

I needed to brief Colonel Waters and was thankful when he picked up the phone right away. I took a few minutes to fill him in on the accident while I had him then finished up by telling him how Zach had shown up on our doorstep.

"Jingle all the way, Major. It sounds like you have your plate full. You haven't seen Major Mitchell, have you?"

"Oh…no, sir. Why do you ask?"

"He's been MIA in the office today," he said. "I have a tasker for him, but since I can't find his ass anywhere, I'm drafting an MFR instead."

"I'll be able to help you once this is taken care of if you need me, sir."

"You're not the one I want for this job, Duvall.

However, in light of Major Mitchell's absence, would you care to expand on your statement from your office yesterday?"

"What do you mean, sir?" I didn't want to rat out Major Mitchell unnecessarily.

"Major, I know there was a skirmish. I want to know the specifics. Now."

"Yes, sir." I blew out a breath and then filled him in on what happened in the office. I had to start and stop and then start again due to his elevating anger and colorful use of expletives, some of which I had never even heard before. He had quite an imagination.

"Bison biscuits, Major. Why the hell didn't you tell me this yesterday when I asked you?"

"Because I thought it was best at the time, sir," I said.

"Next time, Major, let me be the one who decides whether or not it's the right time," Colonel Waters bit out.

He hung up, and Ana chose that moment to bring me the ball with Needles hot on her heels. Her hair stood up on one side where Needles had licked her, but she was full of giggles and joy. Hard to believe her daddy was dead on my front porch. When my name was called, I gathered the twins, and we went inside.

Sammie was standing by the stairs with her head hanging low. She squared her shoulders the minute she saw the twins and pasted a smile on her face.

"You okay?" I asked.

She nodded before reaching down and picking up Ana and taking Ryan's hand to help him up the steps. "I don't want these guys to see anything they shouldn't, so we'll hang out upstairs for a while." She angled her head toward the front door, and I knew she was trying to keep the kids from seeing their dad in his current state.

"I'll let you know when everything's clear." Outside the front door, Desio was taking the blanket off while Dr. Mann helped from the other side to make sure it didn't fall over. I didn't see Cassy anywhere.

"Where's Cassy?" I asked.

"She's in her room making phone calls," Sammie said before she disappeared around the landing on the stairs.

Walking to the front door, I saw the ME technician walking a hand truck to the porch to transport Zach. Once Zach was settled onto it, they walked him to the van.

"Will he be going back to the MEs office for good?" I asked.

"Yes, we're going to make sure there is adequate security for him so this doesn't happen again," Desio said. "Do you have a few minutes to read over the police reports from yesterday and sign them?"

"Sure," I said. "Would you like something to drink?" I grabbed water from the fridge and held it up.

He shook his head and went to the dining table where he sat diagonal to me at the head. Reading through the paperwork, I felt the table moving where he bounced his leg under the table, and I smiled, remembering the other night in the sedan.

"See something funny, Duvall?" he asked.

"Are you nervous, Desio?" I asked—my face a mask of innocence.

He gave me a blank look, but then his face cleared, and his mouth kicked up at the corner. This time the smile reached his eyes. I felt my stomach do flips, and it was like we were sixteen all over again. Desio *was* attractive—if only he weren't such an uptight ass.

"Were you able to move on the people who had Zach? Or did they bring him to us before your guys could do anything?" I asked.

"We got stuck obtaining a search warrant," he said.

"I hesitate to tell you, but I spoke to one of them on the phone this week," I said.

"They called you again?" he asked.

"Umm, not exactly. When they called me for ransom money the first time, I copied their number and called them back yesterday. The man I spoke with on the phone tried to sell Zach back to me. It was we—"

"You called and spoke with them, and you're just now telling me?" he ground out.

Uh oh. "Yes?" I said. "Dr. Mann and I think it's a front for other stuff, but the listing is for Benny's Mattresses on Edmonson."

Desio jotted that down in his notebook while we waged a small staring contest—I don't know who won. I went back to reading the report and signed the bottom line, and no sooner had the pen left the paper than Desio grabbed them and was striding toward the front door. He stopped when he reached it.

"Let me know if you hear anything else from these guys. I hate being in the dark. Got it?" He wouldn't look at me and instead looked out the front door.

"I doubt this will happen again since I don't think we were what they planned on. We didn't jump at their commands, so I think they're going to try something else," I said.

He nodded. Thoughts were racing through his head

and across his face. Then, finally, he blew out a breath, looked at me, and added in a hushed tone, "I didn't plan for you, either." Then he waved and was gone.

I turned and walked back into the quiet house and the kitchen, where I gathered my supplies and made a sandwich.

"Would you like something to eat?" Cassy came down the steps when I closed the refrigerator. "I haven't eaten yet today."

"Sounds good," she said. "How'd your talk with boss man go?"

"It was fine. I filled him in on everything Zach related and told him what happened with Major Mitchell."

"What happened?" she asked.

"I must not have told anyone," I mused. "We were arguing in the office when he placed his hands on me without being invited."

"He did what now?"

"It's okay. He won't make the same mistake again. Though if looks could kill, I would be dead and frozen with Zach, right now."

"Uh-huh, little shit. Let him try that when I'm whichu. What'd you do—get 'em in the man chicken?"

Sweet tea flew out of my mouth and all over the front of Cassy. I started coughing and gagged when I tried to inhale.

"What the hell, woman?" She grabbed the towel off the oven door and used it to dry her shirt and shorts while waiting for the coughing to stop.

"Where on earth did you hear that term?" I wheezed out.

"Which one?"

"Ma—man—"

"Oh, man-chicken?" she asked with a grin. "My momma taught me that one, on account I got two older brothers and two younger. Believe you me; there was plenty of man-chicken floppin' all over my house. You know what I'm sayin'?"

"Where'd you grow up?" I asked. I grabbed our sandwiches while she got the chips, and we sat at the table. Sandwiches for breakfast—just like old times.

"I'm from San Fran." She closed her eyes, and a smile spread across her face as she remembered. "My mom, brothers, and I lived in a small house. We were crammed in there, but it was cozy. You know? Not crowded."

"I didn't know you had brothers—tell me about them. Where are they now?"

"Alexander was the oldest, and he was my idol. He lived up to his name, defender of man. He was a policeman killed in the line of duty about five years ago." Cassy sighed. "I miss him every day. Next is Harold, who was named after my momma's brother. He in the Army and lives in Jersey—I go up and see him whenever I can. Then me, and then comes Jerome. He a priest." She roared with laughter. "Oh, the trouble we used to get into when we were kids. The fact that he a priest now is too much. Last is Benjamin. He's the baby. Benjamin stayed in San Fran when the rest of us left. He's studying to be an architect—the boy is a genius."

"Where's your mom? Is she still alive?" I asked.

"She passed away a couple years ago. It was the last time all of us was together, but we email a lot and send awful memes to each other on social media. They the best."

In the spirit of sharing, I opened up a little about myself. "I have a sister named Mellissa who lives outside Seattle in Everett. She and my sister-in-law, Danica, have one kid they adopted."

"No, shit? You got a gay sister?"

"Yes," I laughed. Then I stopped. "We were close growing up, and now she's settled down with Danica, and their daughter, Daisy. I miss her."

We wrapped up breakfast, and I left Cassy in the kitchen to go and let Sammie know the coast was clear if she wanted to bring the twins down. They were in their room with Sammie and Ana immersed in a bowling game with a small ball and some empty water bottles while Ryan was in the process of waking up in the bed.

We all went downstairs and while Sammie went and got their breakfast together, I went to call auto-body shops. When it was almost ten and I was at my desk finishing up the eighth call, my phone rang.

"Okay, lady. You got him back. Now, where's my money?"

"I told you before. I don't have your money," I said.

"Listen, yous, we gonna start following you until you cough up the money. You hear?"

"Good luck," I said. "Maybe you can figure out who's following me." This was all I needed, two tails.

Sammie and Cassy walked into the office when I hung up. "Apparently, we're going to have a tail until we find Zach and the money."

"Do what now?" Cassy asked.

"I think that was the guy who had Zach. He's still

demanding I repay him what Zach took, no matter how many times I've told him I don't have it. When are you going back to work?" I asked.

"I'm thinking of not going back."

"Wait what? When did that happen?" I asked. "What are you going to do instead?"

"I don't know. I got vacation time built up, so I don't need to know right away. I'll still be getting paid, just not puttin' in the long hours, and getting the headaches or stomachaches. That job makes me sick to my stomach, man. I graduated Magna Cum Laude with my Bachelor's in Criminal Justice a couple of years ago. Maybe I'll do somethin' with it now."

"What about law school or something similar?" I asked.

"I thought about that once, and now seems as good a time as any to think about it again. What are we up to the rest of today?" Cassy asked.

"Right now, I'm trying to find someone who can get my car fixed in less than six weeks."

"I gotchu. Lemme make a few calls." She took her phone and went out the back door, Needles trailing behind her. Boo was already out there lying in the middle of the yard, at least until Needles got to her, she was.

"How was your talk with Desio?" Sammie was cleaning the kitchen and Ana stood with the refrigerator door open and her hand in the blackberries. Her face was covered in blackberry juice and Ryan lay on the floor in the hallway making angels on the carpet.

"It was okay. He's very down to business—no small talk."

"Yep, that's his cop face. It's why I didn't take my

trip to the precinct too hard, but I don't trust anyone else to figure out what happened to Zach."

"Oh, yes," Sammie said. "I don't doubt that he can get the job done."

"Speaking of getting the job done. When you guys moved into your parents' house, what happened to all your stuff?"

"Everything's in a storage unit over by Martin State Airport."

"How about we go on a scavenger hunt today and go through the unit and see if we can find anything?"

"What about Ryan and Ana?" Sammie asked.

"They can come with us. Do you have toys and stuff in storage? We can dig through it and see if there are any you want to bring here."

"You would let me do that?" she asked. There was a note of hopefulness in her voice.

"Well, of course, they need something to play with, don't they? They've done amazing without anything so far, but yeah, you can get their toys."

"What are we doin'?" Cassy came in at the tail end of the conversation.

"We're going to Sammie's storage unit to see if Zach left anything we can use. Any luck?"

"Yep, we gonna go see Carlos. He got a shop on Old Eastern Avenue. Owes me a favor."

"Does everyone owe you a favor?" I asked. She thought about it for a second, and I laughed. "I was kidding."

"I know, but yeah, I gotta lotta folks who owe me a thing or two. What can I say? I'm a helpful person."

****

With Cassy right behind me, we drove Philadelphia

Road to Carlos's shop. Billboards everywhere proclaimed their love for the Orioles. The boards have been around for generations and had been there since I learned to drive many years ago. The O's logo may have changed through the years, but my loyalty to them never did. I could be at Ali Al Salem in Kuwait or walking the streets of New York City, but when I saw another fan sporting their Oriole pride, I always asked, "How 'bout them O's?"

We reached the shop on Old Eastern, and Cassy and I went to meet Carlos, a very flirty man. He effervesced about my beauty while alternatively asking about my car for close to ten minutes until Cassy called it off so we could get moving.

Cruising in Cassy's unairconditioned car, we drove with the windows down and the wind blowing our hair. We cranked up the '90s Hip Hop and sang along with Salt-N-Pepa as we pulled onto Eastern Boulevard. Before we hit the drive-in on Eastern, we turned left into the storage yard.

Sammie checked us in, and we wound our way into the labyrinth of white units covered with blue roofs and blue doors lined with black trim. I wondered if we would need breadcrumbs to find our way back out when Sammie pointed out her unit. Cassy pulled under the overhang and eked out as much shade as possible.

We spilled out of the car like ice cream running down your arm and while Sammie unlocked the unit, I got the twins out of their car seats. Once the garage-like door was rolled up, it was plain to see she was in a hurry when she dropped everything off. There was no organization anywhere, which says a lot coming from me.

The inside radiated heat and was painted white. There were scuff marks covering the walls from the constant rotation of people in and out of the unit. A pair of eight-foot, brown, particleboard bookshelves filled with toys and books sat propped up on the right side.

Next to the bookcases on the right was a file cabinet while a sofa lined the back wall with collapsed cribs propped on the left side. A small dinette table with chairs was planted in the middle of the unit, and the remainder of the space was full of boxes and suitcases.

"How long has all this been in here?" I asked.

"Since we moved to my parents' house a few months ago. I asked Zach if we could keep any toys with us because the kids needed something to keep them occupied. They cried at my parents' house when I didn't have anything to help keep them quiet. I swanny, I think that's why Momma had such a hard time when I came back after he died. I couldn't help it—these guys were bored. I didn't blame them. I was bored too, and we were only there a few short hours."

"Okay then," I said. "I'll start with the file cabinet. Cassy, do you want to go through some of the boxes in the corner? Sammie, you find toys for the kids, though it looks like they got started without us. Does that sound okay? Once you get them occupied, you can help us with the boxes."

Sammie shuffled off through boxes and toys while clearing a path to the bookcase. I stepped over boxes, small appliances, a small brush and dustpan, and a stack of magazines. When I got to the file cabinet, I pulled the top drawer open. Empty. *Damnit*

The next drawer held a jewelry box which I opened and found lint and a few coins rattling around. I put that to the side and looked through everything underneath. There were a lot of bills and notices for money due, but nothing else.

Finished with the file cabinet, I turned to where the kids sat inside a circle of toys, with Sammie outside the circle rummaging through cartons at her feet. I grabbed a few boxes next to Cassy, put them on the table, and combed through them.

Cassy sat diagonal to me, rifling through her containers while surrounded by more. She resembled a goddess in a garden, except it was boxes and not flowers, and there was sweat dripping down the side of her face.

An hour and a half later, we still hadn't come up with anything. Not only was it hot, but the kids were getting cranky, so we decided to wrap things up and head home.

The kids got into a fight over a toy while we were packing things away along the back wall of the unit. It just showed you how tired and overheated they were. Wrestling with the toy and each other, they collided with the bookshelf, and it started rocking.

"Look out," I cried.

I reached Ryan first and grabbed him, and Sammie snatched up Ana just before the bookcase tumbled forward, and the toys cascaded to the floor of the unit, spilling onto the concrete outside. The baskets fell off the top and scattered in the circle of toys where the kids had just been sitting. One landed with a clang outside the unit, and crumpled papers scattered and flew everywhere.

While Cassy set the shelf back upright, I scanned the papers I picked up from the basket, and Sammie occupied the kids outside with a game.

"Hey, Laci, what's this?" Cassy asked. She handed me one of the crumbled-up pieces of paper.

"A paper," I said with a big grin. Cassy's reply was her middle finger. "It's Zach's writing. Looks like a bunch of notes and numbers in shorthand." Reaching back to my high school business class, I could only recall snippets of shorthand, but it was nowhere near enough. "I didn't know he knew how to write like this."

"I know shorthand, but this here is some kinda weird-ass gibberish. I'll look at it again when we back at the house though," Cassy said.

We gathered up the remaining papers that spilled out, and after scanning for a basket, I grabbed the one that landed next to Cassy's car. The keys in it came flying out and hit Cassy in the ass. I snorted, but then she picked them up and put them in her pocket.

"Hey—" I said.

"These'll be fine right here," she said.

Ana came racing around the corner of the unit just then, arms pumping, and ran to the toy she and Ryan had been fighting over. In the blink of an eye, she nabbed it and wrapped her arms around it, which was when Ryan realized he missed it and started to wail.

"Y'all, we're done." Sammie stashed the toys she picked out in Cassy's trunk, and we piled everything else back in the unit. After we locked it and were back in the car, we agreed to hit Groov's drive-through and grab lunch before going home. Sammie fed the kids on the way, so all she had to do was get them upstairs, washed, and down for their naps.

We scattered to our activities once we got home and agreed to meet after the kids were asleep. Needles went to the backyard, and since I spent enough time in the heat this morning, he was on his own. Back inside, Cassy was coming downstairs with a laptop tucked under her arm. She sat down at the kitchen table.

"What are you doing?" I asked.

"Lookin' up law schools."

"You settled on law school then?" I asked.

"I'm considering it."

"Do you have money for school?" I asked.

"A bit that my momma left me. I'mma have to work, but I don't want to be a cop anymore."

"Well, room and board are taken care of as long as I'm here," I said. I was more than happy to have her stay with me, no matter where Sammie ended up.

"Thank you, that takes a lot of pressure off me, you know? What kind of jobs are out there for tired cops?"

"We'll brainstorm once we wrap up this ordeal with Zach and once you have a school picked out."

Thirty minutes later, Sammie joined us, and we sat at the table and ate and discussed everything.

"Sammie, did you know of anyone by the name of Thomas Thornton or Thomas Wheaton?"

Sammie gave me the deer in the headlights look. I waved my hand in front of her eyes, and she didn't even blink.

"How do you know that name?" she asked.

Cassy and I glanced at each other. "I was called down to the morgue and asked to ID him. You know him?"

She nodded. "It's Zach's brother."

"What?" I asked.

"Did you know he had a brother?" Cassy asked.

"Hell no," I said. "The asshole never told me

anything. Why didn't Zach talk about him?"

"Because he's supposed to be dead already. Like from years ago dead already," Sammie said.

"Oh shit," I said.

"Did he look young? Old?" Sammie asked.

"He looked to be about my age or perhaps a little older. Not like he had been in a freezer somewhere for decades on end if that's what you mean."

"So, he died recently," Cassy said.

"Can you see what your partner knows?" I asked.

"I'm on it," she said. She whipped out her phone and stepped out back while dialing her partner, Amaré.

"That's not even the strange part," I said. "While being interrogated, Desio asked me when was the last time I saw Zach. He said they received an anonymous tip someone had recently seen me with him."

"What did you tell him?"

"I told him the truth—that it's been at least fifteen years since I last saw him. When he signed the divorce papers."

"I wonder who called in the anonymous tip? Do you think it was Floyd or Janis because you came to see them last week without asking first?" Sammie asked.

"I guess anything is possible, but I think Desio would have told me if it had been one of them. The thing is—just because Zach saw me doesn't mean I saw him. You know? What did Amaré say? How did he die?" Cassy came in from outside, and I pounced on her with questions.

"They don' know yet, but they think it's poison," Cassy said.

"Oh, lovely. How'd he get it?" I asked.

"Water bottle."

"Prints?"

She gave me a deadpan look. "Now, how the hell would I know that? You know what they say about poison, though—it's a woman's choice of killing." Cassy said.

"Great, this is all the ammunition the police need to pin it on me. Between this and my career choice, I'm a prime suspect."

"If it could be you, it could be anyone," Cassy said.

"Did you say you knew how to read shorthand?" I handed Cassy the small stack of papers for her to look through.

"Yeah—before I was a cop, I did a stint as a court reporter."

"Really?" I asked. "That sounds interesting."

She was shaking her head before I finished. "Boring as hell, man. I only got traffic cases and the dull-ass white folks who couldn't park worth a damn."

"Why were they in court?" Sammie asked.

"Now that is the million-dollar question," she said. "They all thought they didn't need to pay. That the cops were out to tag their ass. Said it was a conspiracy or some shit. Naw, y'all white folk just can't park. It ain't that hard, man. Overall, I liked it, though. Hunh, maybe I'll think of doing that again to help with school. It definitely is less stressful. I could use some boring in my life."

Cassy pored over the shorthand and jotted down a few notes while Sammie and I ate and chatted, waiting for her to finish up. Suddenly, Cassy stood up and grabbed the key from her pocket and slapped it on the table between us.

"Safe deposit or locker key?" she asked.

"Is that what Zach wrote in the papers?" I asked. I reached for the papers before her. "Did he sa—"

"Naw, I just remembered where I seen one before. This here is gibberish. Some of it's shorthand and some of it's his version of it. Even the shit I can read don't make no sense."

The key was square-bodied, but other than that, it was normal. It was brass plated and worn off in places and topped off with a piece of black string.

"Have you seen this before, Sammie?" Cassy asked. Sammie shook her head while staring at the key on the table.

"What about his shorthand? Do you understand his version of it?" I asked.

"I remember seeing him writing stuff down, and these papers match the kind he used to keep in a folder beside the bed."

"Did you guys have a box somewhere?" I asked. "It could go to a storage locker too. If it weren't so hot, I'd say let's go back to the storage place, but that's too much even for me."

"None that I know of, but I'm learning that there's a lot I didn't know about him."

"I think there's a lot that both of us didn't know about him," I said. "I think one step in finding more about him is to go to Benny's Mattresses and see if we can dig anything up."

"You just gonna walk in the front door and expect them to talk?" Cassy asked. "Hunh—I wanna see that."

"I wasn't planning on seeing anyone," I said.

"Now what now?" Cassy asked.

Chapter Eleven

The house was quiet with no dog barking and no screaming from Cassy, Sammie, or even me. Boo heard me roll over and stretch and bounded onto the comforter at the bottom of the bed. I knew she was hungry, but it was nice just to lie there and stare at the ceiling: no demands, no deadlines, no meetings, nothing. I could get used to this... *Nah.* I rolled out of bed and went to get ready for my morning. Shorts, a shirt, and shoes were the wardrobe for the day.

Since we were planning to recon at Benny's tonight, I stayed home from work this morning. I would run over to the office later today to check in with Colonel Waters.

Needles greeted me when I dropped a kiss on the top of his furry head and Boo did her bit and smacked him through the gate. Secretly she liked him; she just didn't want him to know it.

While I was outside with Needles, Cassy called to me from the kitchen, "You want coffee or tea?"

"Now, you already know the answer to that question." I joked with her when I passed through the screen. She was returning the jug to the refrigerator. "Any sign of Sammie yet?"

"Naw, not yet, but I heard moving around in the room."

The kids liked peanut butter toast and it was the

norm on lazy mornings, so, I got the stuff together and set to work. Before it was finished they were downstairs and sitting on the floor in the living room. Sammie closed the back door so Needles wouldn't eat it out of their hands again.

"Sammie, your job is to contact your folks again about babysitting while we head to Benny's Mattress tonight."

"Oh, crap," Sammie whispered. "Are you sure this is a good idea?"

"Well, the alternative is that you stay. Would you rather do that?" I asked.

"I didn't say that." She rushed on, "This is just new to me, and it's terrifying." She stuck her thumbnail in her mouth.

"Flashlights are in my A-Bag in the hall closet upstairs. I'll grab it and see if there's anything else in there we need."

We discussed a few more things before we went our separate ways to get our items and bring them back. I called Carlos about my car, but after a bunch of laughter when I asked about it, I decided to leave it up to Cassy from now on. I remembered Colonel Waters had my zoom lens, and after I called over to him, I hopped in Cassy's car to get it.

I entered his office after knocking and hearing the familiar command.

"Good morning, sir."

He was standing at the filing cabinet rifling through some papers, but he closed the drawer and turned toward me.

"Good morning, Major, glad to see you here. Here's your lens. Thank you for letting me borrow it for a little while. It came in handy on our vacation." He handed me the lens, and I packed it into my bag.

"Glad I could help, sir."

"You're out for the day?"

"I am, sir. Are you okay, sir? You don't sound like yourself."

He turned his head toward me, and his shoulders drooped. He opened his mouth to say something but must have thought better of it because he closed it without saying anything. At sixty, Colonel Waters was past retiring and should have been enjoying Hawai'i right about now, but he chose to remain when the Air Force asked him to, just like I did.

"We've known each other a long time, haven't we, Major Duvall?"

"Yes, sir." I remembered the first time I worked with him. We met on my first deployment about twelve years ago.

"I'm tired, Duvall," he began. "I'm tired of the politics that come with the job and the position. I'm tired of the endless hours and nights wide awake wondering how my people are doing, be it here or in the theater. I've been doing this a long time, Major, over thirty-five years to be exact. I've watched the Air Force change over and over, but I don't know if I have it in me to watch it change again."

"I understand, sir."

"Do you?" he asked.

"Yes, sir, while my time is dramatically different from yours, I have seen the Air Force change, too. The world is also changing, sir, and the Air Force has to adapt. I don't agree with all the ways it's changing, but I believe most are necessary, sir."

He gestured for me to take a seat in front of his desk, and I sat down.

"I've been getting pressure from Command where you're concerned," he said.

I snapped to attention in my chair. "Concerning me what?"

"Someone's creating noise and making threats in some very important people's ears. I worry for you and your career, Major."

"What's being said, sir? Do you know who's saying these things?"

"It concerns the situation with Zach's death. There's grumbling that you did it— not that I believe it, Major." He held his hand up to hush me since I opened my mouth to tell him otherwise. "Now, Duvall, I know you had no more to do with his death than I did, but I'm not who matters. The scuffle you had with Major Mitchell in the office this week only added fuel to the fire."

Shit. I couldn't imagine anyone trying to pinpoint Zach's death on me. Who would do such a thing? Floyd and Janis were the only ones I could think of who disliked me enough.

"Sir, I have been trying to retire for five years, and I've been coerced and conned into staying in. So, maybe this time, I let them 'push' me out or tell them where they can put the threats. If I need to, I have ears of my own that will listen to me, sir. As for Major Mitchell the other day, he's just upset because his wife left him, sir." I hoped I convinced Colonel Waters I was confident in my standing with the Air Force. I didn't want him to know I was scared out of my wits.

"How do you know that?" he asked.

"It's common knowledge here in the office, sir. Mitchell has made a lot of enemies, and they aren't above greasing the wheel of gossip."

"I would hope that you would be above things such as this, Major."

"I never said I participated, sir, just that I listened," I said. "Do you know how I can get a hold of his ex-wife? I don't want to ask him, but I think it would benefit us to speak to her. How much information is Mitchell coming up with in his investigation? Has he met with you about what he knows?"

"Let me see what I can do, Major. In the meantime, it might be better if you avoided Major Mitchell." He didn't have to tell me twice.

****

With the kids kissed goodnight and hugs all around, we loaded into the car and set out for West Baltimore. Cassy knew these roads like the back of her hand and took us down the maze of city streets instead of hitting the interstate. At one point, I think I even saw a llama in a storefront window.

People are funny. Like the three of us—never in a million years would I have put us together, yet here we were. Three entirely different lives crashing into each other at a random time and place.

I had a small connection to Sammie, but we were never friends, and I'm pretty sure Zach bashed the hell out of me to her at some point. Now I'd call us friends—closer than friends. Life knocked on my door and gave me the best four gifts I could ever have gotten.

We found a spot in the library parking lot on Edmonson and walked down the street to the mattress store. Benny's neighbors were a muffler shop and a tobacco store, and I hoped none of them liked to stay late. We packed for every contingency that we could imagine, but you never knew what would happen in these things.

"You okay?" I asked. Sammie's eyes were as big as saucers as she took in everything.

"I'm doing this for my babies," she said while nodding. "I have to keep telling myself that."

My gun was tucked in the back of my jeans where I could easily reach it, and Cassy assured me hers was within reach; Sammie held the taser. She didn't have the confidence for a gun yet, and that was a breeding ground for disaster.

The lights were off in the muffler shop on our first go-round, but they were still on in Benny's. When we passed the alley behind Benny's, red eyes winked at us where a couple of guys stood smoking. The smell of marijuana was one I never got used to, and it wafted toward us in the dead air.

"What is that?" Sammie asked.

"Shhh," Cassy whispered. We were even with the men and didn't need the unwanted attention. I didn't know if these guys knew what we looked like or not, but now was not the time to find out they did.

As we turned the corner of a neighboring street, a car backfired behind us, and we jumped out of our skin. Unfortunately for me, I was the closest to Sammie because she pulled out her taser and shot it in one fell swoop, and boy did I go down like a gangster witness dropped off a bridge wearing cement shoes.

"Oh, no!" Sammie exclaimed from the end of a long tunnel. She rushed over to where I lay flat on my back on the sidewalk and started shaking me. "I'm so sorry," she said. "I'm so sorry," she told Cassy. There was nothing to be done but wait until the fire in my veins stopped.

Sammie paced back and forth behind me, and Cassy eyed the cars that drove by. We got a few looks while we waited, but no one moved in our direction.

"What the hell, Sammie!" I asked the minute I could think straight.

"I'm sorry, Laci, I'm so sooo sorry. The car backfired, and it scared me, and I thought it was someone shooting at us, and I was scared, and I wasn't thinking, and I pulled it out, and I didn't know the trigger—did you know the trigger just has to be lightly touched? I had no idea. I thought it was like a gun where you have to put some real effort into it for it to work, but I barely touched it, and it went off. I had no idea it would go off that easily." She stuttered to a halt. Cassy and I glanced at each other when Cassy turned her shaking head toward me.

"Are you okay?" Cassy asked.

"Yeah, I'm fine," I said, "I just need a bit to get straight in the head again." I was up on my feet, but I tripped over a pebble on the sidewalk. When I finally stopped watching my feet, a white van pulled out of the alley where the smokers had been. Emblazoned on the side was a cartoon of a man with a bald head falling onto a cartoon mattress and the words Benny's Mattress written around him in red. I turned away once I saw the picture, hoping he hadn't seen my face.

"Come on, let's go back and see if the smoke shop has closed," Cassy suggested. We retraced our steps and walked past the alley. Glancing to our left, I saw the lights were off in the small strip mall alongside

Benny's. We kept going until we got to the end and turned around again. This time on our way back, we walked slower so as not to draw attention, so of course, that's exactly what we got.

Five yards from where we turned around, a car rolled up next to us, and a college-aged kid stuck his head out the window.

"Hey, hot stuff, how much for an hour? It's my birthday—give me a treat?" I glanced at Cassy, who looked pissed, then I looked at Sammie, who hadn't heard a thing the kid said. We tried to stay the course, but they rolled right along with us. Finally, we got to the alley and walked in, and lucky for us, he took that as an invitation and hopped out of the car and pursued us, and he brought along his buddies. Once we got to Benny's, we pivoted and faced our pursuers.

"Aww, c'mon ladies. We promise a good time."

"We thank you for the offer, but we're going to pass," I said.

"I don't think you understand," the birthday boy sneered. "We're not giving you an option." He pulled a knife out of his jacket, and Cassy barked a laugh. The boys looked at her like she was nuts, and I was beginning to have doubts about her sanity myself when she continued to chuckle.

"Oh lordy, y'all white boys make me laugh," she said. "Listen, kid, why don't you go back to your room and your birthday cake you left there and celebrate, okay?"

"Oh, listen to the big one. She thinks she can tell me what to do." He mouthed off to his friends and they chuckled along with him.

"I don't *think* I can do anything, but oooh, lookie

here," Cassy said. "This here badge I got for the BPD reminds me it's illegal to solicit a prostitute, and this gun"—she pulled her Glock from her holster—"helps me enforce the law when man chickens try to break it. Now, who wants to be the first for Miranda rights? Anyone?" They turned tail and fled before she got to the Miranda rights. "Damn, I never get to have any fun."

"That was awesome, Cassy!" I hooted when they were out of sight. "I can't believe you did that."

"I can't believe that just happened." Sammie stood there with her mouth hanging open.

"Aww shit, that was nothin'," Cassy said. "What d'you suggest we do now?"

"Let's go around back," I said. We darted down the rest of the strip mall until we reached the end and retraced back to Benny's. The only light was from the road as we stalked in the shadows, hugging the walls. Outside Benny's door, I set to work on the lock.

"You know this illegal, right?" Cassy asked.

"It's only illegal if you get caught," I said. I heard her snort from behind me while I was busy at work. I tried to block out the voice in the back of my head questioning the legality of a B&E, but I knew there were answers here somewhere, and right now that surpassed any niggling of guilt I had.

I inhaled the musty air, full of weed, urine, and trash around us. Cassy held her phone close to the lock so I could see what I was doing, but I didn't have the heart to tell them I'd never done this before and only read about it. I figured someone needed to have confidence.

After about five minutes, Cassy grew suspicious.

"Do you even know what you're doin'?" she asked.

"Not a clue," I answered. "They make it look so easy on TV."

"Damn woman, you wastin' time. Gimme that."

"Do you know how to do it?" I asked.

"Hell no, but I can't be any worse than you."

"Both of you hush," Sammie hissed. "Give it to me. I'll do it."

"How do you know how to do it?" Cassy asked.

"Do you know how many times those two kids have locked me out of the house? I had to learn—it was a matter of survival."

"Why didn' you say so before?" Cassy asked.

"Because no one asked me, and you all seemed to know what you were doing. Who was I to argue?"

"Sammie, you have a lot to contribute to this family. Speak the hell up," I said.

"Don't talk to her that way," Cassy retorted.

"I'm trying to be encouraging," I said.

"You think that's encouraging? Yo—"

"I'm in." Sammie interrupted us and stood with a big grin beside the open door and the dark interior.

"Great job, Sammie," I exclaimed, with a smile that matched hers.

We stepped inside and jumped in unison when the door slammed shut behind us. Thankfully, Sammie had learned her lesson out on the street and kept her taser in her pocket.

An emergency light in the right corner of the room lent a hint of green light that reached us at the door. There wasn't much by way of mattresses back here; they must be in the showroom. The area was empty except for packing boxes lining the wall to our left, a desk, and several filing cabinets in front of us and along the wall to our right. The building looked bigger from the outside.

Cassy motioned me into the showroom with a Sir Walter Raleigh flourish, which left me no choice but to go first into the showroom. The streetlight standing sentry outside the front window showed the large space, and I took it in with one swift glance. The room was crammed full of mattresses on metal bedframes that almost lay on top of each other. The beds butted up against a back wall covered by mirrors.

Years of recon had prepared me for moments like this. Dressed head to toe in black with shoes that silenced our footsteps, we didn't make a sound when we walked into the showroom.

We cleared the door into the exhibition space just as the lights came on behind us in the office.

"Ohhh, mercy," Cassy whispered. I knew how she felt.

"Scatter," I breathed.

Cassy and I took off, but Sammie stood frozen in place. I ran back, clasped her wrist, and dragged her with me toward the wall of mirrors. The voices were getting closer, so I dropped like a lead weight under the first bed I could find, hauling Sammie down with me. I stuffed her under the bed on my right, then I rolled under the bed across the tiny aisle. I could barely see her, but I held my finger to my lips to make sure she maintained radio silence. I didn't know where Cassy ended up, but she could take care of herself as she showed us outside tonight.

"I told ya, them dames don't know nothing," a man said.

"I know what you told me, but I'm not convinced. There's no way his wife didn't know nothing," man number two said.

"Which wife? Man's got two of em. Geeze, them women. They didn't want 'im." Man one again.

Their feet passed right in front of where we lay, and Sammie flinched. I prayed she could hold out a little longer. Beyond Sammie on the other side of the bed, the men disappeared. I hoped Cassy wasn't back there, but no sooner had that thought occurred than Cassy dropped on the other side of me, and army-crawled under the bed to my left. She held her finger up to her lips and shushed me, and I gave her an amused look.

"I wished like hell I got Zach to fess up where he put that money," said man number one.

Sammie's sharp inhale broke into the silence, and I pivoted my head toward her, where I held up my finger again to shush her. She nodded her head from behind her palm-covered face.

The feet walking toward the office door came to a halt about ten yards away. I held my breath as I watched those feet, but they continued into the office after a heart-stopping minute. Another five, and the lights blinked off. I gestured for the girls to remain in place as I slowly crawled from under the bed without a sound.

I stepped into the shadows against the wall and hid while also feeling my way until I reached the office door. I placed an ear against the swinging door and pushed it open with one finger so I could stick my eye to the opening. The light that spilled onto the office floor didn't reveal anyone inside, but I knew the tricks.

Instead of going in farther, I retreated to the same place the men disappeared to.

Turns out they'd gone to the bathroom. While inside I scanned for a way out and found a small twelve inch by twelve inch window at least six and a half feet up the side of the cinderblock wall. Leaving the women's room, I checked the men's and got the same result.

I clung to the shadows leaving the bathrooms and tiptoed back to the showroom, where I dropped under the bed I previously occupied. Sammie turned saucer eyes toward me, and I signaled again for her to remain quiet while Cassy lay with her eyes closed on my left. I settled in to wait indefinitely because I didn't think we were alone. Ten minutes later, the door to the office began to make its outward trip, confirming my hunch, and I watched a pair of shoes appear in the shadows.

Chapter Twelve

With a flashlight, they peered under beds on the far side of the room. *Oh shit*. If they made it to our side of the showroom, we were screwed. I tried to think of a distraction that could get us out from under the bed and into the office, but I had nothing.

I looked over at Cassy, and her eyes were as big as Sammie's. I tried to mouth to her for help, but it was no use; that damn light kept getting closer and closer. When the light reached our row the door to the office swung open.

"You done yet, L—?" man number two asked.

"There ain't no one here," man number one interrupted him. "I done told you that already. Them dames ain't gonna show up here and break in. One's a cop, for God's sake."

"Fine, then you can tell the boss."

They continued to argue while they walked back into the office. Once I calmed my nerves, I snuck out from under the bed. I put my ear to the swinging door, then nudged it open with my finger and peeked through. The door slammed shut after the men stepped outside.

"They're gone," I whispered.

"You sure?" Cassy asked.

"As sure as I can be without pushing the door to outside open. Come on—we haven't finished searching the place yet."

"How we plan on doin' that?" Cassy asked.

"You do look out in the office, while Sammie and I run through the files to see if we see anything of Zach's. We know his writing."

"Okay." Cassy went and stood by the back door we came in. She didn't push the door open but kept her hand on the doorknob and her ear to the door, just in case.

"Come on, Sammie, let's see what we can find."

I ran through the file cabinet with my penlight, and Sammie rifled through the desk next to me, with hers. There wasn't anything in the cabinet except invoices and receipts and contracts with various places in the city. The top drawer was locked, so I put Sammie to work on it while I took over searching the desk.

"Holy shit," Cassy exclaimed from across the room.

I glanced up at Cassy to see what she was talking about, but she had her eyes latched on Sammie at the filing cabinet.

Holy shit. "Who the hell keeps money like this in a simple locked drawer?" I asked. Sammie just mutely stared at the handfuls of money in the drawer. "Just shove it all back and lock it."

"I don't have a key."

"You can't lock it back?" I asked.

She shook her head. "I only learned one way—not the other."

"Then just shove it all in and close it, and maybe they won't notice."

Cassy snorted from across the room.

"Let's get out of here," I said.

I took a deep breath while Cassy stuck her head out

the door. She waved us out and thankfully the lot was empty of people and cars. We jumped again when the door slammed behind us and locked.

We made it down the street and into the car in one piece. My adrenaline was high, and I had an urge for sweet tea.

"Who's hungry?" I asked once we settled in the car.

"Now we talkin'. What do you want?" Cassy rubbed her hands together.

"Tacos, we passed Taco George a block or so back," I said.

"Ohhh yeah, count me in," Cassy shouted.

"Who?" Sammie asked.

"Only the best Tijuana-style tacos you've ever had," I said.

"Tia, who?" Sammie asked.

On Edmonson we backtracked a couple of blocks and pulled into a dimly lit parking lot. Taco George was a hole in the wall with exceptional food. We placed our order and sat down to wait. The place was deserted— which was surprising because the line was always down the block and halfway through the next one during the day.

"Well, we learned that it's money Zach took, we're not the only ones looking for it, and we almost had the name of one of the men who kidnapped Zach."

"Not a bad night's work, but where do we go from here?" Cassy asked. "We gotta find where Zach stashed the cash before they do."

"We need to find where that locker key goes," I said.

"Now, how do we go 'bout that? Do you know

how many of those things there are in Baltimore? We talkin' thousands," Cassy said.

"I think we start here in West Baltimore. That seems to be where all the action is centered," I said. "The other issue is Zach was stationed in many places—who's to say this is local?"

Cassy let out a low whistle that perfectly summed up the mess of our current situation.

"I can look at our bank and see if they have safe deposit boxes or storage lockers that Zach could have put something in." Sammie said.

I nodded and turned for the counter since our food was up then. We then dove into the best midnight snack around. There was nothing like tacos and sweet tea at midnight to make you feel alive.

****

The bank manager had never seen the key before and assured Sammie that they didn't have anything for Zach like that. After some pressure from us, he said he would keep digging and would let her know if something was found.

We returned Sammie and the kids to the house for naps, then Cassy and I began the task of tracking down storage lockers. By noon we had driven to half of our list and still hadn't come up with anything. We'd checked the bus station, train station, airport, and we were now checking the storage places that rented small lockers. We passed Benny's, and I noticed right away the yellow tape splashed across the front of the store.

"What happened? Why is there a yellow tape?" I asked.

"Beats the hell outta me. Imma call Amaré. Maybe he'll know." Cassy pulled into a spot in front of a corner deli, and I went in for snacks and drinks. When I came out, she told me he was on patrol right now, but would swing by so we could all talk in person.

I divvied up the drinks, chips, and some chocolate, and we snacked while we waited. A few minutes later, a BPD squad car pulled in, and an African American man got out. This was my first time seeing him and boy, did he leave an impression. A whistle escaped my lips before I knew it and Cassy swung her head over to me.

"What?"

"That's Amaré?" I asked.

"Yeah, why?"

"Cassy, that man is gorgeous." He was Cassy's height, maybe an inch taller, with broad shoulders and not a stitch of hair on top of his head, but he was sporting a full beard. In terms of tea, this man was unsweetened and strong as hell.

"Naw," she said, "that's just Amaré." She got out of the car and approached him, and the smile he smiled at her could have melted the polar ice caps. After a few minutes, I swung open my door to join them, but they stopped talking when I walked up. Cassy had me by three inches, and this guy wasn't far behind her. He stopped and looked down at me, and I stuck out my hand.

"Hi, I'm Laci—"

"This here the woman I been tellin' you about," Cassy said.

"No shit?" he asked. "You're nothing like I pictured." He scanned me from head to toe, and I looked down at my toes to see what he saw. Yep, just me. I gave him a full smile back.

"Nice to meet you. I heard all the stories, so it's

nice to put a face to the name. Did you tell him what we wanted to know?" I asked Cassy.

"Yeah, a body was found early this morning at Benny's Mattress, white dude, early to mid-fifties. You know him?" Amaré said.

"Not personally, but there were two of them last night," I said.

Amaré's eyebrows shot up. "Last night? I think you left something out of your explanation, Cass."

"Well, I ain't gonna be responsible for you getting in trouble for talkin' to us. I tried to keep you out of it. You welcome."

"Nothing happened," I said, crossing my fingers behind my back. "We got into Benny's, and then we got out. That's all there was to it. We didn't take anything."

"How'd you get in?" he asked.

"Ummm…"

"Day-um, you ladies are full of surprises."

"Yes, we're lovely. Now, what about the guy they found?" I asked. He laughed again.

"You'll have to ask the ME about—"

"Of course." I smacked myself on the forehead. "I'll ask Dr. Mann."

"She knows the ME?" Amaré asked Cassy.

"Baltimore County Medical Exa—" Dr. Mann answered.

"Good morning, Dr. Mann." I interrupted his spiel because I was in a hurry. "Did you do an intake of a white male in his early fifties today?"

"Uh-oh, yes, why?"

"What happened to him? How did he die?" I asked.

"I don't know yet—we're still prepping him for the autopsy. Do I want to know why you want to know?"

"Yes, yes you do. Can you call me when you know something?"

"Will do."

"Nothin' yet?" Cassy and Amaré joined me back at the car.

I shook my head while staring off, trying to figure out who the guy was. Was he one of the people that called me? No time like the present to find out. I dialed the number of the guy who was trying to blackmail us.

"Whatta you want?" he barked.

"Is that any way to answer your phone?" I asked.

"Listen, lady; I gave you back your guy, so if you ain't returning the money, then wouldja leave me the hell alone? Now, look what you made me do. I ain't suppose to be using the profanities and now look at me."

"What happened? Who was the dead person at your store?"

"How you know 'bout that?"

"Let's just say I have my ways," I said.

"Your cop friend, ain't it? Now, we don't want no trouble from the fuzz. We run a legit business and keep our nose clean."

"You call kidnapping Zach keeping your nose clean?" I asked. Cassy climbed in the driver's seat and Amaré returned to his patrol car. She raised her eyebrows at me in question, but I gave her a slight head shake.

"He owe us money. When someone owes us money, all bets are off the table."

"What was the money for?" I asked.

"He was going to the jewelers. Something for his old lady."

"I beg your pardon?" I was dumbfounded. "This is all about jewelry?"

"Beats me. I just know he asked for the five-hundred grand."

"Five hundred thousand dollars?" I asked. "Where is it now?"

"Now, how the h— How should I know? He wanted the money, and he signed to pay us back. Only now e's dead and we out five hundred Gs."

"How did Zach die?" I asked. "Did you do it?"

"How the hell should I know? No, I didn't do it. Just stay away, lady. Once we get our money, we'll leave ya's alone." He hung up.

I turned to Cassy, not believing the conversation I had just had. "The mattress guys don't have the money, they didn't kill Zach, and there is $500,000 floating around out there somewhere that Zach borrowed. Benny's guy says it was to buy jewelry, but I don't know anything about that. This is the first I've heard it."

"What?" Cassy exclaimed.

"I don't think Sammie will like this at all."

"Damn skippy."

****

Cassy and I got home from our morning out, caught Sammie up on everything, and dropped our question about the jewelry in her lap.

"Did you know anything about the jewelry?" I asked. She shook her head from side to side, eyes wide open.

I sat back on the coffee table and tried to think of another question, but the truth was, I was as baffled as anyone. I didn't understand any of this.

When my phone rang in my bag, I went to the table by the front door to answer it. "Major Duvall."

"I need you to come down to the station," Desio said.

"Well, hello, Detective, can I ask why you need me to come down? Again?"

"The DA has a warrant for your arrest," he said.

"They what now?" I asked. "Based on what?"

"Duvall," he began in a weary voice. "This is over my head. I volunteered to call you so you wouldn't have to hear it from someone else. You can come down here voluntarily or they'll send a squad car to get you."

I was in shock. Never have I come under suspicion for anything remotely close to this.

"How much time do I have?" I moved into the bathroom by the front door—I didn't want Cassy and Sammie to hear for fear of what would happen.

"I can give you a couple of hours, but no more," he said, his low voice carried across the line and right down my spine.

"Do I search for you, or will this be conducted by someone else?" I asked.

"It will be me, so let me know when you get here. I'll meet you out front of the building."

"Okay," I said.

Cassie and Sammie were chatting in the living room when I went upstairs to call Colonel Waters. Instead of reaching him right away I left a message with his receptionist to have him call me the minute he got in. I stood in my closet and called a car service while I numbly stared out the window. The mystery SUV pulled into place, and for once, I didn't give a damn. I finished changing, and my phone went off.

"Duvall, what's the emergency?" Colonel Waters asked.

"Sir, I wanted to give you a heads up that I am leaving for the BPD. They intend to arrest me for the death of Zach and his brother," I said.

"Peanut butter and jelly, Major!" he shouted. I knew how he felt.

"Yes, sir, I was given a heads up by the detective in charge of the investigation and asked to report ASAP."

"Is this the same detective, Duvall? Do you trust him?"

"Yes, sir, it's the same. On any other occasion, I would say yes, but right now I don't have an answer."

"I'll be on the horn with JAG immediately when I hang up. After that, I'll be in touch."

"Thank you, sir."

"Don't thank me yet. Let's get you out of this first," he said.

I hung up with him and went downstairs where Cassy and Sammie were in the backyard. I stuck my head through the screen and told them I had to meet Desio.

"He not comin' here this time?" Cassy asked.

"No, he's in the middle of something, and I agreed to meet him. I'll be back as soon as I can." It wasn't an out-and-out lie, more of a leaving a lot out of the telling, scenario.

Chapter Thirteen

The car pulled up to the Baltimore City Police Department and I paid the driver and texted Desio that I was there. My legs were shaky when I reached the steps which would take me to the front door. I pasted a smile on my face and began the climb to the top where Desio stood. I refused to let him see how rattled I was.

"Nice to see you again, detective."

He just peered at me and gave a jerk of his head—a facsimile of a nod.

"Nothing to say? No gloating? After all, you've got what you want. A viable suspect." I was baiting him, and he knew it. There was no reason why I should be the only one uncomfortable here.

"Damnit, Duvall," he interrupted me when I was next to him. "This is not what I wanted," he ground out.

My eyes snapped to his and what I saw there made me want to cry—the bastard did care. He reached for my arm, but I snatched it away. If he touched me, I would fall apart right then and there.

Instead, I went around him, and he fell in step behind me. When we got to the building, he reached from behind my right shoulder and opened the door. Once inside, I prayed for the first time in probably twenty years.

Desio guided me through the maze of desks until we reached one on the far side of the room. He pulled out the chair in front of an officer who was studying the paperwork in front of him.

"Laci Du—" The officer turned his head, and I was face to face with Amaré. "Long time no see, Ms. Duvall," he tried to joke, but I wasn't feeling it.

The process wasn't as bad as I thought it'd be. Somehow, I kept my face neutral and my voice calm. I was glad Amaré was the one who took my name and my photo—I don't think I would have done as well with someone else.

There were a lot of steps in the process, and every time I made a move, I found myself bumping into Desio. The third time I stopped apologizing, and about the fifth, I stared at him, but it didn't even phase him. He was immune to hostility from perpetrators, and I was no exception.

Finally, after what seemed like hours, they took me to the cell where I would be spending my free time. There were a few women in there already, and I listened to Desio confront the officer attending us and yell at him about how I was supposed to be alone.

"Desio, it's fine." He turned his head toward me, and I nodded.

At the door of the cell, I waited for the young officer to open it so I could go in. Once inside, the door clanged shut behind me, but I didn't turn around. The footsteps fading in the distance drew my attention to where Desio marched down the hallway like he had the devil on his heels.

An empty cot was along the wall to my right so I headed there and sat down and waited to see if it would collapse with me on it; it didn't. My fellow cellmates watched me from their positions on the wall across from me, and it was relatively quiet despite the noise coming from the precinct beyond the door.

"What brings you in?" a forty-something bottle-blonde sporting a black eye and wrecked hair asked me from the left end of another cot. She sat apart from the other women on the wall facing me. I thought she was with them, but their body language told me they didn't want anything to do with her.

"Just a misunderstanding," I said.

"Ahhh, same here, a *misunderstanding*," she said. Her gap-tooth grin held a hint of an edge.

She got up and meandered around the twelve-foot square cell, with each circuit bringing her closer to my feet, which I had crossed in front of me. When she got close enough, she kicked my feet out from in front of her and kept on going. I didn't place much stock in it, but I closed my eyes to narrow slits—pretending I was bored. On the next pass, she kicked me higher on the calf, and the third, she kicked my knee, and I was finally getting angry.

I rearranged my feet to a position with them under me in preparation for what I knew was coming next. When she got to me this time I was ready. She drew her leg back to kick me and I rammed my foot as hard as I could into the knee that held all her weight, and I heard it crack as she went down with a scream.

She lay there screaming and writhing in pain for about three minutes before anyone from beyond the doors bothered to check on the noise. When he saw her, he rushed inside the cell. The women and I glanced at her and each other, and then we looked away.

"What the hell happened?" he asked.

When the screaming woman didn't answer, he

turned to the other women along the wall and asked them. They claimed to have their eyes shut and missed the entire thing. He swiveled his head to me next. "I assume you'll give me the same story?" he asked. I shrugged my shoulders, crossed my arms over my chest, and closed my eyes.

He left the cell and went to the door of the office area, where he yelled for someone to come help him. Together they helped the whimpering woman to her feet, and they were not gentle with her either. When he finally told her to can it, I think one of the ladies across the way snorted. On their way out, they pulled the door shut behind them, so we had quiet.

"Thank you," one of the women said.

"You're welcome." I didn't know which one it was, but I nodded and kept my eyes closed.

In the silence, I thought of Zach and tried to recall our happier times. Sightseeing in Italy or making love in Paris. The beginning days when we lived in San Antonio in a small apartment and tripped over each other constantly. We both saw the writing on the wall when I came home from my last deployment, and we didn't naturally settle back into our routine. We were at each other constantly and miserable to boot.

"Duvall." The officer at the cell door called my name.

He indicated that I needed to come with him, so I got up and walked over. I expected them to cuff me when leaving the cell, but he turned and walked away instead, assuming I would follow.

"Where are we going?" I asked. He didn't answer, but I didn't expect him to either. I followed him through the maze of men and women in cubicles and desks until we reached an interrogation room. He opened the door and ushered me in.

No one else was there, and I paced over to the one-way mirror and back again. I was on my third go-around when the door opened, and Desio came in with Amaré behind him; they looked miserable.

"Have a seat, Major Duvall," Desio said.

I raised my eyebrows but did as he asked by pulling out a folding chair and dropping into it. My shoulder blades hit the back of the chair in a slouch I felt to my core.

Desio sat across from me, and Amaré had a notepad and a recorder with him. He pressed the record button on it before Desio got started and we got down to business. Opening the folder in front of him, he pulled out a picture, flipped it around, and pushed it over so I could see it.

"Have you ever seen this man before?" Desio asked me.

"No, I have not. Who is he?"

"He's a homeless veteran. Found outside Benny's Mattresses," Desio said.

This is the man that Amaré told us about—I had to fight every instinct to glance over at him. "Why do you think I know him? You think I'm on a killing spree and hitting anyone I can?" I asked.

Amaré reached his hand up to cover what looked like a smirk, but I couldn't be sure. Desio opened his mouth to give me what I was sure was going to be a set down, when suddenly he changed his mind.

He took another picture from his packet and placed it on the table in front of me.

"This is Thomas Wheaton, right?" I picked up the

picture. This was Zach's brother, but they didn't look alike. I could see the resemblance to their mother though.

"Yes, do you recognize him?" Desio asked.

"If you mean other than seeing him in the morgue with you, then no."

"Did you know Zach had a brother? Did you ask Sammie about him?"

"No, I didn't know he had a brother. Yes, I asked Sammie and she said she knew he had one, but he was supposed to have died in high school."

Desio jotted down some notes and opened his mouth to ask me something else, but there was a commotion from outside the room. A thundering voice I knew very well filled the void, and in the background was the distinct whine of Ryan. Sammie was here too.

"What the hell is goin' on here?" Cassy boomed. She slammed the door open which ricocheted off the wall. "This is your meeting? Where's your lawyer, woman?"

I glanced back at Desio. "How did she know I was here?"

So quick, I almost missed it, he winked at me. But before I could recover, Cassy yanked me up by my arm while Sammie stood on the other side of her with Ryan squalling. Ana had her thumb in her mouth but reached for me from Cassy's arms the minute she saw me.

"I can't tell you how happy I am to see you here," I said. I collected Ana, who settled herself on my hip right away like it was made for her.

"Oh, I bet I can. Come on, we bustin' you outta here," Cassy said.

"Wait, what? How are you getting me out?"

She put her hands on her hips. "We posted bail, woman, c'mon."

I turned to look at Desio who was standing behind me and caught my and Cassy's play-by-play. He was looking down at the table at his files, but I could hear the gears turning.

"Am I free to go, Detective Desio?" I asked in a quiet voice.

"Yes, there's nothing more I need to ask now," he said.

He glanced at me, holding Ana, and an unfamiliar feeling pulled at me. I didn't have time to think about it because Cassy pushed me toward the door and Sammie swooped in the minute I was out. She gave me a hug with Ryan attached, and I stood there with my hand stuck to my side in Sammie's embrace.

Desio spoke with Amaré while Cassy gestured at them both as she contributed her two cents to the conversation. When Desio looked at me, our eyes connected, then Sammie let go of me, and I stumbled with the force of the release. I caught myself against the doorframe, and Cassy was on me the next second, taking my arm again, and steering me out of the room.

Walking to Cassy's car, I brought in air while slowly enjoying the smell of Ana and the fresh night air. It was going on ten at night, so not nearly as late as I thought it would be. This had been a long, emotionally exhausting afternoon but tired as I may have been the questions began the minute my door closed.

"What was jail like?" Sammie asked.

I told them the story of the woman in the cell and the resulting actions I had taken, and neither one said anything.

"I didn't know you could do that," Sammie whispered.

"It's not something I like to do. Ever. Violence is never the answer. But she pissed me off, and I knew there was no talking to her. I know her kind."

"Damn skippy," Cassy said.

"Right before you got there, Desio asked me if I knew the man who had been killed and left at Benny's. He was a homeless veteran. So apparently, I'm the go-to now for local murders."

The rest of the drive was made in silence. Even the twins understood the need for quiet and dozed in their car seats. When we got home Sammie needed help getting the twins ready for bed, so we all assisted her. Boo was on her pillow but raised her head with a meow when I finally got to my room. I stroked her fur for a minute before heading into the bathroom, where I showered the jail cell smell off me and shampooed my hair like five times.

I lay next to her and petted her again while my mind was a buzz of activity. Was there something pertinent about this homeless man? What about Thomas Thornton? Where did he fit into all of this? I finally fell into a restless sleep with that thought in my mind but woke up a few hours later. After I flipped and flopped for a while, I finally got my bunny slippers on and went downstairs to get something to eat and drink.

With my head buried in the fridge, I thought I heard a light tapping on the front door. I wasn't sure if that's what it was, but I went to the peephole to look anyway. I probably should have been more surprised than I was when Desio's profile showed up in the small window.

I unlocked and opened it and leaned against the door jamb with my hands crossed over my chest. "Desio, what brings you out this early in the morning?"

"I haven't been to bed yet, Duvall. I wanted to see how you were doing after your visit."

I blinked at him a couple of times then stepped back. "Would you like to come in?" I wasn't sure what he would do, but my mind flashed back to that wink, and I knew why I had asked. He quietly crossed the threshold and followed me into the kitchen. "Are you hungry? I was getting out leftovers when you knocked. I think I have enough we can divvy up between us."

"Sure, food sounds good," he said.

I grabbed the meatloaf and mashed potatoes and heated them before we headed to the table with a couple of waters. After taking a few bites, I looked up, and he was watching me.

"Are you going to tell me why you're really here, Antonio?" I asked. "What else did you want to know? I didn't know the man at Benny's from Adam. And as far as your anonymous tip, I hate to beat a dead horse, but any way you look at it, it's still been at least fifteen years since I last saw Zach. But just because that's when I saw him last doesn't mean that's when he saw me last. We could have been in the same auditorium or building, but that doesn't mean I knew he was there."

Desio remained silent through the rest of the meal. When I stood from the table and gathered our things to put in the dishwasher Desio got out of his chair and walked silently across the carpet.

"You know the strong silent type is only sexy in the movies, right, Antonio?" I asked him when I flipped off the kitchen light.

The house was quiet except for Needles settling back down on his bed in the kitchen and the air conditioner coming on out back. The light was on above the stove, and the streetlamps filtered into the home office as we walked toward the front door.

"How come you never got married?" I pulled the door open and asked what had been on my mind. We stood frozen in the stream of light that entered through the storm door.

He looked at me in mild surprise and shrugged his shoulders.

"You know a conversation usually requires two participants, right?" I asked. He grinned. "There, you see, I knew you had it in you." I playfully punched him in the shoulder.

"You're a puzzle, Laci," he said. The intimacy of the moment led us to speak in hushed tones. "I see glimpses of that girl from long ago, and then you change in the blink of an eye. I'm left wondering which one is the real you?"

"I'm one and the same, Antonio," I said, "but life has made me wary. I've had to develop a thick skin because I've seen things that no normal person should ever have to see." I closed my eyes, recalling too many faces that I couldn't help.

His hand on mine drew me away from my thoughts, and I realized he had drawn closer and reached out to hold it. I grasped it like a woman drowning in the ocean. It had been a long time since someone held my hand in comfort. He didn't say anything. Instead, he just looked into my eyes, and neither of us moved. My face hovered below his chin, and the temptation was more than I could handle right then.

I moved the last fraction to his chin and laid my lips against the whiskers which formed throughout the day. I leaned my head back to where I could see his eyes looking down at me, but I didn't move the rest of me. Instead, I waited to see what he would do.

His response was pensive and surprising. He leaned over and kissed my temple, above my eyebrow, inhaling while he did it, just like he used to all those years ago. Then he retreated, letting my hand go and reaching for the door.

"I could have given you a goodnight kiss at the precinct, Detective," I told him, with a touch of humor in my voice. He huffed a small laugh and relaxed his shoulders. "Goodnight, Antonio," I said with a finger wave.

He raised a hand in silent farewell. Once he was gone, I retreated to my room to contemplate the weirdness my life had suddenly become.

****

"Whachu doin'?" Cassy asked me from her place at the doorway of my home office.

"I'm trying to find information on Thomas Thornton," I said. "There's no social media presence and no record of him anywhere. It's like he doesn't exist."

"Well, Sammie done told us he was supposed to be dead. We could go to that club and ask around," Cassy suggested.

"Good idea," I said. "I'll let Sammie know what we're doing."

Sammie chose to come with us, so we dropped the twins off with her parents. We figured this way we would make it in time to avoid the lunch crowd.

The Purple Peacock lived up to its colorful namesake. It was purple everywhere except for black trim work and black doors. Inside the club, the color theme continued—purple painted floors and purple glittered booths. The bar was black and there were a few stragglers despite no one being on the stage.

A man about my height was at the bar wiping it down and stacking glasses. He had black hair and brown eyes and I'd place him in his mid-thirties. He eyed us as we approached, and I sensed he was taking us all in and putting us in categories.

That's okay. I was doing the same to him. He reminded me of a sweet tea that's been mixed with lemonade—for those people who couldn't decide what they liked.

"We don't have any openings." He spoke with a strong Baltimore accent.

"Well, that's good since we're not looking for a job," I said. He raised an eyebrow but kept further comments to himself. "We're here to find out some information."

"What makes you think I'm willing to give any?" he asked.

Cassy reached into her back pocket and pulled out her badge, laid it on the bar, and slowly pushed it over in front of him with the tip of her index finger. He picked it up, looked at it, turned it over in his hands, then glanced at Cassy and the rest of us before letting out a sigh.

"Fine, what do you want, Officer Davis?" he asked. We hadn't gone over what to ask, but I wasn't worried about Cassy; she knew what to ask. I glanced at her, but she hadn't taken her eyes off him.

"Can you tell me if you recognize this guy?" Cassy held her hand out for Sammie to give her the phone. She scrolled through it looking for a picture of Zach.

Once she found one, she put it in front of him and he picked it up and nodded his head. "Yeah, but it's been a couple months for him, too."

Sammie deflated next to me, but we'd deal with that later. "Was he here often?" I asked.

"Eh," he said, giving his hand a waffling back and forth motion, "sometimes yes, sometimes no. Depending on how he and his partner were doing with their odd jobs. He was here a lot when business was up; down, eh, not so much."

"Partner?" I asked.

"Yeah, at least that's what he called him."

"What was the partner's name?" I asked.

"Thomas something or other."

"Thomas Thornton?" Cassy asked.

"Yeah, that's it," he said.

Cassy dropped an f-bomb, and I stared at him, speechless. I glanced at Sammie, and she stared at the bartender with large eyes.

"So, the dead guy in your dumpster was the partner to this guy in the picture?" I asked.

The man's face cleared like he just put two and two together.

"Yeah, how about that," he said.

"What was their business? Did they say?" Cassy asked.

"Not that I ever heard," he said.

We said our thanks to him and walked back out to the car, and the conversation erupted the minute the doors closed us in the car.

"So, Zach knew Thomas was alive, and they were partners. Zach never mentioned him?" I asked Sammie.

"Nope, he told everyone his brother was dead," she said.

"I wonder what the partnership was," Cassy said. "Did Zach ever mention a side job?"

Sammie shook her head in the back seat.

"Zach never spilled his secrets when he was alive and now that he's dead, that's not likely to change," I said.

****

We exited Route 40 in Middle River and passed the manicured lawns into well-established neighborhoods that stood the test of time. There were bungalows, Victorians, ranches, and a Mediterranean here and there to spice things up.

Sammie's parents' house was a dated ranch with a wide lawn. On one side there was a newer two-story and on the other was another ranch, made about the same time as her parents'. A small patch of corn stood behind the house to the left, and a newer but not brand-new sedan occupied the small carport. The walkway was slim and made of white granite rocks and something else and led to a sedate front door painted navy blue.

"Did you grow up here?" I asked.

"No, we moved here when I was twelve and Daddy got a job at Martins." She slowed her pace as we walked up the driveway. "This is where I graduated from high school, where Zach picked me up for our first date, and where I received the news that he was dead." She finished the last with a sigh.

A concrete porch slab, painted green, was at the back of the house, covered by a tin awning. The tinkling of a wind chime strung up on the porch broke through the air. In the middle of the backyard was a very large weeping willow, with vintage tin chairs scattered under it in the shade. The tree took up most of the backyard.

We followed Sammie up the small wooden steps where she opened the door without knocking and walked into the house. Old furniture polish and memories smacked me in the nose when I stepped inside, and I was taken back to my grandmother's house before she died. I felt the tears well up when I took it all in and I closed my eyes, and for a second, I could hear my grandmother's voice.

I was the last to enter the living room since I was still hesitant to meet the couple that had driven Sammie away from my house those first couple of days. The mutinous look her mother was sporting was the same one she wore that day, too.

"Daddy, this is Cassy and Laci." Sammie began the introductions. "Cassy is a new friend who is a Baltimore City policewoman, and you remember Laci from…" She ground to a halt.

"It's okay," I said. "It was a rough few days in the beginning." Sammie nodded her head and bit her lip. "Hello, Mr. and Mrs…?" *Shit, what was their last name?* I turned my head to Sammie for her to supply the name, but she was trying to assure Ryan that he was okay.

"Williams," her dad barked out.

"Oh, nice to meet you, Mr. Williams—Mrs. Williams." I nodded at each of them.

"Yes, well," her mom sniffed. "Come in and have a seat, why don't you?" She turned, and we followed as a group over to the sitting area of the room. The orange curtains hanging at the front windows cast a yellowish-orange hue into the living room. The furniture polish smell was stronger here, where it mingled with the faint smell of mothballs and vanilla. A cream-colored sofa scattered with small maroon flowers stood in front of the curtained window on the center of the back wall, and there was a recliner for her dad alongside a wingback chair for her mother.

On the wall opposite the recliners was an old cabinet. Chances were it was a record player or eight-track player—my grandparents had one just like it. Behind that wall were steps leading to a second story.

We sat on the couch while they settled into their chairs and waited for us to speak into the awkward silence. I glanced next to me at Cassy, who was messing with the cuff of her shorts and wouldn't look up. On the other side, Sammie was trying to shed Ryan, who refused to get down.

I noticed the absence of toys in the house for the twins—no wonder they came to us when we walked in.

"So," her mother spoke first. "You're Zach's ex-wife."

"Yep, that's me," I said.

"I can see he did much better for himself the next time around," her mother said.

"Momma," Sammie said. There was a touch of warning in her voice.

"Well, honey, what do you want me to say?" she huffed. "I swanny—in my day when a couple divorced, the original was never seen or heard from again; they definitely weren't friends."

I opened my mouth to speak but was speechless for once. "It's okay, Sammie, she's right. You were much better for Zach than I ever was," I said. "Mrs. Williams, I hadn't seen or spoken to Zach in fifteen years," I began. "We were friends of a sort, but not the type you would call up out of the blue to catch up on old times. I wished him nothing but luck when we divorced, and there were no feelings of love or sorrow when we signed the papers. Zach loved Sammie and—" I stopped because her dad snorted at my comment. My head swung his way, and I was curious what would cause that reaction.

His gaze met mine, but while mine was curious, his was mad. "The only one that man loved was himself," he said.

"Daddy—" Sammie began, but he halted her with his raised hand.

"I'll have my say for once, and I won't repeat it," he said. "That man only cared for one person—himself. I have seen much in this world from my time in Nam to your birth, to these children. I have seen the worst of humanity, and I have seen the best. These two, right here, are the best." He pointed to the twins. "Zach wasn't worth a hill of beans. The fact that he could deny what is as plain as the nose on my face is an abomination, especially knowing his family. One only had to see those two children with him to see the resemblance, and I told him as such. Now you tell me he owed the mob, Sam? I wish I could tell you I was surprised, but I'm not. That man wasn't worth the shit God used to make him with."

"Daddy!" Sammie's mouth fell open in shock.

"You're speaking badly of my kids' father in front of my kids."

"Don't I know it? Those two are the only good thing that man did the entire time I knew him. How quickly you forget the way he used to talk to you—like you weren't worth his time."

"Yes, at the beginning, he did, but he stopped."

"Why do you think he stopped?" he roared.

"What did you do, David?" Sammie's mother asked. Her hands fluttered to her throat like the delicate wings of a butterfly, but that's where the resemblance stopped. This woman was about as delicate as a Sherman tank.

"Not as much as I wanted to, I'll tell you that much. I merely straightened him out on a few things one afternoon while Sammie was at work. I may have said things a little strong, but he wouldn't have listened otherwise. I just made sure he understood what would happen if he didn't straighten himself out soon."

"Oh, Daddy."

Sammie stood and walked into the kitchen. Cassy and I joined her where she leaned her stomach against the counter. Her face was covered by her hands, and she rocked her head side to side, but there weren't any tears. I stood next to her in front of the refrigerator, and Cassy stood on the other side by the microwave. I leaned into her, and she raised her head.

"What's wrong, Sammie?" I asked.

"I'm just so embarrassed," she said.

"Why?" Cassy asked.

"Because my dad decided I couldn't handle my husband and he needed to do it for me."

"Aww, Sammie, that's not why he did it," I said.

Pamela Kyel

"Then why?"

"Because I imagine it was hard to see his little girl hurting and not do something about it. Did you confide in your dad about Zach?" I asked.

"No, but he was around us when we first got married," Sammie said. "We lived in the attic for the first few years, so I could get my feet under me after leaving bodybuilding. Then we moved to Montana when Zach got assigned there. Y'all know we recently moved in here again."

"Zach never kept his opinions to himself, did he?" Sammie shook her head. "I know it's hard after all this time to find out your dad stuck his nose in, but do you know what I would have given to have someone care like that when I was married to him?"

"Damn skippy," Cassy said. "My dad never stuck around, and I woulda given everythin' I owned to have one."

She lifted her head, and there were tears in her eyes. "Thanks, you guys, for helping me see what I missed." She headed back into the living room to where her parents and kids were.

I turned toward the refrigerator covered with pictures of the twins and the Williams's travels, coupons, and business cards. One particular card caught my eye.

"Cassy!" I reached out and yanked it off the refrigerator and shoved it in front of her face. Her eyes grew huge while she read it.

Chapter Fourteen

"Thomas Thornton," she exclaimed. "Why the hell they got a card for him if they worked together?"

"I think we should find out," I said.

Sammie was on the floor when we entered the living room, with Ryan in her lap, while Ana played in her grandpa's lap. I hoped he would be around long enough to take as good care of the twins as he had of Sammie. He looked up and caught my eye, and in that instant, I knew he was thinking the same thing, and something in my heart eased at the connection to him. These people cared a hell of a lot about their daughter and grandchildren.

I sat in the seat I left earlier and turned to her dad. "Mr. Williams, has Sammie told you I'm trying to find out what happened to Zach?" When he nodded, I kept going. "Can you tell me what you know about this man?" I held up the business card from the refrigerator.

"He came by a few months ago while Zach and Sammie were gone. Asked if there was anything that needed to be hauled away or cleaned up. Zach and I had just finished cleaning out the attic and taken it to the dump, so I didn't have any pressing needs right then and told him as much. He insisted on giving me a card, and I stuck it to the fridge and forgot about it. When Zach saw it a couple of days later, he hit the roof. I asked him what was wrong, but he never told me, just said not to trust the man. I guess I forgot to take the card down. Why?"

"That's what we're trying to find out. Zach didn't give you any indication he knew the guy?" I asked.

I watched him close his eyes and go back to when he met him. I knew he was doing it because I did the same thing. "Right after our conversation, I saw him pacing out front of the house while on the phone, and he was angry. I didn't catch any of it, but I could see him gesturing, and when he finished, he got in the car and stormed off as mad as a hornet."

"Thank you, that helps," I said.

"What's this about?" he asked.

"Do you trust me, sir?" My heart was in my throat. When we walked in a bit ago, he was full of hostility toward us, but I was leaning on the one shared glance we'd had.

"What kind of a que—" her mom began with her voice full of indignation, but he held his hand up to stop her talking. He didn't take his eyes off me, though.

"Yes, ma'am, I do," he said.

"Then know this, sir. I'm doing everything I can to take care of Sammie and the twins. They and Cassy have become my family," I said. "Someone needs to be held responsible for this, and until I know who it is, I won't stop. I will stake my word and my reputation as Special Agent Major Laci Duvall, that we will get this figured out, so Sammie and the twins are safe."

He nodded, and that was that. Then, he picked up the remote to the TV and turned it on. We were on our own now, but I noticed he put it on cartoons for the twins.

"I wanna see your room." Cassy was practically

bouncing on the couch.

"Oooh, me too," I said. I was trying like hell to bring my racing heart back to normal. We jumped up and followed Sammie to her room upstairs.

"Oooh, my eyes." "Now, that is a lot of pink," Cassy and I exclaimed when we walked in.

"You two, hush," Sammie said. There were tears in her eyes, and she was wiping them away with the sleeve of her T-shirt. "Thank you, Laci, that means a lot. Now let me hug your neck." She wrangled me into a hug and squeezed the stuffing out of me. See, little but mighty.

"We'll talk about what we've learned when we get home. For now, let's just enjoy a teenage girl's pink room and remember back when we were all young and innocent. Do you still have your plug-in telephone? Mine was clear."

I plopped down on the bed and bounced around like a teenage girl. I planned to think through things on the way home, so maybe I could come up with some kind of solution to this mess by then.

An hour or so later, we headed to the door with the twins, alongside her mom and dad. Sammie and Cassy put the kids in their seats, under the direction of her mother, and her dad stepped over next to me.

"Special Agent?" he asked. He kept his eyes on the activity by the car, but he was alert while waiting for my answer.

"Yes, sir," I said. I followed his lead and kept my eyes on the car. "Air Force OSI."

I saw his eyebrows rise in surprise when he turned toward me. I don't think much caught him off guard, but I managed to do it all afternoon. "What about you, sir?"

"I was Army, Radioman."

"Oh, shit," I said. Realizing I cursed, I instantly apologized. "Sorry, sir."

A big grin transformed his features, and I could see the resemblance to Sammie in that smile.

"You understand, so you are excused," he said. "Many people don't understand the job or the stress of being a radioman, and most don't want to. Zach didn't want to. The fact that you know, and you realize, is a compliment to you and who you are. Zach didn't deserve you either."

It was my turn to give him a huge smile. He saw it and winked at me, and on impulse, I gave him a hug and a kiss on the cheek. When I pulled back, the look of shock on his face was priceless. I turned and walked to the car and bid a quiet goodbye to her mother.

****

We got home in time for Sammie to get the kids lunch and put them down for a nap, and I made sandwiches for us to snack on while we talked and mulled over what we learned.

Once the twins were asleep and Sammie rejoined us, I slapped the business card in the center of the table. "I don't believe for a second that he left that card at your parents' house by chance, Sammie."

"You think he did it on purpose? But why?" she asked.

"He wanted Zach to find it," Cassy said. "He wanted Zach to know he had been there. But I thought they worked together—did they have a fallin' out?"

"I think so, but what would cause Thomas to threaten Zach? Was Zach into something that Thomas wasn't, maybe?"

"Could it be something with work?" Cassy asked.

"He wouldn't be allowed to give information to someone not in the Air Force. Which I know doesn't mean he wouldn't do it, but I have a hard time seeing Zach cross that line," I said.

"Drugs? You said he had a stake in some marijuana stocks," Cassy asked. "What if Zach had somethin' that he wasn't sharin' with him? Didn' have to be Maryjane—could be anything."

"I know Zach had his faults, but I don't see him coming to blows over marijuana. He gave up his rights to it once he was forced to. At least as far as I know he did. I can talk to Colonel Waters and double-check that."

"Do you think Thomas knew what the mystery key went to?" Sammie asked.

"Did Thomas know about the money, do you think?" Cassy asked at the same time.

"Both of those are really good questions," I said. "If we only knew how to find the answers."

We stood up to clear the table when I heard the quiet knocking on the front door and knew who it was right away.

"Good afternoon, Desio. What can I do for you?" I opened the door and swallowed my heart in my throat. I hadn't seen him, or spoken to him, since the night we'd shared that quiet moment. It had been like a dream.

"Afternoon, Duvall, I have a few questions concerning Zach Wheaton and the activities he was involved in," he said. "I also have Zach's death cert for Mrs. Wheaton."

"Come on in." I waved with my hand and followed

him to the dining room. Cassy and Sammie stopped in their tracks when they saw him coming down the hallway. I was behind him when he stopped and saw them, but I kept going and bumped into his back. I might have been noticing the way his jeans fit and failed to stop when he did, but I wasn't sure.

"Desio is here with more questions; you guys okay with that?" I spoke from behind him since we were still in the hallway.

The girls nodded and we parked it in the living room. Me with Desio on the loveseat and Cassy and Sammie across from us on the couch.

"Mrs. Wheaton, I have a few more questions for you, if you could, please."

Sammie nodded. Her white-knuckle grip on her coffee cup was the only indication she was nervous. I hoped she didn't pass out.

"I know I asked you this already, Mrs. Wheaton, but I have to ask again. What can you tell me about Zach's friends?" Desio asked.

"It's okay, detective. I've thought about it since the last time, but it doesn't change anything. I didn't know his friends. I don't think he had any. I mean, he never mentioned any to me the whole time we were married—what about you, Laci?"

Three sets of eyes turned toward me, and my mind went blank. "We were married for five years, and I can count how many of his friends I met on one finger. We shared co-workers, but who he hung out with, there weren't any I ever met."

"From what I've been able to ascertain, he had a side job working as a handyman," Desio said.

"Handyman? Doing what?" I asked. My voice was

neutral. This wasn't my first time interviewing while being interviewed.

"Odd jobs and the like. We're still looking into it, but we have a possible lead. I also want you to know Mrs. Wheaton, his tox screen states he had codeine and marijuana in his system at the time he died. Do you know anything about how these two interact with each other?"

"No," Sammie said.

"It can kill a man," Cassy interjected. I swung my attention to her. "I seen it before. Once."

"Officer Davis is correct. The combination is volatile and can cause respiratory distress, coma, and even death. But that's not what killed him."

"Then what the hell killed him?" I asked.

"Ricin," Desio said.

"What?" Cassy and I said at the same time. However, mine was more of a yell.

Desio nodded his head. "Dr. Mann said ricin popped up out of nowhere on the blood sample he sent out. We believe someone mixed it with the marijuana, which means he never knew it was there. There was enough in him to kill three men. Whoever did it wanted to make sure they got the job done. Did Zach show any signs of being sick when you saw him last, Mrs. Wheaton?"

"I'm not even sure when I saw him last. What is ricing?" Sammie asked.

"Ricin is made from the remnants of castor beans. Castor isn't prevalent here in the East, but it grows in the southwest United States," Desio said. "What car did Mr. Wheaton drive?"

Sammie shook her head. "He and I shared mine.

The last I saw him was when he went to work the day before he died. He could have slept in the bed, but it's just as likely he didn't. I reckon he could have been with anyone. He wasn't one to keep the horse in the stable."

"Was he having an affair?" Desio asked. He glanced at me, and I knew he recalled our earlier conversation.

"I had my suspicions, but suspicions don't amount to a hill of beans unless I have something to show for it. I told Laci I felt he was ready to leave at any time. He didn't bond with the twins, and he accused me of cheating, but I told him that dog won't hunt once the DNA test came back. They were his, and it was all there in black and white."

Desio jotted that in his notebook and then placed his hands on his thighs and stood. No one spoke when I walked him to the front door. I returned to the living room where Cassy and Sammie still bore stunned reactions from the news.

"So, what do we think?" I asked.

"Ricin? That shit ain't nothing to mess with." Cassy scrolled through her phone in search of fast information on it. "Five hundred micrograms can kill a man, and if Zach had enough to kill three men, then damn. I'd like to know who hated him enough to put that much in him."

"Ricin isn't something you can pick up at the feed store, though. Castor can only grow in certain climates here in the United States," I said. "Why didn't Dr. Mann notice it in Zach's system right away?"

We looked at each other, and none of us had a good answer. I picked up my phone and dialed and put it on speaker for all of us to hear.

"Baltimore City Me—"

"Dr. Mann, can you tell me how come you didn't spot the ricin right away?" I asked.

"Good afternoon, Major Duvall. I didn't spot it because I wasn't looking for it. That's honestly the best answer I can give you. I'm sorry I wasn't very thorough at first glance. The report just came through. How did you find out so soon—I've only had the body 24 hours."

"Wait, Dr. Mann, I'm talking about Zach. Who are you talking about?" I asked.

There was a long pause. "I was referring to Thomas Thornton."

"Holy shit—" Cassy exclaimed. "There ain't no way that's a coincidence."

Feeling like someone had just yanked the rug out from under me, I stood there trying to understand it all. There had only been a handful of suspected ricin poisonings in the world, and now here were two within a week of each other, and the bodies were relatives. Cassy was right; there was no way this was a coincidence. I'm surprised Desio didn't arrest me again while he was here.

****

"I think we need to return to Benny's," I told Cassy and Sammie the following morning. We were standing around the kitchen while the kids watched cartoons.

"Why?" asked Sammie.

"Well, I think we're in the market for some beds and mattresses. Am I right, Cassy?"

"Yes!" Cassy pumped her fist in the air and jumped.

"And this will be the perfect chance to ask the owners some questions. In a legal way, of course," I said.

"Sammie, we'll take the twins with us. I mean, how much trouble can they get into in a mattress store?"

The twins ate breakfast while we cleaned up, then we all loaded into Cassy's car and made our way to Benny's. Cassy cranked up the hip-hop, and we cruised 695 with the windows down and the music up. At one point when I glanced in the back seat, I swear Ana was bobbing her head along to the beat. She was wearing mini sunglasses that matched Sammie's even to the blue eyes behind them. It got me thinking about Zach and the twins and how they would never know him, and it made me sad.

Before I knew it, we pulled into the lot in front of Benny's then strolled through the front door with me toting Ana and Sammie holding Ryan. The salesman was busy with another couple in the back by the bathrooms. I glanced that way and handed Ana to Cassy. "I'm going to go pee," I said.

"Okay? Knock youself out?" she said. She grabbed hold of Ana and frowned at me.

I stepped away from her and walked through the store to the restrooms. I leaned toward the salesman when I walked past, and once I reached the restroom I texted Cassy, letting her know why I had gone. When I came back after a reasonable amount of time, I found her and Ana bouncing on beds while Sammie stood with Ryan awkwardly glancing at the office door, sometimes toward the bathroom, and often at the front door.

"Don't you want to try one out, Sammie?" I asked. "I'm buying."

"I'm okay," she said.

While Sammie was hesitant to participate in the festivities, Cassy bounced from bed to bed to bed with Ana a step behind her, giggling like mad. When she was splayed out spread eagle on her sixth bed, a man came out of the back, took one look at us, and muttered, "Oh shit."

My face lit up. "Hello there, my name is—"

"I knows who you are," he said.

"Well, seeing as how you know me, might I get your name Mr....?" I left the question hanging to see if he would fill it in. In terms of sweet tea, this guy's attitude yelled, left out in the sun too long, but his physical presence was all milk tea. He was also not thrilled we were there. So, instead of giving his name, he crossed his arms over his barrel chest and beer belly and eyed all of us.

"Listen, lady, what the he—what are yous doin' here?" he asked.

"We have some questions concerning Zach. It seems you know more about his extracurricular activities than we do, so we need some assistance," I said. "That's his wife Sammie." I pointed to Sammie holding Ryan and if it were possible, she looked more miserable than before. "We're also here as honest-to-God customers. Cassy has been sleeping on a yoga mat in my spare bedroom, so I'm treating her to a bed. You may just get our business if the price is right. I mean, I'm not paying five hundred grand for one, but if it's reasonable, then we'll talk."

The customers and salesman in the other corner

stopped and stared at us, and I thought the guy talking to us would explode when I mentioned five hundred grand. Just then, a third man came out of the back room.

Now, this guy was a freshly brewed iced tea, hold the sugar. He was early 50s and graying in all the right places. What? I can look. He was also a direct contrast to our guy. Ours was tall and massive, but this guy was small and mighty, kind of like Sammie.

"Is there a problem, Luca?" he asked in a no-nonsense voice. So, that was the big guy's name, Luca.

"No, sir, Mr. Zucca," Luca said.

"Pumpkin?" I slapped my hand over my mouth, but it was too late. Mr. Zucca's head swiveled to mine, and if looks could kill, I would be dead. "Sorry," I said. I held up my hands in defense. "It's automatic."

"*Parla Italiano?*" The scowl remained firmly in place.

I held up my fingers about an inch apart. "*Un poco.*" I flashed a Cheshire grin. It all came back to voices and languages for me.

"*Va bene,*" he said and returned to the office. The look on Luca's face was priceless.

"What'd he say?" Cassy asked.

"Very good," I said. Luca confirmed it a heartbeat behind me. He looked at me, and I shrugged. Eh, what could you do?

"Now, about Zach, did he have anyone else with him when you made your transaction?" I asked.

"Just the first couple trips. Then he came alone."

"What did he say whenever he came alone?" I asked. "Did he ever refer to the other guy by name?"

"Wasn't a guy—was a dame," he said.

"Really? What was her name?"

"Dunno, he never told me."

"What did she look like?" I asked.

"Always covered up, scarf, hat, and glasses. Like she was hiding something," he said.

"Well, we know it wasn't you, Sammie. Did Zach give a reason he came alone when he did?" I asked.

"Nah, just said she was busy."

"Did they seem to get along?" I asked.

"What do I look like, Oprah? They looked fine to me," Luca said. "Now, you gonna buy something, or do I ask yous to leave?"

"Okay." I rubbed my hands together, ready to get this business over with so we could move on. "Cassy, did you find one you liked? Sammie, did you?"

"Hell, yeah," Cassy said.

We spent the next forty-five minutes purchasing and filling out paperwork for the mattresses and bed frames. I finally talked Sammie into one instead of the lumpy one I knew she had been sleeping on in her room. When I told her we would move the other over so the twins could share, I finally convinced her. We were turning to leave when Luca asked about delivery.

"Oh, I thought you knew where to deliver to," I said. His eyes grew large, and he turned bright red. "Do you need me to write it down?" I asked.

"No, no, no," he said. "I'm good."

****

Sammie called ahead to give Floyd and Janis a heads-up that she was coming. We decided that since we were out we would speak to them about Thomas. Next, she called her parents to meet us at a local park to hang out with the kids, which they readily agreed on.

But when we pulled up to Glendale Park, only her dad was there to meet us.

"Where's Mom?" Sammie asked.

"Reading group started up today, so these rascals have just got me today." Her dad was crouched down to greet the twins. Ana went willingly, but Sammie needed to pry Ryan off. "If we're not here at the park, we've gone to get a treat up at the fast-food place," he said.

We took Goucher to the perimeter of the Country Club of Maryland and entered through the security gate. Zach grew up with a silver spoon in his mouth and never lost the taste for it.

This afternoon they were expecting Sammie, but they were getting all of us—this should be interesting. The sight of a stressed-out classic muscle car in this neighborhood could get the community security called on you if you weren't expected. The door was opened by the maid I met the last time.

"Hello again—do you remember me? I came with the detective?" I asked.

The maid didn't answer but glanced at Cassy and the rest of us, then silently opened the door for us to come in. We followed her down the hallway, and the Persian rug that covered the tile floor silenced our footsteps.

The maid showed us to the same room from when I visited with Desio. The furniture was leather, and you could smell the beeswax polish in the air, in addition to the musty smell of old parchment from the shelves filled with books.

Zach's mother was again in the wingback chair by the fireplace, and his father stood next to it with his arm resting on the mantel. I wondered if they practiced their positions.

I was struck immediately by the resemblance of Zach to his father. I didn't know why I never noticed it before. Perhaps it was the scowling he was giving us that highlighted the likeness. His mother's eyebrows shot to her hairline when we passed by the maid and entered the room.

"Sammie, I did not realize you were bringing others into my house." Floyd rebuked her immediately.

"I'm sorry," Sammie said.

"I'm not. It's nice to see you again, Floyd—Janis," I said.

I sat on the edge of the couch I occupied before, with Cassy next to me and Sammie on the other side of Cassy. Sammie was wound so tight she would break if you touched her—with stiff shoulders and a brittle smile pasted on her face.

"I know you're surprised to see me here again so soon, but we have reason to believe that someone saw Thomas and Zach together recently, and we wanted to know if you knew about it?" I asked.

"Why would we tell you that?" Floyd snapped.

"Because Zach may have stolen five hundred thousand dollars, and we're trying to discover if they were in it together," I said. "We're also trying to find the money, before the mob boss he borrowed it from finds it."

"Yes, well, we knew what we had in them," he sniffed.

"Tell us about them," I said. "How old was Thomas compared to Zach?"

"They were twins," Janis said. "Zach spoke with us only when he wanted money, which we made clear we would not do. Thomas has been out of our lives since he was…" She showed a bit of emotion for a second, but it was hard to tell because she wiped it off her face the minute it crossed. "We lost Thomas many years ago, and that is all I will say about that."

"What could Thomas have done that you cut him off?" I asked.

"At one time—"

"Janis," Floyd interrupted. She held up her index finger in much the same way Sammie's dad had done to her mom.

"After high school, Tommy was involved with some common criminals who he helped perform some extracurricular activities that landed him in jail for a short period."

"You cut him out 'cause he was in the pokey?" Cassy exclaimed.

I covered my laugh with a cough as Floyd opened his mouth to respond, but he was so astonished by Cassy's outburst that nothing came out.

"He assisted in the murder of an innocent person," Janis said. She spoke like a robot. She was removed from the room even if her body was sitting before us. She blinked, and the look of a mother mourning was instantly gone. Replaced by the cold woman I had always known. "We had hoped that Zach would turn out different from his brother, but we quickly realized we were sadly mistaken. When he chose his career and then married against our wishes, he sealed his fate, and we wrote him off also."

"You wrote off your remaining son because he married me?" I asked. "You told me when I was here with Detective Desio that you saw them a couple of

Easters ago." Neither one responded to me calling out their lie. "So, you've never seen your grandchildren, Janis?"

Sammie colored and averted her eyes, then shook her head. My head swung back to his parents—I couldn't believe what I was hearing. Janis studied the low-lying coffee table between us and rolled her shoulders forward in defeat. She then turned and almost spoke to Floyd but decided against it.

I reached into my pocket, grabbed my phone, and scrolled to the picture of Ana and Ryan covered in lotion for their chickenpox. Smiles covered their faces, and I remembered the sound of Ana's giggle when we put the cream on a particularly ticklish spot. I laid the phone on the table with the picture toward Janis. I pointed to each of the kids when I named them.

"This is Ana, and this is Ryan. They were recovering from a bout of chickenpox. I think it was close to the last day before the spots began to disappear."

Janis's shoulders slumped, and she fought herself to not look at the picture, but I saw her glance over at it, then quickly look away. This was one stubborn woman. I picked it up and scrolled to the video I had taken of Needles licking Ana and the delicious giggles that poured out of her. I pressed play once I placed it on the table, and it was too much for Janis to resist. She turned her head and watched it, and I saw the tears pooling in her eyes. I glanced at Floyd, but he had turned his back to us and stood staring at the bookcase in front of him, pulling out a book here and there. I heard the video restart and saw Janis staring at the video with longing. Nothing got to a woman more than seeing and hearing her grandchildren.

"That's enough," Floyd interrupted.

"No, it's not," I bit out. "Would you like to see another one, Janis? Sammie has a phone full of them, and you can see their birth pictures. You coul—"

Floyd stalked across the room, grabbed my phone, and reached his arm back to throw it, then caught himself. He dropped it back on the table and stood up. "It's time for you to leave."

"I think that's probably a good idea," I said. I stood up, and Cassy and Sammie were a heartbeat behind me. "But just know this, your grandchildren are innocent. They didn't choose Zach, and they didn't make him an asshole. He did that on his own; maybe he even had a little bit of help." I raised a single eyebrow as the insinuation sunk in. "Why don't you think of all you're missing out on? Those twins are the only—" I stopped at the look on his face. "You didn't know they were twins, did you? Yes, they're twins, and yes, they're Zach's. Sammie has the DNA test to back it up. You believed him, didn't you? He told you they weren't his, and you believe him." I shook my head. "One last thing; when was the last time you saw Zach?" I waited ten seconds. "I'd wager it was when he came to you asking for five hundred thousand dollars, wasn't it?" When Floyd's face turned stormy again, I knew I was right.

We took ourselves out of the room and silently walked the length of the hallway to the front door before proceeding outside. Before closing the door, I pulled Cassy aside. "Take Sammie to the car. I want to find the maid and ask her something."

"I gotchu," she said and passed through the front

door.

I took the corner and went to the kitchen to find the maid, and lucky for me, she was where I thought she'd be. I stepped quietly into the kitchen.

"Excuse me." I interrupted her lunch preparations. When she looked at me, her eyes went wide in fright. "It's okay," I said. "I just wanted to know if you've seen the Wheatons' other son, Thomas, here lately?"'

She nodded her head but didn't give any specifics. I think she was too frightened to speak.

"Has he been here since I was here with the detective?" I asked.

She nodded her head again but didn't answer.

"Thank you. You can call me if you hear anything, okay? Zach was my husband a long time ago." I turned to go, but I heard her quiet answer.

"I remember."

I glanced back, reached over, and placed my hand on top of hers, and gave her a squeeze. "If you need anything, anything at all."

She nodded, and I heard the recognizable sound of footsteps in the hall.

"Oh shit," I said.

She waved me over to a door in the pantry and opened it. It led to the garage and what I hoped was the exit. I grabbed the handle on this door and found myself on the far side of the house. I skated the wing and came out on the other side of the lawn where I took a hesitant step to the front of the house. I hoped the girls had thought to drive away. My phone beeped with a text from Cassy.

—*Down the street.*—

I jumped the hedges and landed by the road. Then,

glancing right and left, I took off toward the security gate and came to a halt about forty yards away when Cassy came up a side street. I jumped in the car, and we drove out of the neighborhood and turned toward the park to pick up the kids.

"So, Imma gonna make a wild statement here. I think Zach and Thomas were in this together, and Zach somehow wound up with the money," Cassy said. "Which left Thomas holding the bag. Who's to say 'Tommy' didn't kill Zach? I mean, his momma done told us he killed someone already."

Chapter Fifteen

There was quite a mixture tonight outside the Purple Peacock—since the club was coed dancers tonight. Women sporting tiaras and bridesmaid shirts alongside a group of soccer moms out for a night on the town. Then there were frat boys, old men, and boys barely out of high school.

"Let's go over our jobs," I said. "My job is to question the bartender while Sammie charms the dancers in the back, which leaves Cassy to make her way outside to check on the crime scene. If we finish our assigned duty early, we come back and help the first person we see right away. If any of us runs into trouble, we alert the others ASAP with a text or phone call."

Once the doors opened at ten, we were ushered in along with the crowd—the bouncers didn't spare us a second glance. We scanned the club from the back and found a secluded tabletop in the shadows and made a beeline for it. From here, we could see all our means of escape and the positions we were to take up.

Directly in front of us and spilling over to the left was the "dining" area where customers mingled at bar-tops and smaller tables with chairs.

The bar was to our right across the room, about thirty yards away from us, and the bartender was the same guy from the other day. He was busy with people's orders, and tonight he had help in the form of a tall, well-built man dressed in a black shirt, tie, and pants. His right ear sported an earring that caught the light when he turned his head; he didn't smile. This tea was definitely bitter.

Beyond the bar area was the door Sammie would use to speak to the dancers and see if she could get any information. We were counting on them talking among themselves about the tragedy that recently happened here.

"Should I get us a drink to help us blend in?" Cassy asked.

"Sure," I said, "I could use something tonight. I'll take a Mai-Tai, easy rum. What do you want, Sammie?"

"Umm, I've never had anything with alcohol before." Cassy and I both stared at her. I suddenly realized how quiet her life must have been before we came into it, and I didn't know if that was good or bad.

"Make that two," I said. She nodded and took off across the room, and I watched the number of eyes watch her go.

I returned my attention to the room—taking note of the customers, and to my surprise, I recognized someone. Seated in the left corner in a purple glitter vinyl booth was Luca.

"Well, well, well," I said. "Look who we have here." I tilted my head in his direction, and Sammie followed my gaze.

"Oh my gosh." She gasped and her hand flew to her mouth. "Isn't that—"

"Yes, yes, it is. I'll be right back. Stay here and wait for Cassy to get back."

I sauntered across the room, nodding at soccer moms and fending off more than one pick-up line. When I reached the glittered half-moon booth, I slid in across from Luca. The look on his face was priceless.

"Aww, lady, whatta you doin' here? Can't a guy get a moment's peace from you?"

"I'm not here to harass you. I just thought I'd come over to say hello. I'm here with my two friends—I'm sure you remember them." I turned and gave Sammie a finger wave, and she gave a small wave in response. Cassy joined her just then and I switched my focus back to Luca.

"Hello. Now can you leave? I don't want my night ruined by you dames."

"Oh, we're not here to bother you—you just got lucky. We're here to qu—" Cassy interrupted me when she nudged me with her hip and placed my drink in front of me. She then pushed Sammie into the booth next to me, leaving herself on the end.

"Aww, man, how do I get this bad a luck? You dames are crampin' my style." I didn't know he could whine like that.

"Oh, are you here trying to get a date with one of the dancers?" I asked. I couldn't tell under the low lighting, but I was pretty sure he flushed. "Ooh, which one? Maybe we can help you out."

"No, no, I got all the help I want from yous."

He clammed up as the lights began to change and the music ramped up. The DJ had the bass cranked, and I could feel it run through my feet on the floor.

The first dancer came out dressed in feathers and little else. Her blonde hair was piled on top of her head where more feathers were attached. Her shoes were at least six inches tall. How on *earth* did she walk in those things? Next, an African American woman dressed like a disco ball joined the first girl out on the stage. The lights glinted off her mirror covered bra and booty shorts and reflected all over the room. Her shoes rivaled the first one's in height but were clear with lights in the heels. The last one out was petite but well-endowed, and she received the most encouragement from the crowd. Her shoes weren't as high, and she dressed in a simple bikini which she spilled out of, but the men loved it.

"So, which one is she?" I asked. He glanced at me but crossed his arms over his chest and rested his elbows on the table. He switched his attention back to the dancers and ignored us altogether.

"How long until we get to work?" Cassy asked. She was eyeing the crowd and moving to the music. I could tell she was raring to go.

"Now's as good a time as any," I said. "You ready, Sammie? You didn't bring your taser, did you?"

Sammie jerked her head around, glancing at Cassy and then back at me, her eyes large in her petite face. Yep, I guess this was as ready as she would get. Cassy slid out, and I nudged Sammie to get her out of the seat. They went off to their assignments and I grabbed my drink and moved to the bartenders.

I leaned on the bar with my drink in front of me and placed my elbows on the mirrored surface. I was waiting my turn for the bartender when the man in black approached me—checking out all that he could see. I fought the urge to look down at my V-neck T-shirt to see what he was seeing, but I kept my eyes on him.

"You finished?" I asked. He raised his eyes to mine, and then he scanned me again, this time going slower and focusing on my breasts. I was getting fed up and was ready to put him in his place when Cassy sidled up next to me. The bartender looked at her and did the same process.

"Yo, up here, ma' man." She pointed to her eyes, and he finally finished by looking at her face. He raised his eyebrows at the two of us, and you could see him incorrectly connecting the dots, but I didn't straighten him out. If it got him to leave off the hassle, I was all for it.

"What can you tell us about Thomas Thornton?" I asked. Now that we knew the last name, it would help considerably. My eyes traveled over to Luca, who had been joined by his uncle. I wondered if he called him in for reinforcements against us.

"Uh-oh," Cassy said. I glanced at her, and she was looking at the bartender.

"What? What's wrong?" I asked.

"I don't know nothing about that," he assured us.

"'Bout what?" Cassy demanded.

The guy we talked to the other day walked up, and he didn't look to be in too great of a mood. His nametag read, Adam Wilhite. Our guy in black whispered to Adam, who looked over at us and inclined his head so he could leave.

"Why are you here again?" he asked. He pinched the bridge of his nose and let out a deep sigh.

"We asked about Thomas Thornton, and youda thought we screamed boo. Why is that?" Cassy asked.

"All of us are on edge about people dead on the property," Adam said.

"Did Zach ever come alone? Was there a dancer he confided in here?" I asked.

"Sometimes he came alone. Sometimes he came with Thomas. Sometimes he came with a woman."

"What did she look like—this woman with Zach?" I asked.

"Don't know. She was always covered up—scarf, sunglasses, sweats, hat."

"How'd you know it was a she?" Cassy asked.

"Let's just say there were things any breathing man would notice," he said.

I opened my mouth to ask another question when the music in the club changed, and the lights stopped strobing. Everyone looked around at everyone else, wondering what was going on.

"What the hell?" Cassy asked.

"Ladies and gentlemen," the woman's booming voice spoke over the speaker. "The Purple Peacock has some new talent we'd like to introduce you to tonight. She's new—"

"Oh shit," I said, "Where's Sammie?"

"...so be sure and give a rousing hello to Miss Calliope..." The lights came up and ran in a circle around the club. The spotlight was shining every which way, then landed in the middle of the stage where a petite blonde stood in a trench coat, with the front clenched shut in her hands. On each side of her were the male dancers doing their thing—gyrating and jumping and everything.

Suddenly, another blonde erupted from the curtains along the back and sprinted for the front of the stage, where she promptly fell into the audience. Cassy and I took off for the stage to remove Sammie from the tangle of the front row. We made it to the middle of the crowd before the bouncers nabbed us and hauled us back. I wasn't above punching someone to save her, but I never got a chance. We were deposited in the back of the bar and shoved outside, and the last thing I saw was Zucca striding for the front row. We tried to get back inside right away, but the doors were locked and guarded by big bouncers.

Around the back, next to the door, was the infamous dumpster with the crime scene tape still attached. When Cassy disappeared inside, I stayed and looked at the police tape covering the dumpster and immediate area. I understood now why Cassy was quick with her task, but I still took pictures of the location and placement of the two-ton dumpster. I was crouched down getting pictures of the ground when a bouncer strong-armed Cassy out the door.

"Didn't you show them your badge?" I asked.

"Yeah, but they said we overstayed our welcome, or whatever the hell that means."

"Where's Sammie?"

"Waitin' for us at the car."

We circled the club and came out front where Sammie stood beside the car with Zucca and Luca. She looked dazed and confused, but that wasn't outside the norm for her, bless her heart.

"Are you okay? We tried to get to you, but the bouncers hauled us out the door," I said. "What on earth happened?"

"I'm okay. I got stuck in the back when the dancers left, and I got scared."

"Do you got everything you took back whichu?" Cassy asked.

Sammie shook her head. "No, I dropped my phone an—"

"We will get your phone," Zucca said. He pivoted on his left foot and walked back into the club with Luca on his heels.

"Mr. Zucca came and got me off the floor. Of course, the bouncers were unhappy, but they took one look at him and backed off."

"Hunh— I bet they did," Cassy said.

"Did you get anything from the dancers?" I asked.

"They knew the name, but none ever spoke to him," she said. "I didn't get the chance to ask them about Zach, though. I'm sorry."

The sound of music spilling into the parking lot drew our attention, and we turned toward Zucca coming back. I didn't see Luca anywhere.

"Here are the items that belong to you, Mrs. Wheaton. I don't know what happened back there, but I am sorry. Did anyone hurt you?" he asked. "Why were you back there?"

"No, I'm okay. No one hurt me. Just scared the livin' daylights out of me."

"We were trying to ask questions about Thomas Thornton. Do you know the women?" I asked.

"Yes, I own this place."

Cassy let out a low whistle, and I couldn't have agreed more.

"So, you know about Thomas's death. Which we're unclear on. What can you tell us?" I asked.

"Why do you want to know?" Zucca answered my question with one of his own.

"Because he was related to my ex-husband and Sammie here's current one," I said.

"Thomas died before the ambulance got here."

"He was in the dumpster?" Cassy asked.

Zucca nodded but didn't say anything.

"Who got him out?" I asked.

"The man from the company that hauls away my trash," Zucca said.

"Did you talk to him?" Cassy asked.

"No," he said.

"How did no one see anything? Aren't the cameras fixed?" I asked.

"Yes, they work, but none are pointing at that general location."

"Now that's...interesting," I said. "Why have the cameras then?" My arms were across my chest, and I tried to intimidate him into telling us more, but I got nowhere. I guess if you were a crime boss, you can't be intimidated by just anybody. "What can you tell us about Zach and his visits here? Who was he with?"

"I pay no attention to the day-to-day comings and goings in the club. I keep my nose out of the goings-on and am well occupied with other things."

"Then how come you knew about Thomas?" Cassy asked.

"I pay particular attention when someone dies at my place of business." Nothing seemed to faze him, and he had an answer for everything.

"Well ladies, as I'm sure to be receiving a phone call from Desio shortly, I suggest we head home," I said. I knew when to call it quits in the face of the mob.

Zucca turned for the club's front door then disappeared inside, while we piled in the car and took our place on the interstate headed home. I went over the events of the evening and the information we had gathered.

"Why would someone kill Thomas Thornton? I would have thought the only one to do that would be Zach, but he was already dead." I asked.

"Obviously we missin' something somewhere," Cassy said.

****

I let an excited Needles out of the kitchen when we got home, and he followed me into the backyard where I sat on the patio. Sammie was upstairs changing her clothes, and Cassy hit the can the minute we stepped into the house.

I wished I'd had the chance to ask more questions of Zucca. Finding out he owned two businesses where dead people recently showed up wasn't a coincidence in my book. Then add in he's the Italian mob—I found it interesting no one questioned him regarding Zach and Thomas's murders.

"Amaré told me Desio on his way over here," Cassy said. She stuck her head through the opening in the screen and saw me sitting in the dark.

"Where's Sammie?" I asked.

"Talkin' to her folks. Wanted to check on the kids, so she called 'em real quick." Cassy sat down beside me on the outdoor couch, and we stared into the yard.

"This just gets more and more confusing, Cassy."

"True dat," she said.

"Why doesn't Zucca seem more concerned about a death on his property? And why isn't he under suspicion?"

"I don't know. I wish I did, though."

"You would think the local mob would be on everyone's radar, but he seems to slip right under it.

Possibly getting away with murder in the process," I said.

"We had the mob in San Francisco. They flew under the radar and strictly adhered to *cosa nostra*," Cassy said.

"What is that...something thing?"

"Yeah, *our thing*. It's a mafia thing—describes their hobby. They was there but were quiet."

Sammie stuck her head through the screen and the rest of her quickly followed. She took a seat in the chair to my right.

"How are the twins?" I asked.

"They're fine. Momma and Daddy said they had a blast with them tonight and thanked me numerous times for letting them stay overnight again. I'm thankful for the break, to be honest, especially after the club."

"You okay? Howdju get stuck backstage?"

"I have no idea. One minute everyone is there, and the next, it's just the bouncer and me. I asked him where they went, and he didn't answer but just pointed to the stage."

I was about to reply when I heard the doorbell ring.

"That can' be Desio; he don't ring the doorbell," Cassy said.

An impatient Desio was on my front porch when I pulled the door open. "Trying something new, Desio?" I asked him with a twinkle in my eye. He didn't find it funny.

"Duvall, I need to speak wi—"

"Yeah, yeah, I know. It's concerning Thomas Thornton. Come on in." I waved him into the house where Cassy and Sammie stood inside the back door. "Do you need all of us?"

"Yes, I'd like to speak to you all individually. I'll be in here," he said and indicated the front office with his pencil. "Officer Davis first."

Divide and conquer must be the agenda tonight, so I went back outside, and Sammie came and sat with me while Needles lay at our feet.

"Do you miss the kiddos tonight?" I asked. I tried to keep our minds off what was to come.

"A little, but at the same time, it's nice not to worry about them waking me up early, especially after staying up late tonight."

Our excursion to the club hadn't lasted long, but it was going on midnight. Cassy joined us again, and Sammie went and took her turn with Desio. I tried to breathe into the humidity while focusing on the cicadas outdoing themselves tonight. The singing in the trees was drowning out the road traffic in front of the house.

"How'd it go? What's he want to know so I can be prepared," I asked.

"Jus' your standard questions, with a little 'I'm disappointed in you Officer Davis' thrown in for good measure. He tryin' to threaten me to go to my superior, and I told him to knock hisself out, that I'm on my way out anyways and there ain't nothing he can do about it."

"Oh, boy, I bet that went over well."

"Yeah, well, he irritated me," she said. "He tryna to find out why we interested in all this shit. I told him that girl in there deserves to know what happened to her husband."

I nodded my head in agreement. "You don't need to wait up for me. I don't know how long it will take or if he'll even let me stay here. I foresee a return to jail in my future."

"How the hell you figure that one? We all in this."

"I know, but I'm the one whose ex-husband and former brother-in-law are both dead. So, yeah, it wouldn't surprise me if he does. I'll let you know before I go."

"True dat, but it's also Sammie's husband and brother-in-law," Cassy said.

"He wants you next, Laci," Sammie said from the screen.

"You okay?" I asked. She nodded her head. "Why don't you go upstairs and try to get some sleep? Cassy can fill you in on what we talked about, and if I'm here in the morning, we'll discuss everything over breakfast."

"If you're here?" Sammie asked.

"I'll explain. Come on," Cassy said. She took Sammie by the arm, and together they went upstairs, and I went into the office to face the inquisition on my own.

Desio was looking less than his stellar self when I walked in, and right away I felt bad for him, even if he was here to take me to the station. He was in the wingback chair with his forehead resting in the palm of his hand on the arm of the chair. I took a second to look at him and somewhere buried beneath all my anxiety were the butterflies at seeing him again. If only my life had taken another path. What would we have become? Would we have become anything together? I could sit and brew like tea all night, but I made my choice a long time ago and now I lived with my choices.

"Do you need some water or something, Antonio?" I asked.

He put his hand down and looked at me through

unfocused eyes, and then they cleared. "Water would be good, thanks."

I grabbed water from the fridge, handed him a glass, and set mine next to the chair I took. "Well?"

"I think I have a pretty good idea from speaking to them. They claim you couldn't have killed either one of them, but I know how partial they are to their hero," he said. I opened my mouth to refute that, but he held up his hand to keep me quiet. "I know you were looking into Mr. Wheaton's death, but I also didn't anticipate the death of Mr. Wheaton's brother."

"None of us did," I mumbled. "I'm here to find out what happened to Zach. To me, it's no coincidence that Thomas Thornton and Zach both died of ricin poisoning. I questioned Zucca about Thomas, but he had nothing to say."

"You spoke with Mr. Zucca tonight?" Desio froze me in place with the look.

"I thought you knew that already," I said. "Cassy and Sammie didn't tell you?"

He shook his head.

"Well, shit." He raised an eyebrow at my remark. I shrugged and took the plunge and filled him in on our night, but I didn't tell him any of the information we obtained from the bartenders. He wasn't the only one who could keep secrets.

When I finished, he leaned back in the chair with a muscle ticking in his jaw. The last time I had seen him like this was when I ended our relationship twenty years ago.

"Was Mrs. Wheaton, okay?"

I nodded. "Yeah, Zucca was swift-moving and took care of everything. I have some more questions for him about Thomas and Zach, tho—"

The storm gathered in an instant across Desio's face. "You are not to go anywhere near Mr. Zucca or that establishment. If I find out that you have, I will put all three of you behind bars for obstruction of police business."

"You can try, but I wouldn't recommend it." My voice was calm, but my insides were screaming.

"Oh, you wouldn't?" he said—his tone reflecting mine.

"Where is the professional courtesy, Desio?" I asked with steel in my voice. "What happened to working together? Zach was a member of the military. So am I. It's my job to investigate until I get the answer." I forgot in an instant the information I wasn't sharing with him.

"You realize I could arrest you right now, don't you? In this case, you are a person of interest, and I could haul your ass in for interference," he snapped. I didn't even know he knew the word ass, let alone how to use it, and I felt a gurgle of laughter coming up. I quickly squelched it, but not before he saw it. "You find that funny, Duvall?"

I shook my head, but it gurgled up again, and I snorted. Another storm crossed his face and I snorted again. I held up my hand while I tried to control myself.

"I'm sorry, Antonio."—*snort*—"I don't know what's come over me."—*snort*—"I think it's the stress, and I finally have a release, but oh Lord, I didn't know you knew that word." I glanced at him, and he looked ready to blow his top. So, I regained control and looked at him again. "What do you want to know, Desio?"

"Where were you this morning and afternoon?" he

Pamela Kyel

asked.

I let out a long breath. Was this the time to tell everything I knew and hope that he would do the same? "This morning, I bought a mattress from Luca at Benny's Mattress, then I went with the girls to see Zach's family, and tonight we went to the Purple Peacock to talk to the bartender and the dancers."

"Why did you go back to the Wheatons'?"

"To get information from Janis and Floyd about Zach, and his twin, Thomas."

"Did you learn anything new?" he asked.

"We learned that Zach approached them asking for money, roughly five hundred thousand dollars and that Thomas killed someone when he was younger and spent time in prison because of it. I'm sure this is something you already knew, but it was news to us." I closed my mouth, debating again how much to tell him. "The maid told me that Thomas has been to the house since you and I were there."

"Is that important?" Desio asked.

"I think so," I said. "Janis lied and told us they haven't talked to Thomas since they kicked him out. It makes me wonder what else they lied to us about."

Desio sat and chewed on that for a few minutes before he heaved himself up from the chair. I followed him to the front door. I wasn't sure if I was sad or relieved to see him go.

Chapter Sixteen

I jogged down the stairs the next morning and left a note for Cassy in the kitchen, asking her to call Carlos about my car. Sammie was on the couch in the living room, and she wasn't alone. In her left hand was her coffee cup and her right hovered over a gray body curled up in her lap. Sammie's face was a network of confusion.

"Do you need me to get her?" I asked.

"No, it's okay, it's just…well…what do I do with her?"

"What do you mean what do you do with her?"

"I've never had a cat sit in my lap before," she said.

"Never?"

"My mom was allergic, and Zach didn't like cats."

"Oh yes, I remember now. I got Boo before the ink was even dry on the divorce papers. Just gently pet her; she'll let you know if she likes it or not. Where's Cassy?"

"She hasn't come down yet, and I haven't heard any movement from her room either. I don't think she's much of a morning person. Where are you off to?"

"I've got to run to the office, but I'll be back as soon as possible. What time do you need the car to get the twins from your parents?"

"Not until after lunchtime—this way, they'll be

back in time for naps." She gave me a crooked grin and a finger wave as I turned toward the front door.

"Enjoy your quiet," I whispered.

The drive to the office was short and to the point, and when I got there the parking lot was empty except for a black SUV in the back corner with no one in it. That's odd. I vaguely remembered seeing it here before, but then as Cassy reminded me, I'm sure the company made more than just the one.

My steps slowed when I walked down the air-conditioned hallway. Special Agent General Joseph Carroll's picture held the place of honor in our hallway of comrades who were no longer with us. General Carroll was responsible for establishing the Air Force Office of Special Investigation. Former FBI Director J. Edgar Hoover loaned him to the Air Force to establish an investigative and counterintelligence body.

General Carroll and others hung under the OSI motto, "The Eyes of the Eagle," and there were too many that I knew personally. I lightly traced my fingers over the four we lost after my last tour and vowed again to do better by them.

****

I was hip-deep in Zach's records when I was interrupted by a perfunctory knock on my door and Colonel Waters entered. I was on my feet at attention when he reached my desk, but he waved me to relax. I sat down in my chair, and he took the seat across from me.

"I'm glad to see you here, Major. No harm done from your excursion to jail, I take it?" Colonel Waters asked.

"No, sir. No harm done," I said.

"Any luck with Zach's records?"

"I'm not sure, sir." I filled him in on the death of Thomas—Zach's brother. I didn't know if there was a connection, but I figured it couldn't hurt to catch him up on everything.

"Do you know what Anne Carson looks like, sir?" I asked.

"Not really, no. Why?"

"Zach was seen with a woman at Benny's Mattress and again at the club. I'm wondering if they renewed their acquaintance. Do you think you could set up a meeting for Anne and me?"

"I'll see what I can do," he said.

"How has Major Mitchell been lately?" I asked.

"He's been pretty quiet. Plugging away, trying to dig up information on Zach and his activities before his death. He's left his SUV in the parking lot for a couple of days. I'm not sure why."

"That's Mitchell's SUV, sir?"

"Yes, I saw him getting out of it yesterday morning, but it's sat there ever since," he said. "Well, I'll leave you to your work, and I'll alert you if I can get a meeting with Anne."

I left shortly after my conversation with Colonel Waters, and while I was going to my car, I slowed down outside of Major Mitchell's office to see if I could hear him, but all was quiet in there. I knocked on the door, and he told me to enter.

"Did you get a new SUV, Major?" I asked.

"Oh, no, I've had that one for a while. I just had a wax job done on it, though. Damn birds outside my apartment won't leave it alone. It's one of the only things I got in the divorce settlement."

Once in the parking lot, I looked again at the SUV in the corner. Even while driving away from the building, I looked again at the SUV in my rearview mirror. There really was no way to tell if this was the same one or not.

I was almost home when Colonel Waters texted me.

—*Tomorrow morning, nine o'clock, the coffee shop on the corner next to Golden Ring.*—

Cassy and Sammie were in the dining room eating when I got home and joined them at the dining room table. "You'll never guess who I have a meeting with tomorrow morning?"

"Who?" they said in unison.

"Mrs. Neil Carson, also known as Anne, the ex-wife of Major Keith Mitchell."

"Why you meetin' with her?" Cassy asked.

"Because of her relationship with Zach. I'm sorry, Sammie, but I need to hear her side of the story about the affair with Zach."

"I know," Sammie said, "and I realize I shouldn't be hurt, seeing as how he's dead and all, but it leaves a hole in my stomach."

I reached over and held Sammie's hand for a moment. I knew the feeling she was experiencing. I had felt it myself on numerous occasions where Zach was concerned.

"Any news on my car, Cassy?"

"Oh, yeah, it's ready," she said.

"Awesome. Let me change clothes, and we'll go.

Twenty minutes later and we were at the auto-body garage. We walked in and Carlos started gushing on our beauty and how we were the sun and moon and stars walking into his body shop. We laughed—and he knew, we knew, he was laying it on thick, and he laughed with us.

I went home while Cassy and Sammie took off for her parents' house. Mr. Kirby, who I shared the fence in my backyard with, was checking his mail when I pulled up.

"Good afternoon, Mr. Kirby," I greeted. "How goes the farm?"

He laughed at my greeting when he turned to speak to me. "Good afternoon yourself, Major Duvall. We're doing just fine. Let me know when you're ready for a tour," he joked.

Hmmm. "I have time for one now if you do?"

His eyebrows rose in surprise. "Sure, come on over. I was just cleaning the aquariums, so you get them fresh and riled up."

Once parked, I walked around the end of the row to his house, where he waited with the door open. I said hello to his wife, who was cleaning up the kitchen before following him upstairs where we entered the sanctuary of all things that slither. I stopped at the door. It's not that I minded snakes. It's that I minded a group of them, even when contained.

Boo was bitten when we lived in California a few years ago. Damn rattler was hiding under the drain spout cover—lucky for her I was home at the time. I swear those things sound nothing like what you think they should sound like.

He took me around and showed me his prize albino, which was marked like a calico cat. It was white with organic patches of the usual brand of snakeskin color scattered over his body; actually, very pretty.

"Do you know much about snakes indigenous to this area?" I asked.

"What do you want to know?"

"What to look out for in my backyard?" I said.

"Mainly the Eastern King Snake. They're harmless to humans but can go after anything else."

"Where do they hide? I have that huge bush in the corner of my backyard, and I'm trying to keep the cat out of it."

"That's a Burning Bush," he said. "You haven't been here yet for the fall. It'll come out bright red and orange."

"How do you know this?"

"I'm a closet botanist." He grinned.

"Oh wow, can you tell me what you know about ricin? It comes from a plant, doesn't it?" I leaped on the unexpected opportunity. How did I not know this already?

"Castor plant is what it's from—also where we get castor oil. It's not native around here but found in Arizona and New Mexico. Once the castor oil is withdrawn, part of the leftover "mush" is used to make ricin."

"Can anyone do it?" I asked.

"*Mmm*—It's a lengthy process, but I'm sure the internet is ripe with information about how to make it. Why?"

"I've got two cases of death by ricin poisoning, and I'm at a loss of how it got there."

"Were they sick leading up to their deaths or was it immediate? Ricin diluted in water can take a few days to process."

"How does it work?"

"It messes with the proteins and cells we need and use to survive," he said.

"For one of them, he ingested enough ricin to kill three men. How much does it take to kill someone? Can the amount speed up the process of death?"

"It depends on how it entered the body, but overall, it would take a couple of days to kill. If you eat it, you get serious nausea and an upset stomach. If inhaled, you'll have issues breathing, and your lungs fill up with fluid. I've read it takes about 500 micrograms to kill someone. How come I haven't seen anything on the news about it?"

"I think the police are keeping it hushed to prevent a panic," I said. I added his information to the category in my mind called, "information I'll need if I'm ever on Jeopardy," and headed home.

I should call and chat with Dr. Mann and see what he could tell me about evidence of symptoms of the ricin in Zach and Thomas. Sammie didn't notice anything off about Zach's behavior.

Needles greeted me from the kitchen when I walked in and leaned down to kiss him on his head and open the gate. His excitement was contagious, so I took him to the backyard, and we threw the ball around for a bit in the humidity, before going back inside and getting water.

Cassy, Sammie, and the twins were walking through the front door when we came in and Ana ran up to me for me to pick her up.

"Hiya, toots," I exclaimed and tickled her until she giggled.

"I'm going to take these guys up and get them down for naps. I may sleep a little with them if it's okay with you guys?" Sammie asked.

Cassy went off to her room too, and I stayed downstairs with Needles to work on my laptop. I sat in the wingback chair in the office and looked up anything I could find on Anne Carson when I heard a tapping at the front door. I knew that tap, and I was surprised to see him here.

I opened the door, and Desio was standing on my front step. "Hello, Desio, I'm surprised to see you. What do you want?"

"Can I talk to you?" he asked. There wasn't a trace of a smile anywhere.

"Okay." I waved him in, and he followed me into the front office.

"We have the report back on Thomas Wheaton alias Thornton. His tox screen lists ricin, marijuana, and codeine in his system." He watched for my reaction, and I knew why. That was the same diagnosis that Zach had gotten.

"Do you think that someone gave it to both of them and then killed them? Or could it be a copycat?" I asked.

"Yes, they both had this cocktail in their system, but both have another factor that could contribute to their deaths," he said.

"That they're related?" I asked.

"In addition to that," he said. "You and I both know there's another way to look at this."

"You've lost me, Desio, because I fail to see any other factor because I know you're not talking about me." He didn't say anything, just kept his eyes on me, waiting and watching. I crossed my arms across my chest and turned the tables on him. "Have you talked with Zucca? Have you hauled his ass in for questioning as you have mine? What's his excuse for two dead bodies appearing at two of his businesses?"

I was getting mad. There was a double standard here, and it pissed me off.

"I know you're mad, Duvall, but I can only go with the evidence, and yes, a lot of that points at you."

"Like what, Desio? What is the evidence against me for Thomas? What is the evidence against me for Zach? I think you're bluffing, and I'm going to call you on that bluff, but what I don't understand is why? Why do you have me tagged for this? Are you still angry after twenty-plus years that I picked Zach? Are you so angry that you would arrest me for two murders I didn't commit?"

I remained where I was, but I looked at him hovering over me. I wanted to see his face when he admitted he was here for me. He was mad, too. His eyes were the color of steel, and the muscle in his jaw was ticking. Good, I hoped I made him as mad as he made me.

"I came because you griped about professional courtesy, Duvall," he bit out, "and I'm extending it. Yes, you're a suspect. Now I'm leaving before I say something I'll regret. Don't leave town." He stormed down the hallway and slammed the front door behind him.

I sat there for so long that Sammie and the kids came down from their naps, and I was still there. Cassy followed shortly, and still I didn't move. I wasn't mad anymore. I understood Desio was doing his job, but the double standard was pure BS. I knew he wasn't still angry about my fateful choice all those years ago, I think I just needed to hear him say it, but then he hadn't.

"What are you doing in here?" Cassy asked. She stood at the door to my office with one hand propping her up on the door frame.

"Desio came by while you guys were upstairs," I said.

"Uh oh, something tells me it wasn't to ask you out."

"Are you crazy?"

"Just you wait. It's only a matter of time," she said.

I looked at her like she had lost her mind. "Cassy, I can bet you that you will go out on a date before Desio and I ever do."

"From your mouth to God's ears." Cassy kissed her fingers and pointed to the ceiling.

"What's going on?" Sammie joined us in the office.

"Desio came by," I said. "Guess who's now officially a suspect and asked not to leave town?"

"You're kiddin'?" Cassy asked. "What the hell?"

"According to Desio, in addition to the ricin, Thomas was found with marijuana and codeine. I apparently gave it to him before I killed him."

"You can't make this shit up," Cassy said.

****

Boo and I turned in once my teeth were brushed, and I was changed for bed. It wasn't until I heard Needles baying from the kitchen that I realized how quickly I had fallen asleep.

Rolling out of bed, I reached the landing empty-handed, again. *Damnit*—I hadn't thought to bring a weapon with me—my skills were getting rusty. I crept the rest of the way down without a noise. I reached the hallway outside the kitchen and looked to Needles for guidance. But instead of giving me an answer he tilted his head to the side in question.

I didn't know what to do next when I heard what Needles must have heard—a metallic clang from the backyard. At the window beside the dining room table, I moved the blinds and peered into the backyard.

"Laci?" Cassy asked.

"I don't think it's her," Sammie said.

"How the hell would you know?" Cassy asked. Her voice was full of curiosity, and she was no longer whispering.

"Because the door to her bedroom was closed."

"That don't mean nothin'. She coulda closed it behind her when she left—you know how she is."

What the hell did that mean? At this point, I gave up all hope of catching the intruder. Anyone with ears could hear these guys from two blocks over. I might as well have a little fun, so I backtracked to the bottom of the stairs and waited. I didn't have to wait long.

"I don't think we should go down there." Sammie was getting closer to the living room.

"Why not?"

"Because, what if it's a burglar, and what if they have a gun?"

"Oh damn, I left mine in my room—" Cassy said.

I knew it was now or never and leaped from behind the living room wall and yelled as loud as possible. Cassy didn't disappoint. She let out a lung-filled scream that was cut short by the volts of electricity shooting through me. *Shit.* It felt like my soul was on fire. Again. The electricity was shooting out everywhere so fast, I didn't know where it started or where it stopped. I went down to the sound of Cassy's roaring laugh ringing in my ears.

"I'm so sorry, Laci." Sammie's agonized voice reached me from above my head. "It's just that—"

"I'm not. That was the best thing I seen since you did it the last time," Cassy said through her tears of laughter. "I didn't get to laugh last time on account of the place, but damn."

I flipped her off and then turned to Sammie. "Ish okay, Shammy. Ish my fault." Something was seriously wrong with my tongue. I rolled it around in my mouth and stuck it out at Cassy.

"Damn skippy," Cassy said. Then she flopped down on the bottom step and held her sides, tears streaming down her face. I couldn't help it. I started to chuckle, and soon we were gasping like idiots.

"Why are you down here?" Sammie asked.

"Needles was baying, and I came to see what it was. I just moved the blinds and peeked out when I heard you guys on the stairs. They must have heard you too because they're long gone. Why are you two down here?"

"We heard Needles, too," Sammie said.

"Yeah, she was in with me when we heard it, so we came out. Thought you were still asleep."

"How many cartridges do you have left now, Sammie?" I asked. We were running out of weapon options for Sammie. She shrugged her shoulders, and I rolled my eyes in non-surprise. "Enough partying— let's try and get some sleep. I need to prepare myself for this meeting in the morning."

We trudged upstairs together, but I knew it would

take a lot of breathing exercises to get me back to sleep tonight. Between the meeting in the morning with Mitchell's ex, someone running through my yard, and trying to figure all this out, my adrenaline was running high, and sleep ability was low.

The truth of the matter was I was afraid of failing—failing these women, failing my boss, failing my country. All of it. Yes, this was my day job, but this case was personal. These people counted on me in more ways than one. To provide a roof over their heads. To be family.

Family. That alone meant more to me than anything. It never held much appeal to me until these women showed up, and now I didn't want to let them down.

They would yell at me if they knew what I was thinking, but I set the standard for myself and I had to live up to it.

I grabbed my laptop off the bedside table and propped myself up in bed since sleep wasn't happening anytime soon. Doing a quick search, I found a newspaper wedding announcement for Anne Carson née Mitchell, where she and Eric Carson were married in Las Vegas.

An hour later with a molehill of notes in a document, I finally closed my computer. It was going on one in the morning, and I needed to at least try and get some sleep before I met Anne in the morning.

Chapter Seventeen

The coffee shop was typical of its kind. Umbrellas on the outside with people underneath them working away on their laptops and notepads before the heat came and ushered them all inside. I glanced at the sky and noted a few clouds, but none that would change the day's forecast—yep, still hot and muggy.

The smell of roasted beans hit me the minute I stepped inside, and it packed a punch. I looked over the smudgy picture from the online paper and scanned the shop for anyone remotely close.

In the corner in the back, far from the windows and the eyes of customers, sat a woman not much younger than me. She had a cup of something on the table in front of her, and she looked down her nose as she scanned the shop every few seconds.

"Anne Carson?" I asked. I held my hand out for a shake, but she only nodded her head. "Can I get you something to eat or another drink?"

"No, I'm okay." Her voice was strong—like a cup of strong hot tea, artificial sweetener on the side. Her strawberry blonde hair was straight and back in a ponytail that dragged over her right shoulder. She wore a sweatshirt despite the heat predicted for the day and perched on her nose were tortoiseshell rectangle glasses with blue eyes behind the lenses. She pushed them back up when I sat in front of her, blocking her view from anyone who would see her.

"Thank you for agreeing to meet me," I began. "I have so many questions. I guess my first is, how did you know Zach Wheaton?"

"Zach and I deployed together when I first came in, but I knew him years before."

"How long ago was that?"

She sat there and looked at me, and I felt myself being assessed like a side of beef.

"I know who you are," she said.

My eyebrows hit my hairline, and I immediately sat back in my chair. "It's not a secret," I said. "I'm Special Agent Laci Duvall. Didn't Colonel Waters tell you it was me?"

"Oh, yes, Colonel Waters told me. He didn't have to tell me you were Zach's first wife, though. I already knew that. You never knew about me, did you?" she asked. She had a way of pinning you in place with her eyes. That's okay. This wasn't my first time playing this game.

"Were you among Zach's comfort women that showed up when I was gone?" I asked. I pinned her back with the same look she gave me. She didn't like that. She pressed her lips together, and hostility poured out of her.

"I don't have to be here talking to you; you know that, right?" she asked.

"Then why are you here?" I asked. I tried to keep a tight rein on my temper, but she was pushing all my buttons this morning, and we had just started.

"Maybe I wanted you to know about Zach and me." She arched an eyebrow and crossed her arms over her chest.

I swallowed what I wanted to say. I needed to get her to talk. I didn't have the time to waste on catfights.

"Okay, now you've told me, but I stopped caring what Zach did fifteen years ago."

"Then why are you asking around about what happened to him?" she asked.

"Because it's my job," I said. "When someone kills a US military member, it's my job to find out what happened. When did you see Zach last?" I figured it couldn't hurt to change the subject right then.

She frowned. "I don't know. When Keith told me, it was his way or the highway, I guess."

"Speaking of Major Mitchell, how long were you married?"

"Fifteen years. I've known him since high school though."

"Did you date in high school?"

"Yeah, we started dating when I was a senior in high school. He was graduating from college but hadn't left for his master's program."

"So, there are four years between you?" I asked, and she nodded in reply. I was mentally trying to do the math. "How long have you been divorced?"

"Two years," she said.

"How long ago did you get remarried?" I asked.

"Last year, but just because I was married for fifteen years doesn't mean the marriage lasted fifteen years. I should have pulled the plug long before I met Neil. Keith and I did fine when we were first married, but he wasn't enough for me, if you know what I mean."

Well, I didn't see that coming.

"Where are you originally from?" I asked.

"I'm from Arizona, born and raised."

"Oh, that's right, Major Mitchell said his family is out there. He was trying to visit when Colonel Waters canceled his leave."

"Yeah, his folks still live over in Yuma," she said.

"Would you say you and Major Mitchell get along now?" I asked.

Her eyes slid away from mine. I could tell that she was deliberating something but had no idea what it was. "He didn't want the divorce, but I did. So, take from that what you will. I do think he's following me. Keith kept our SUV, and I sometimes see it outside my house in the middle of the night. I know it's ours because the back-right window is tinted differently due to an accident. He isn't trying to hide that he's there either— he wants me to know it's him. I'm about to call Colonel Waters myself and report him."

"Why didn't you tell him when he called you about meeting me?" I asked. After a long silence, I tried again. "So, you haven't seen Zach since when? Someone said they saw Zach with a woman who matched your description." She didn't need to know that I was exaggerating the truth a bit.

"I don't know who would have told you that unless you're making it up right now. Which knowing what I experienced with AFOSI wouldn't be a stretch for you."

Yep, we're done.

****

I slammed my hand down on the dining room table in frustration the following morning and immediately felt bad when the breakfast dishes jumped. Ryan scrunched up his face, prepared to let it rip, and even

Ana was startled. Sammie immediately distracted Ry while I worked on soothing Ana, but Cassy sat with her thinking face on across from me.

"Tell me again from the beginning?" Cassy asked.

"Anne went out of her way to sidetrack me on her relationship with Major Mitchell. She mentioned he had a black SUV, and I don't know why she bothered telling me that."

"What about the black one that been outside here?" Cassy asked.

"Oh shit," I whispered. "How did I not put that together?" I slapped my hand across my forehead. "That's it. That's who's been parked outside. That's who hit me. She told me he kept the SUV, and he told me the same thing. I wonder if she was trying to tell me it was him without telling me it was him. But why would she do that? She didn't answer my question about if she'd been with Zach. She said what she wanted me to hear, that it had been years, but I think she went with Zach to Benny's people. I need to think of a way to ask her about it again. I wonder if Benny's uses cameras outside."

I went upstairs to shower and change into my uniform while also changing my mental state for the task at hand. I left the bathroom in my towel when someone tapped on my bedroom door. I pulled it open to find Sammie standing there chewing on her thumbnail.

"What's up?" I asked.

"That detective is here to see you again."

"Shit, doesn't he take a day off?" I asked. "I'll be right there. Give me a few to get dressed."

I swiveled my head at the bottom of the stairs

around ten minutes later, looking for anyone, but the place was empty. Cassy and Sammie were on the porch watching Desio talk with Mr. Kirby at the mailbox. I pushed open the door, and the girls turned to look at me.

"Is he here for Mr. Kirby or me?" I asked.

"He said he was here for you, then he seen Mr. Kirby and walked over to him," Cassy said.

Swallowing my opinion of the situation, I stalked down the sidewalk and joined the two men where they stood. Mr. Kirby saw me first.

"Good morning, Major Duvall," Mr. Kirby greeted. Desio turned around and watched me approach while eyeing my OCP uniform.

"Morning, Jonah, how are you?"

"Just fine. I was just explaining to Detective Desio here our conversation from the other day." I couldn't tell if Jonah was trying to fill in for me or if he was scared I would be angry because he was talking to him.

"You could have asked me about it, Desio," I said.

"I'm here to do just that, Duvall, among other things," he said. "Thank you, Mr. Kirby. If I have any more questions, I'll let you know."

It was all I could do to walk civilly next to Desio and not stomp on ahead. Something was up if he was here asking questions from my neighbors. Cassy and Sammie were back inside, avoiding the eruption threatening to occur any minute.

I went into the front office, paced to my desk, and then to the chairs and back. "You want to tell me what you need, so I can get to work?" I asked.

He stood with his feet planted shoulder-width apart, and arms crossed over his chest. He was in his

239

standard uniform of jeans and a sports coat. His aviators were in the pocket of his coat, and his holster was at his hip.

"Do you know Anne Carson?" he asked.

I stopped in my tracks at the unexpected mention of her name. "I only know what I learned about her yesterday morning when I met with her for coffee. Why?"

He pulled a picture out of his sports jacket pocket and flipped it around for me to see. "Was this her?"

"Is that her husband, Neil?" I nodded my head while scanning the picture of the couple.

"Yes," he said. He held out his hand. "What time did you meet her?"

"We met at nine o'clock yesterday morning." I gave him back the picture.

"How long did you meet?"

"I don't know…until I got my questions answered. What's this about, Desio?"

"Anne Carson was found dead this morning by her neighbor. She didn't answer her door, and her neighbor was worried about her, so she called the police."

I landed hard on the wingback chair when he told me she was dead, and my stomach rebelled before he finished. I ran to the bathroom and emptied everything I'd eaten for breakfast, then sat on the floor. I thought about the woman I met yesterday at the coffee shop, and I started crying. I cried out of frustration for not being able to figure this out in time and for the loss of another life, even one that didn't like me. Underneath was the realization that I had failed to stop another needless death.

I rinsed out my mouth and gathered myself

together, then went back and faced Desio. I knew he
was here for me. He was sitting on the other wingback
chair when I walked in. "There's a lot you should
know." I sat in the vacant chair and recounted my
conversation yesterday with Anne, including her
hostility toward me. "What did her husband have to
say?"

"He said the last he saw of her was right before she
left to meet you for coffee yesterday morning. He never
saw her alive again. Did you see her leave the coffee
shop?" he asked.

"No, I left before she did, but Anne told me
yesterday that Major Mitchell has been stalking her.
She knew it was their SUV because of a tinting issue on
one of the back windows. How did she die?"

"Why were you asking Mr. Kirby about castor?" he
asked. He didn't answer my question.

"Because that's how Zach and Thomas died," I
said. "I don't think it's a coincidence they both died
from ricin, Desio. There has to be a connection. If
Major Mitchell was stalking me in addition to Anne, the
main question is why?"

"How much was he contributing to the
investigation?" Desio asked.

I blinked at his question. It was both outlandish and
on point at the same time.

"I don't know, honestly. I asked Colonel Waters
once what information Major Mitchell had, but he
didn't know. Mitchell told me he's working on things,
but I don't know what he has, but then he doesn't know
what I have either. Let's run over to the office and see
if he's there. I'll let the girls know I'm leaving—I'll be
right back." I raced up the stairs and burst into

Sammie's room.

"He asked you out on a date, didn't he?" Cassy asked the second I came in the door.

"What? No." I was confused. "We're going to my office to see what information Major Mitchell has on Zach. I wanted to let you know I was leaving. I told you, that ship has sailed. He wouldn't ask me out again if I was the last woman on the planet."

"Wait, when did he ask you out?" Sammie asked.

I just stared at her.

"Oooh, I smell a juicy story." Cassy rubbed her hands together.

"Gotta go." I waved and closed the door, but not before I heard Cassy laughing.

Once in Desio's unmarked car, we made the quick trip to my office. When we got to the parking lot, I pointed to the black vehicle in the corner. "I think that's his SUV."

We got out and I walked around the black SUV. Before I finished circling it, I realized Desio was at the door of the building. I crossed the lot and entered with him and was halfway down the hall when I again realized he wasn't next to me. Instead, he was looking at the pictures and names. I backtracked and joined him in front of the memorial wall.

"Did you know all these people?" he asked.

"I knew Vorderbruggem, Cinco, Taub, and McBride," I said. I spoke their name with reverence. "A suicide bomber killed them in '15. They were all good people."

He nodded and then turned to follow me to Major Mitchell's office. I knocked on the door, but no one answered. I pushed it open and found the lights were on, but he locked his computer, and his CAC card was gone.

Out the window, I saw the SUV pulling out of the parking lot. It was too late to catch him, so I went to Colonel Waters's office and knocked.

"Enter," he barked.

"Colonel Waters, sir, this is Detective Antonio Desio, with the BPD. He came to my house to tell me that someone killed Anne Carson sometime between yesterday and today. Have you spoken with Major Mitchell at all today? I tried to catch him in his office, but he left before I could reach him."

"Holy hell, Major, you mean she's dead?" he exclaimed. "Nice to meet you. I haven't spoken with him—I didn't even know he was here, to be honest. Do you think he had something to do with it?"

"I'm not sure, sir. That's why I wanted to speak to him. Anne told me yesterday that he was stalking her. I figured out it was his SUV sitting in front of my house and also the one that ran me off the road twice." I turned to Desio. "Did you speak to anyone at the coffee shop?"

"The workers from yesterday don't remember seeing her. They remembered seeing you, but not Anne or who she may have left with."

"Colonel Waters, has Mitchell turned anything over to you regarding Zach's death or the investigation?" I asked.

"No, Major, he's avoided me since that debacle of a meeting last week."

"I can tell you." Tech Sergeant Ballou, who worked with Mitchell, stuck his head in the open door behind us. "Or rather, I can tell you he had nothing on it."

"What do you mean?" Colonel Waters demanded.

"Sorry, sir," he said.

"What led you to believe he didn't have anything?" I tried to soothe Colonel Waters's biting remark.

"He was obsessed with his ex-wife, Major. He hated Major Wheaton. He's been holding a grudge for years."

"How do you know this?" I asked.

"I've worked with him every assignment since I enlisted, ma'am. Not by choice, mind you, but by the sheer dumb luck of the Air Force. I been in for twelve years, ma'am, and the only time I haven't seen him was when he deployed.

"When his wife cheated on him with Major Wheaton, he was madder than a hornet. When you get Major Mitchell to drinking, he talks a lot, and there ain't nothing he won't talk about."

"What did he have to say about Zach?" I asked.

"Kept talking about how he'd make him pay. How he stole his wife and how he, Major Mitchell, couldn't stand the sight of his wife no more. This here was years ago. More recently, he didn't talk much about Mrs. Carson, not since she up and married her new husband. I think it took the sting out of Major Wheaton's affair."

"So, you know he had nothing because…?" Desio asked.

"Oh! Yeah, he had me shred a bunch of papers, and I was reading through them, and it was a timeline of his association with Major Wheaton. He mapped out when they met up and when his wife ran around with him. In the middle of the papers for shredding was a note that she had called him. I remember 'cause I took the message myself. She wanted him to call her back."

"I didn't know they were on speaking terms. That wasn't the message I got from her when she told me he was stalking her," I said. "How long ago was this message?"

"Now let me see, it was right about a month ago at the most," he said.

"Do you know if they met up?" Colonel Waters asked.

"No, sir, I don't know if they ever did. I never seen them together after the divorce."

"Why didn't you tell us this sooner?" Colonel Waters barked at Ballou.

"Well, sir, no one asked me. It's right there in my records where I've been assigned with him." Ballou replied.

"Fine, that's all we need right now," Colonel Waters said.

Desio's phone went off, and he stepped out into the hallway, and I continued my talk with Colonel Waters.

"Sir, why did you cancel Major Mitchell's leave to go home?" I asked.

"Because he wanted to help his mother around their house and yard. I get she's not as young as she used to be, and apparently, he's been going and helping her for years, and this year was no different. I told him until he solved Zach's murder, no one is going anywhere."

"Her yard? That's a random excuse," I said. Then it hit me. "Unless it's true." I remembered Desio speaking with Jonah, and then I jumped to my conversation with him on plants. *Oh shit.* "Is Major Mitchell into plants himself, sir, or was it merely helping out his mom, do you know?"

"I have no idea, Major, why?" he asked.

"Something just occurred to me," I said. Desio walked back in, and I filled him in on our conversation about Major Mitchell. "Jonah, my neighbor, is a botanist junky, and he told me ricin comes from the southwest of the United States. States like Arizona."

"Jesus and John," Colonel Waters said.

"When was Major Mitchell in Arizona last?" Desio asked. His eyes were alert, and he focused his attention between me and his notebook, where he was making notes all over.

"I don't know," I said, and Colonel Waters agreed he didn't know either.

"That's a big leap, Duvall," Desio said.

"I know, Desio, but what else do we have to go on right now? Even the smallest information can be useful in the right hands."

We said goodbye to Colonel Waters and returned to Desio's car. "How did Anne die?" I asked. This was one of many questions swirling inside my head.

"The neighbor found her with a gunshot wound to the stomach, and she bled out. There was no pooling on her backside, though, which indicates—"

"That it wasn't a suicide." I finished for him. "Where was her husband?"

"He was fishing with some friends at the shore—his story checks out. He had to come home when we contacted him about her death."

"No chance of him having someone do it for him?" I asked.

"We didn't see any need for that line of questioning just yet."

"Let's speculate for a second, why don't we? Major Mitchell has family in Arizona that he can get castor seeds from—just bear with me." Desio opened his mouth to disagree, but I held him off. "Who's to say that he isn't still bitter about Zach and Anne? That would take care of Zach and Anne and link them to Mitchell, but how is he linked to Thomas?"

"I think I should ask Anne's husband, Neil," Desio said.

"Do you know where to find him?"

"He's currently being questioned at the department, but he stopped talking and is asking for his lawyer now. They called me while we were with Colonel Waters. How much stock would you put into what Sergeant Ballou said?"

"I have no reason to doubt him. I'm chalking it up to anonymous information right now." I shook my head when Desio turned toward my house. "You may as well turn around and head to your office—you're not doing this without me."

He glanced at me out of the corner of his eye, and I crossed my arms over my OCP. There were a lot of horns honking when he made a U-turn in the middle of Route 7, but the stubborn man didn't notice.

Chapter Eighteen

At the BPD headquarters, we found Neil Carson in an interrogation room by himself. They were waiting on his lawyer.

I didn't know what to expect from Neil, but he wasn't anything I pictured. He was like Major Mitchell in size and appearance—brown hair and eyes, etc. It looked like Anne had a type.

He was younger than Mitchell, but not by much, and wore rectangular glasses which made me think of an old professor of mine in college. He pushed his glasses up when we walked in, and his hair looked like he'd recently raked his fingers through it. His eyes were red and swollen, and I felt mine tearing up just looking at him.

"Mr. Neil Carson?" I asked and he nodded. "I'm sorry for your loss, Mr. Carson."

He nodded again but cast his eyes down to the table. There was a sharp knock on the door behind me, and I stepped away so Desio could answer it. It was Neil's lawyer. A tall man of middle years who towered over the rest of us.

"Hello, Neil," he began. "May I have a few minutes to speak with Mr. Carson alone, Detective Desio?" he asked.

Desio agreed, and we stepped outside the door. "The lawyer's name is Mr. Vass. He's well known in the area for his kindness and his excellent winning record."

We waited in silence. I looked around us and down the blue and white hallway, anywhere but at Desio. When I did glance at him, his eyes were closed, and his shoulder was propped against the door frame. After about fifteen minutes he knocked, and we went back in, and immediately got to work.

"Mr. Carson, this is my associate Special Agent Laci Duvall of the Air Force Office of Special Investigation. She's helping solve the case concerning your wife, Mrs. Anne Carson."

"What does the Air Force have to do with a civilian?" Mr. Vass inquired.

"It's called Analyses of Competing Hypothesis (ACH). I'm gathering all the information I can that will lead me to a conclusion as to what's happened. I believe Mrs. Carson's death touches on another case I'm working on for the Air Force, and until I reach a conclusion that shows me it wasn't, I'm here."

Mr. Vass nodded and whispered something to Neil. He then turned back to us and told us to proceed with the questioning.

"Mr. Carson, can you tell me when you last saw your wife, Anne?" Desio began.

"Umm, I saw her the morning she died. She was on her way to meet someone."

"What day of the week was that—do you remember?" Desio asked.

"It was Tuesday, so yesterday morning I guess," Neil said. "Wow, yeah—sorry. My days are mixed up right now. I left shortly after her to meet up with my buddies. We were going fishing over on the shore."

"How has she been acting lately?" I asked.

Neil shrugged. "Not any different than usual, I think."

"Was she gone a lot?" Desio asked.

"Umm—not really. She'd been spending time with a girlfriend lately. They'd gone out of town a month or two ago."

"Do you know if Anne was in touch with her ex-husband?" I asked.

"No, she wouldn't do that," Neil said. "She hated him."

"We just came from my office where I received this." I placed the replica of the note Sgt Ballou had taken from Anne, on the table between us. "It reads, 'Anne Carson wants you to return her call.' One of the Tech Sergeants in our office took her call and jotted this down. It was found with papers to be shredded. The date is last month."

Neil opened his mouth and closed it. He turned to Mr. Vass and whispered something to him, and they went back and forth for a few minutes behind a notebook. "—damnit." Neil was sweating, and his face was red.

"I need another moment with my client, please."

"Five minutes." We got up and left. Again, we stood in silence, but Desio opened the door without knocking once his watch hit five. We interrupted their conversation, and Mr. Vass looked ready to have a kitten.

"It's fine, Henry. I'm ready," Neil said.

"My client has decided to give a testimony in return for immunity," Mr. Vass said.

Desio thumped his pen on the notepad in front of

him, then nodded.

"Anne was seeing her ex-husband on the side. I knew it and didn't do anything about it," Neil said.

"How did you know?" I asked.

"Anne was not subtle when she decided I wasn't enough for her. You can check Mr. Vass's records—I was beginning divorce proceedings."

"So, you would have a perfect reason for wanting her dead then," I said.

"Why would I want her dead when I could divorce her? We had nothing to gain from each other. Anne grabbed some money from the mob and planned to leave the country. I was trying to get the divorce finalized before she left," he gushed.

"Even more reason for you to want her out of the way," Desio said.

"You said Anne stole the money? Did she do it alone?" I interrupted the chain of questions for one of my own.

"No, she was working with some other guy. Something with a Z—" he said.

"Zach—" I said. "You say it had a Z, but you knew it was Zach Wheaton. The man she had an affair with a long time ago. My ex-husband."

"Yeah," Neil muttered.

"What do you know about the money? Where is it?" Desio asked.

"I don't know where it ended up. Anne and Keith were supposed to get it from Zach, but he hid it, and they couldn't find it."

"Is that why they killed him?" I asked.

"Yes," Neil said.

"Is that all you need?" Mr. Vass asked.

"What do you know about Thomas Wheaton, alias Thomas Thornton?" Desio asked.

"Who's he? Is he related to the dead guy?" Neil asked.

"Yes," Desio said.

"How did you know Anne stole money with Zach?" I asked.

"I found out she was having an affair when Keith told me. I didn't know about Zach until I confronted her about Keith, but she asked if I was talking about Zach." Neil stared at his hands on the table. He spoke with a lot of emotion in his voice, but I couldn't tell if it was anger or sadness. "She laughed when I confronted her about Keith and was giddy that she could juggle three men. She seized the opportunity to brag to me about it all. She knew we were over, but she didn't know I filed for divorce already. She mentioned the money when I asked who Zach was. How he was a friend from long ago and, 'sorry, but we're running away together.' I never realized she had it in her to be that cruel, but I never wished her dead—just wished I was."

"That's all for now," Desio said, "but we retain the right to ask further questions. I suggest you not go anywhere, Mr. Carson."

We got up and left the room to go to Desio's office. My heart was heavy for Neil Carson. I wasn't a fan of Anne's, but even I couldn't have guessed how mean she was.

Desio's office was small but larger than the cubicles where the patrolmen sat. Bookcases lined the room, and they were full of books and binders. There was a picture of him and his brothers on one of the shelves, and I went over and picked it up.

It was from ten years ago I'd say. When all the brothers were young and together. I turned to see Desio reading over his notebook.

"Well, we know who killed Zach and why," I said. "We need to find Major Mitchell to corroborate the story. Let me call Colonel Waters to see if he's returned to the office."

Colonel Waters told me he hadn't come back, and while I was on the phone with him, Desio's desk line went off.

"Dr. Mann needs us at the MEs office," Desio said once we both hung up.

"How come?"

"He didn't say why, but he did say that he's been trying to reach you, but no one's answered. He asked if we could come right away."

My phone didn't read any missed calls, so I wondered what number he'd been trying. Leaving the office, I waved to Amaré and followed Desio out to his car.

****

We pulled up to the ME's office and parked in the spot for police cars. I was out before Desio, and it took everything in me not to run and track Dr. Mann down.

Once inside we went in search of Dr. Mann and found him in the exam room with a very large, very dead individual. I stopped in my tracks at the door and refused to go any farther. Desio turned toward me with a look of confusion on his face, but then his face cleared, and I watched him try and hold back his grin. I stuck my tongue out at him.

"How on earth are you a Special Agent when you can't stand the sight of blood?"

Pamela Kyel

"My specialty is in other areas that don't involve…this." I gestured at the body. "I'll meet you in his office."

I walked down the hallway to Dr. Mann's office which smelled just as bad as the room I just left. On the sideboard were instruments and in the middle of the room stood a medical tray stand with more autopsy instruments. I was thinking of questions to ask Dr. Mann when someone pushed the door open behind me. I thought it was Desio and Dr. Mann, but Major Mitchell stood there with a gun pointed at me.

"It's about damn time I have you alone," he said. He turned the lock on the door behind him without taking his eyes off me. It appeared I was on my own for this.

"How did you know I was here?" I asked.

"I think I'll just let that remain a mystery," he said.

"I'm glad you're here, Major. I have some questions for you." I crossed my arms over my chest to hold myself together—this was a new one, even for me. "We just met with Anne Carson's husband at the police station. He had some interesting things to say. Why did you kill Zach?"

"I think I'll let you wonder about that while you're dying." He cocked his pistol, which was surprisingly steady.

"He double-crossed you, didn't he?" I asked. "You and Anne had it all planned out."

"Yes," he said. "Anne convinced Wheaton that she wanted to start an affair again, and he believed her." He threw back his head and laughed, but the gun remained steady. "She was so convincing that he would have done anything for her. His brother spooked him

254

somehow, so he took the money and ran."

Mitchell paced the room; the gun was constant and steady in its deadly accuracy.

"What happened to Anne?"

"My poor Anne." He hung his head and dropped the gun to his side but returned it a heartbeat later.

"You killed her because Zach took off with everything."

"*Yes*. She ruined everything. She was sleeping with him, too. It was only supposed to be me." Mitchell's face was red, and there was saliva running out of the corner of his mouth as he raged. "She ruined everything. If she had just stuck to the plan, we would be free from this place."

"I can see why you loved her; she was very pretty. She told me she was concerned about you following—" I stopped because someone was banging on the door to our room.

Mitchell swung his head to the door, and I lunged for him and tried to kick the gun out of his hands. But, instead, when I grabbed his arm, he swung it up and out of the way and discharged it into the ceiling above us. The pounding on the door continued with more effort.

"You may as well give up, Major. There's no way out," I said.

"The only way I give up is if you go with me," he said. "I'm going to use this on you"—he waved his gun at me—"and then I'm going to use it on myself. You see, you're the last of the line." He raised the gun to fire it at me, and I upended the medical tray stand to my left. When the instruments clattered to the floor, he covered his ears as the sound reverberated around us.

On the other side of the room, I ducked behind Dr.

Mann's desk. Gunshots replaced the pounding on the door from the other side, and Major Mitchell threw himself over the top of the desk and crashed into me on the floor. The contents of the desktop flew everywhere, and the gun skittered across the tile floor and went off. Something whizzed past me while I fought Mitchell, but I couldn't afford to stop.

His arm was around my neck in a headlock. I knew my air supply was limited, then my training kicked in. I threw my head back and nailed him in the nose with my skull, and he screamed in pain and released me enough for me to catch a breath, but he was back in full force a heartbeat later. Another gunshot went off while I grappled with his arm around my throat. *Jesus, what the hell were these doors made of?*

"Why won't you die?" Mitchell spoke from beside my left ear.

I reached up and raked my nails across his arm to try and get him to loosen up again, even if just a hair. His arrogance was his downfall. He kicked back his head and laughed after my nails went through the skin on his arm, but it was enough for me to wedge my chin in, and bite down with everything I had. I felt the skin give way, and the rush of blood came to the surface at the same time he threw me off and away.

The lock on the metal door finally gave, and Desio rushed in with his gun ready. He saw the blood pouring from my mouth, thought it was mine, and rushed over.

I spat out the chunk of arm I held in my teeth, and when Desio saw it, he turned his head to Mitchell, curled up in the corner in the fetal position. He kicked the gun out of the way and walked around him with his weapon still drawn.

When he circled behind him, Mitchell lunged for me, so Desio shot him in the kneecap, and he went down again. I closed my eyes and turned my head, but it was too late. I emptied my stomach right there on the floor of the ME's office.

Chapter Nineteen

Three days after Mitchell was released from the hospital, he reported to the interrogation room at the BPD. He had cuffs on his wrist and his arm was bound with gauze where I bit him. The hospital wrapped his knee in a cast which he propped on the folding chair next to him, because Desio took out his kneecap and the doctors performed surgery to put in a replacement.

Desio was in the interrogation room with Mitchell, waiting for the Area Defense Counsel (ADC) and Colonel Waters to arrive. Since Major Mitchell's crimes extended over the line of military and civilian territories, we would work together to make the case against him stronger.

Colonel Waters entered with the ADC and glanced at the two-way mirror I sat behind, before assuming his seat across from Mitchell and his counsel. I don't imagine it was easy on Waters to interrogate one of his own.

Desio and Waters began by laying the facts of the case out for Major Mitchell, but he kept interrupting them and inserting his version of events. The ADC tried to quiet Major Mitchell, but after about three tries he threw his hands up in the air and pushed back in his chair—crossing his arms on his chest in disgust. With one last attempt, the ADC made Mitchell clarify that he would not be using his services. This meant that

Mitchell could plead the fifth or confess to everything right here and waive his right to an attorney. He settled on the latter and opened the floodgates.

"Tell me what this is all about, Major," Colonel Waters asked.

"I had Anne back—that's all I ever wanted. My life was nothing without Anne. I wasn't the same after she left me."

"Start at the beginning for me, so I understand this," Desio asked.

"What are you not getting?" Mitchell slapped his palms on the table, and his face was red when he yelled across the table.

Desio was seemingly unphased by the outburst from Mitchell, but there was a noticeable tick in his jaw. "We know about Zach's affair with Anne and how far back it goes. When did you and Anne connect again?"

"Anne and I connected after she married that buffoon, Neil. He wasn't enough for her, and I was perfect," he said. "At least I was until Zach contacted her. After that—everything changed.

"Zach's brother Thomas tried to get Zach to go the straight and narrow, but he refused—he was in too deep. He wanted Anne back, and it didn't matter what he had to do to get her. Anne was with Zach long enough for them to set up the theft of the money, but the bastard double-crossed us and hid everything."

"Why did he double-cross you?" Colonel Waters asked.

"I can only guess. Maybe Thomas finally convinced him. Maybe he knew what Anne was doing. I don't know."

"You don't know where the money is?" Desio asked.

I didn't hear his reply because the door opened behind me. When I swiveled my head, Cassy and Sammie stepped through the door. My troops were here, and I gave them a watery smile when they sat next to me, one on each side. Desio glanced at the mirror, then turned his attention back to Mitchell.

Sammie reached over and picked up my hand and held it while Desio and Waters resumed their questions.

"How did Zach die?" Desio asked.

I squeezed Sammie's hand when I heard her catch her breath. This wasn't going to be easy on any of us.

"I don't know what you're talking about, Detective," Mitchell said.

"I think you do. I think when you visited your parents last time, you brought back a little souvenir," Desio said. "The ricin is from your parents' house in Yuma."

If looks could kill, Desio would be dead right about now.

"When did Mrs. Carson give the ricin to Zach?" Colonel Waters asked.

"Don't call her that," Mitchell bit out. "She set up a night for them to get together for him to use her for her body, and she slipped it into his marijuana. The dumbass didn't know what hit him. All we had to do was sit back and wait. It didn't take long, a little over twenty-four hours, and we dumped him."

"Why did you feel the need to kill Thomas?" Desio asked.

"Ahh, I didn't do that either." Mitchell didn't seem to realize that he was willingly confessing. He was so caught up in pride he didn't know what he was doing. "That was Anne, my wonderful, beautiful Anne; she did whatever I asked her to do. I convinced her that he was a threat to our relationship, and if she didn't quiet him down, he would ruin it all. We were on the trail of the money and almost caught up with Wheaton, but we lost it all at the last minute because of Thomas. He got between Zach and us, giving Zach time to get away. Thomas called the police, so we had to leave."

"What did Major Duvall have to do with any of this? It was you who hit her with the SUV, wasn't it?" Desio asked.

"She was investigating Zach's death and learned about his affair with my Anne. She even spoke to Anne. She knew too much and was learning more with each passing day. She was getting too close. That's why Anne had to go—she was stupid to meet her."

He turned toward the mirror, knowing I was behind it, and in the blink of an eye was on his feet. The folding chair his leg was propped in clattered to the floor in the wake of his lunge at the mirror. He beat the window with his left fist, and his right arm where I bit him dangled by his side.

I jumped out of my chair and Cassy came and stood between me and the mirror while Sammie still clutched my left hand. I glanced at Sammie and tears were streaming down her face.

Desio and Colonel Waters wrangled Major Mitchell away from the window while he spewed his wild accusations. "I lost Anne because of you!" he yelled.

Once he was seated, they tried to question him some more, but he wouldn't answer. He refused to answer any more questions until he'd had dinner.

"Man, that guy is unbalanced," Cassy said into the silence of our room.

Sammie nodded her head but remained quiet.

When Amaré entered the room to escort Major Mitchell to his cell, Colonel Waters and Desio spoke in hushed tones about what their strategy would be going from here. Cassy opened the door for Sammie and me to leave the room, but I took one last look at Desio who stood with Colonel Waters. He was staring into the one-way from the other side.

****

The house was quiet, too quiet, and I was going nuts. Cassy went with Sammie to her parents' house to let them know what had happened. We didn't want Sammie alone after hearing what happened between Zach and Anne. I stayed behind because I anticipated a visit from Desio, but I wasn't sure when it would happen.

Needles and I played ball in the backyard, but I desperately needed the chaos and noise to drown out the anxiety in my head as I replayed the last couple of weeks. I looked for opportunities I might have missed to save them all, but there wasn't anything I could have done differently.

Needles whizzed right by me with his tennis ball and dropped it at the front door. I didn't hear the doorbell ring, but I pulled it open, and there was Desio, looking as tired and worn down as I felt.

"Well, hello, Desio. I wondered if you'd show up."

"Are you alone?" he asked. Okay, I'll admit, I heard Cassy's voice in my head. *I told you he would ask you out.*

"Yes, why? What's up?"

"You want to take a ride with me?" Now Cassy was laughing.

"I don't know. Do I?"

"Trust me. You don't want to miss this."

I mean, I knew he thought a lot of himself, but wow.

"Let me get Needles into the kitchen and grab my bag, and I'll be out."

I put my words into action and was inside his unmarked car in a few minutes. Neither one of us spoke until we reached Route 1 and took the onramp for 695.

"Where are we going?" My stomach was flip-flopping with anticipation.

"I called Floyd and Janis from the office after everything calmed down. They deserve to know what happened to their sons. They asked me to come to see them because they had something to tell me."

"Oh." I tried not to let my disappointment come out in my tone, but he must have gotten a whiff because he turned to look at me.

"Where did you think we were going?"

"I honestly had no idea."

He turned his head to look at me several times until we took the exit for the Country Club of Maryland. He gave our info to the security guard, and we pulled into the neighborhood. When we entered the circle drive, I saw the drapes fall back into place in one of the rooms.

I followed Desio up the path to the front door that Floyd opened this time.

"Detective…you brought company…again."

"Yes, I did, Mr. Wheaton. Laci deserves to be here," Desio said.

We followed Floyd to the same study we occupied before, and Janis was there already. Her eyes swung to her husband when she saw me, but she stayed quiet.

I sat beside Desio, and we waited on Floyd and Janis, who came and sat in the chairs in front of us. Janis looked like she had aged ten years since I last saw her and the dark circles under Floyd's eyes were distinct, along with the pain etched in his jaw, and my heart immediately went out to them.

"What's going on?" I asked. "What's wrong?"

"I'm not sure if you know why you're here, Detective Desio, but I think you may have a clue," Floyd began.

"Yes, sir, I think I do. Do you have the money?"

I let out a gasp from beside Desio, and I saw the answer on Floyd and Janis's faces.

Floyd hung his head. "Thomas came to us after you were here the first time and told us what happened. Thomas approached Zach, trying to get him to leave Anne—he was desperate. He went to Samantha's parent's house; only he wasn't there. He left his card with them, hoping Zach would call him. Zach called him once and yelled at him to leave him alone."

"What was Zach doing that Thomas thought was dangerous?" Desio asked.

"Zach was trying to double-cross Anne's first husband, Keith. Anne convinced him that they were in it together and would be together again once they succeeded in getting the money. They could begin a new life somewhere else. Zach did all the dirty work and met with the mob boss to get the money, and he took Thomas along with him. I think he was trying to show off to Thomas."

"But Anne was double-crossing Zach with her ex-husband," I whispered.

"Where is the money now?" Desio asked.

Floyd went to the bookcase beside the mantel, the one he always hovered over, and removed a large book. He brought it back and set it on the coffee table in front of us. Desio reached over and picked it up and opened it. It was a false book made to look like a real one and inside were stacks of money.

"How did you get this?" Desio asked.

Janis looked at her balled-up fists in her lap and then at her husband. "Zach brought it to us once he learned about Anne and Keith."

"So, you've had it the whole time?" I asked. They both nodded. "Did Thomas resolve things with you?"

"We don't blame Thomas for Zach's death. Tommy came out of prison a different person than who went in," Janis said. "I will live the rest of my life knowing I wronged him."

"I think Sammie needs to hear this from you. Can I have her come here? Can you tell her what you told me?" I asked.

Janis and Floyd shared a look before Janis said, "Yes, I think that would be good. There's something else."

I glanced at Desio, who raised his eyebrows in surprise.

"What else is there?" I asked.

Floyd reached into the inside pocket of his jacket and pulled out an envelope which he handed to me. Surprised at the overture, I reached out, and he placed it in my hand. I opened the envelope, and inside was a marriage certificate with Zach and Samantha Wheaton listed on it. I opened my mouth in stunned disbelief, but I was on my feet, leaving the room to call Sammie the next second. Then Janis stopped me in my tracks.

"Do you think she could bring the twins with her?"

Tears sprang to my eyes. "I'll be sure and let her know who's asking."

****

The maid ushered Cassy, Sammie, and the twins into the library, where we sat waiting in silence. Janis was on alert the minute the twins walked into the room. Her eyes never left them, and her knuckles were white in her lap. Sammie didn't see it because she was terrified.

I got out of my chair to greet Ana, who spotted me and was making a beeline right for me. Ryan was glued to Sammie's side and had a pacifier in his mouth. I glanced at the clock and realized it was prime napping time, which meant this could go either way.

"Sammie, Floyd and Janis wanted to see you and speak with you. But first, I have something for you." I handed Sammie the envelope, and with a curious expression, she opened it up.

"Is this my…?" she asked.

"Yes, you and Zach were officially married after all." The tears poured out of Sammie, and I felt my own gathering in my eyes. "I'm going to sit right here on the floor with Ana at Janis's feet, so we won't miss anything."

I put words to action and sat down in front of Janis so she could watch Ana from where she sat. I kept Ana occupied while Floyd and Janis relayed the entire ordeal to Sammie and Cassy.

Occasionally, I glanced around the room, and each

time I passed Desio, he was watching me. The third time I didn't turn my face or eyes away in embarrassment and just let him see me watching him. He didn't turn away either.

The room fell away, and memories flooded back to long ago. We were seventeen all over again, and our lives were before us. We didn't know what havoc the next year would bring—we were blissfully ignorant. My eyes traced over his face, noticing where he had aged and how it only added to his good looks.

"You done through?" Cassy asked from beside me, and I jumped out of my trance.

"What?" I asked. My eyes snapped to Cassy, and then I scanned the room. Everyone was watching Ana and me, and I heard nothing of the conversation around me. Cassy was keeping her laughter on a tight rein, but oh, she knew she had me.

"We're leaving?" I asked.

"Now, why would you think that?" Cassy asked, her face was the mask of innocence. "Sammie just said she going to the backyard with Floyd and Janis and the twins."

"I'm going to be leaving then," Desio said. "Do you want to get your stuff out of my car?"

"Sure, she does." Cassy snorted and followed us out of the room.

I trailed Desio to the car, and when he opened the passenger side door, I got my bag out. I stood up and turned to him to say something, but he beat me to it.

"Maybe we can take another ride tomorrow night?" he asked.

Pamela Kyel

Before I could reply, I heard Cassy's booming laugh from behind the front door.

"Yeah, I'd like that," I said.

268

A word about the author…

I am Baltimore (pronounced "Bawlmer"), Maryland, born and raised. Life has taken me from Maryland to Montana to Italy and points in between, courtesy of the US Air Force. Being a military spouse, I have had a front-row seat to the workings of the military, and I use that in my Charm City series. www.pamelakyel.com

Thank you for purchasing
this publication of The Wild Rose Press, Inc.

For questions or more information
contact us at
info@thewildrosepress.com.

The Wild Rose Press, Inc.
www.thewildrosepress.com